ADVANCE PRAISE FOR
HOW TO LIVE ON THE EDGE

"A stirring story filled with heart and soul, and one that will dare you to rethink what it truly means to be brave and alive!"

—Mary Rand Hess, *New York Times* bestselling author of *Solo* and *Swing*

"Cancer took Cayenne's mom, it's gunning for her aunt, and she's sure she's next. But as long-held secrets upend Cayenne's world, she learns that defying death isn't about facing down trains or jumping off cliffs—it's learning to live and love with every ounce of your being. Honest and real, *How to Live on the Edge* is a gift to young readers living in the frightening shadow of a genetic curse."

—Catherine Linka, author of *What I Want You to See*, *A Girl Called Fearless*, and *A Girl Undone*

"Told with humor and truth, this story of a young woman navigating loss, devastating secrets, and the reality of her own mortality is made richer for the unique and hopeful bond she shares with her sister, the unfamiliar love she discovers with a family she thought she understood—and the strength she needs to save herself."

—Jennifer Longo, author of *Six Feet Over It* and *Up to this Pointe*

"Scheerger drops us into the psyche of a snarky, irresistible teen who's navigating the dangers of a life-threatening gene mutation. The voice is authentic and emotionally passionate in this headlong page-turner."

—Sherry Shahan, author of *Skin and Bones*

"In Cayenne and Saffron, Sarah Lynn Scheerger creates fearless, compassionate, empowered sisters who, in figuring out what kind of women they want to be, love on the edge and steal your heart like they stole mine."

—Gaby Triana, author of *Wake the Hollow*, *Cakespell*, and *Summer of Yesterday*

D1054124

HOW TO LIVE ON THE EDGE

SARAH LYNN SCHEERGER

carolrhoda LAB

MINNEAPOLIS

Text copyright © 2020 by Sarah Lynn Scheerger

All rights reserved. International copyright secured. No part of this book may be reproduced, stored in a retrieval system, or transmitted in any form or by any means—electronic, mechanical, photocopying, recording, or otherwise—without the prior written permission of Lerner Publishing Group, Inc., except for the inclusion of brief quotations in an acknowledged review.

Carolrhoda Lab®
An imprint of Lerner Publishing Group, Inc.
241 First Avenue North
Minneapolis, MN 55401 USA

For reading levels and more information, look up this title at www.lernerbooks.com.

Image credit: portishead1/Getty Images.

Main body text set in Janson Text LT Std.
Typeface provided by Linotype AG.

Library of Congress Cataloging-in-Publication Data

Names: Scheerger, Sarah Lynn, 1975– author.
Title: How to live on the edge / by Sarah Lynn Scheerger.
Description: Minneapolis : Carolrhoda Lab, [2020] | Summary: Eighteen-year-old Cayenne learns that her long-dead mother left her and her sister a series of video messages; that their aunt, who raised them, has the same gene mutation that caused their mother's cancer; and that she and her sister may also have it.
Identifiers: LCCN 2019008528 | ISBN 9781541578890 (lb : alk. paper)
Subjects: CYAC: Sisters—Fiction. | Breast—Cancer—Fiction. | Genetics—Fiction. | Family life—Fiction. | Death—Fiction.
Classification: LCC PZ7.S34244 Ho 2020 | DDC [Fic]—dc23

LC record available at https://lccn.loc.gov/2019008528

Manufactured in the United States of America
1-47050-47883-9/19/2019

For my siblings (Jessica, Adam, & Daniel)
and our shared history

Chapter 1

There's a curse on the women in my family. We die young.

In the last two generations, not a single woman in my mom's family has lived past the age of thirty-seven. Aunt Tee is still alive and kicking, and the doctors say she's a perfectly healthy thirty-two-year-old, but I doubt the Silk family curse will pass her by.

Just like I doubt it will pass me by.

Which means almost half of my life is over.

I intend to enjoy it.

* * *

I feel the vibrations in my teeth. My feet straddle the train tracks, craving what's to come. The sounds of churning wheels *clackety-clack*ing register in my brain as white noise, strangely comforting, like the sounds of ocean waves or heavy rain.

Train dodging freaks people out. They think I'm suicidal or tripping on psychedelics. No, I do not have a death wish. People don't get that though, and it's a royal pain to try to explain it. So now I dodge alone. Just me and the train.

Sometimes I name the chuggers for company. I'm calling this one Betty.

The track hugs a mountain curve right near the beach. That's my spot. If I stand just around the bend in the shade of the mountain, the engineer can't see me as the train approaches and won't slam on the brakes.

Whir-whir-whir-whir.

I picture Death holding out her bony hand. I accept it, voluntarily placing myself in her grasp. I know it's the vibrations of the train I feel through my feet, but I imagine Death shivering with anticipation.

Whir-whir-whir-whir.

I do get it, why this might seem concerning—some girl waiting to dodge a bazillion-ton train that's moving at fifty-something miles an hour, all while imagining an interaction with Death herself. But I swear I'm perfectly lucid. I just happen to have an overactive imagination and an underdeveloped instinct for self-preservation.

Whir-whir-whir-whir.

God, the anticipation is exquisite. The vibrations and Betty's chugging intensify as she nears the bend. I open my arms wide, letting the wind rake through my hair. I know how to time this. I can do it by feel, by sound, by intuition. For the right kind of adrenaline surge, the train has to get close enough. I close my eyes, and without sight, my other senses kick in. I am one with the wind.

During moments like this, I feel alive. Every cell in my body stands alert, the hairs prick up on my arms, and the endorphins saturate my brain. My insides buzz with anticipation, like I'm harvesting a hive of bees. My heart beats so hard I can feel it in my temples.

Whir-whir-whir-whir.

My grip on reality loosens and I can visualize Death, can hear what she would say to me if she could talk. Her sense of humor is a little off. Can't blame her. Look what she does for a living.

Do you like meatloaf?

Not particularly.

Then what's with these incessant attempts to turn yourself into ground meat?

She's a trickster, eager to confuse me, eager to distract me, knowing that a few-second delay is all she needs to gobble me up.

She narrows her eyes. *If your timing is off, all they'll find is your teeth, scattered in the sand. The impact will decimate you.*

Lovely image, I say. *But stop distracting me.* I won't let her dictate my fate. Curse or no curse, for the moment I'm the one in charge.

I sense the train edging toward the corner, and I bend my legs. Like always, my instinct is to jump too soon. My organs desperately want to break through my skin and escape, but I hold myself back.

For all that banging around my heart's been doing, I swear it stops, so suddenly that it feels like my brain is sending a command, slamming on the brakes. *Discontinue heartbeat. End blood flow to cells.* Right on schedule, just like magic, fear sucks me in, telling me it's nearly time.

Betty's *clackety-clack*ing is so loud I can scarcely think. *Not yet. Not yet. Not yet . . . Now!*

I leap. As I do, the train blasts past, and the force of the wind slams me forward so hard that I lose my breath. I roll over in the sand until I land on my back, staring at the sky. My system is in shock at first, like always. The hive of bees flaps haphazardly

3

within my gut and chest, banging into organs and each other, total chaos. Perhaps this time I cut it a little too close, and there's a distinct possibility I'm not breathing right now.

Death sighs, lazily swirling around as if entertaining me with her own mini tornado. *When will you tire of this ridiculous game of cat and mouse?*

Not till it ends. You know everyone roots for the mouse.

Perhaps. But the cat always wins. Death shakes her head with a forlorn expression, then disintegrates into nothingness.

Boom! My heart starts pumping again, each beat bumping into the next, fighting for first place in line. I make a concerted effort to inhale. At first the breath holds too little oxygen, but gradually the air travels through my blood to my organs, quieting the bees.

I carefully pat my arms, my face, my legs, checking for missing parts or blood. I've lost the top layer of skin on the undersides of both arms. There's sand in my mouth and wedged in the cracks of my eyes, but I don't care. I've cheated Death once again. Nothing makes me feel more alive.

Chapter 2

My younger sister, Saffron, pokes her head into our jack-and-jill bathroom, where I'm standing, shirtless, to disinfect my bloodied arms.

"Uh, privacy?" I remind her. The stinging from the alcohol wipes is making me cranky. There's more blood than I thought there'd be. The scrapes on the underside of my left arm vaguely resemble Hawaii. "This *is* a bathroom, you know."

Saffron shakes her head in disgust as I consider pointing out the plethora of grosser things I could be doing in the bathroom. She steps inside and partially closes the door behind her so that she can point to the tiny lock. "Cayenne, I'd like to introduce you to a bathroom lock. Lock, meet my sister Cayenne. She's somehow made it to her senior year of high school without making your acquaintance."

"Very funny." I contemplate my arms, casualties of my train dodge. I'm not squeamish, but I do like to keep my shirts bloodstain-free. "Do you have a long-sleeved black top I can borrow? Preferably one that will accentuate my boob-age?"

Saff ignores the reference to my breasts. "What, you don't want to show off your latest stunt for our dinner guests? What was it this time, Cay?" She doesn't wait for me to answer. "You tell Axel that if he brings you home in a casket, he'll be next. I'll see to that myself."

I wave my hand in front of my arm, trying to dry it off. "Axel wasn't even with me. Why do you blame him for everything?"

"Maybe because you didn't do any of this crap before you started dating him." This is true. And Axel was with me the first time I train dodged, but truthfully, I think it freaked him out. He didn't want to do it again, saying the train could jump the tracks if the engineer tried to slam on the brakes. Now train dodging is a solo activity.

Still, I'll give Axel credit for awakening this idea that I can look Death in the face and *defy* her. That I can take control of my family's curse. That it doesn't have to define me, that I can define it. That kind of power is addictive. Not to mention an ass-kicking adrenaline high.

Saffron disappears for a moment and returns to throw a dark stretchy top at me. "This argument is not over. Just cover yourself up and stop flaunting your assets."

I catch it, along with a glimpse of myself in the mirror. I can't take all the credit. I *am* wearing my favorite bra.

"You're the best—I don't deserve you."

She must agree, because she wears her revulsion openly. I decide it's not a good look for her.

* * *

Aunt Tee is chasing the Minions—aka my four-year-old cousins—in circles, trying to pin their hair up with bows. She's apparently forgotten the divide-and-conquer rule of wrangling the twins.

I grab Missy's arm as she squirrels past. "Hold up, Buttercup." I kneel down next to her and swivel her shoulders so that she faces me.

"My name's not Buttercup," she says, in that giggling you're-so-silly kind of way.

"I've received orders from your fairy godmother," I whisper in her ear. Tee has captured Maggie by the sofa and is attempting to insert a barrette-bow.

Missy's eyes widen and sparkle. She loves to pretend. "What did she say?" She's trying to whisper but she doesn't quite have the hang of it. Everyone in the room can hear.

"She asked me to decorate your hair for our royal celebration."

"Does she have a treat for me?" Missy knows how to work it, and I can't help but love her for that. She touches her nose to mine, so close that her eyes congeal into one, the optical equivalent of a unibrow. I suspect my Minion cyclops may have been sampling the frosting on tonight's cake. The sugary sweetness to her breath and her purple tongue betray her.

"Hmm . . . let me confer with Miss Fairy Rosetta." I stand on the arm of the couch and pretend to talk to an invisible fairy. "Rosetta's an extraordinarily tall fairy," I explain to Missy. Pretending to listen, I nod at the air. Then I hop down and whisper in Missy's ear. "Bubble gum. That's all she can manage on this short notice."

Missy wraps her sweaty arms around my waist and poses long enough for me to pin her long hair back. Ever the opportunist, she swivels around and holds out her expectant hand. I dig into my pocket for a piece of gum. Luckily, four-year-olds don't mind slightly warm, slightly squashed bubble gum. She grabs it and races over to Maggie to share. The way the Minions love each other melts even my jaded heart.

Tee mouths "thank you" to me. I nod in return. Here's the thing: I sort of owe her. Tee inherited Saff and me when she was about my age, so we're responsible for hijacking her life. These days we do our best to pay her back.

The doorbell rings, and Tee runs to answer it. A moment later I hear Nonna's voice, filled with her usual gusto: "Isn't this a gorgeous night? Just the perfect way to end the week!"

Nonna and Papa Channels are Uncle Luke's parents. Saff and I call them "the Chowders" because when we were little, we kept confusing their name with the soups Nonna brought to pretty much every kind of gathering. They show up for dinner about once a month, though I swear they were just here last Friday.

Partly to avoid Nonna, who's sweet but kind of a *lot*, I head to the kitchen and start chopping bell peppers for Luke's famous chili. Saff's already hard at work at the chopping board, mutilating vegetables with precision.

"I feel sorry for that carrot." I pause my own chopping and honor the vegetable with a moment of silence.

"Yeah, I'm channeling my anger. I'm pretending this is your face." Saff's sarcasm shows she's on the way to forgiving me. She can never stay genuinely mad for long, no matter how hard she tries.

While I'm constructing the perfect sassy yet endearing response, Nonna interrupts me with a perfumed hug from behind. "Cayenne! More beautiful every day."

I stiffen a little. I'm never sure what to say to Nonna. I get the distinct impression that the woman feels sorry for me, since I have no grandparents of my own. It's always made me feel a little awkward.

Luke raises his left eyebrow, as if to say "be polite." I attempt to raise my brow right back, but I'm pretty sure both go up, like always, because Luke's smile breaks through his goatee. I don't mind Luke. Mostly. He's got rules coming out his ears, but he loves Aunt Tee and he always makes Saff and me feel like we're part of his family. He's got to get credit for that. Plus the man makes a mean veggie chili.

I set down the knife and turn to greet Nonna and her entourage. Nonna, Papa, and Ryan Channels all hover in our kitchen. Papa holds a huge loaf of garlic bread, and Ryan carries a fruit platter. This crew comes to every celebration, sporting event, and school function, no matter how small. I wouldn't mind leaving them out of some of our gatherings, but Luke's all about Family with a capital "F," and Tee's all about Luke, so there you go.

Luke's older brother, who we affectionately (behind his back) call "Ryan-the-Reject," is permanently attached to the Chowders. Never cut that cord, apparently. A couple of times Luke and Tee heard Saff and me joking about Ryan-the-Reject, and they got *so* mad. I know it's harsh to call him a loser, but the dude's like forty-three—he lives with his parents, is a professional house sitter, and practically bathes in cologne. His nose is crooked from a bad break years ago. I suspect he had way too much fun in his youth, and he's paying for it now.

We all eat outside, at the table in the backyard, since Southern California is having an extra-mild February. I help the Minions fashion "magic wands" out of straws and show them how to cast secret spells on all their family members, mostly so that I have an excuse to avoid interacting with the adults. Luke can talk about his property management job for hours straight, with his parents hanging on his every word, because the only other excitement in their lives involves Ryan's recent expansion of his housesitting package to include window washing and pet grooming.

I promise myself that even though I've officially been an adult for six months, I'll never be as boring as the rest of them.

After our food settles and we've cast way too many spells involving jellybean rainstorms, Tee sends Ryan to retrieve the purple-frosting-slathered Bundt cake for dessert.

My scraped-up arms ache. I ingest a slice of cake before slipping off to apply some more antiseptic. On my way to the bathroom I spy an envelope propped up on the kitchen counter addressed to Saff and me. How did I miss that?

I don't recognize the handwriting. *Hmm. An early Valentine's Day card?*

I gently tease open the envelope flap and pull out a simple card. It's white, with silvery cursive letters across the front. *A present for you both . . .*

Dearest girls,

Today I wrap a gift I will never see you open. I have asked my best friend, Alicia, to hold this present until the time is right. Go to Alicia's house to open it as soon as possible. I hope you enjoy this gift as much as I've enjoyed preparing it for you.

Sending a million hugs and kisses,
Mom

My hands are shaking. That thick slice of Bundt cake climbs halfway back up my throat and sits there in a hard lump.

My mother has been dead for fourteen years.

Chapter 3

"I'm still in shock." Saffron slips her flip flops off the moment she slides into Gertrude, my ancient Honda Civic.

"Oh, come on. You know dead moms leave love notes all the time. It's a thing." I can't hold back the sarcasm. The Chowders left an hour ago, but the hard cake-lump is still wedged in my throat. I learned how to swallow sadness a long time ago, only somehow it always gets stuck in my throat. At least this time it tastes like confectioner's sugar.

I briefly considered crumpling up the note and pretending I never saw it. But my mother had once touched that paper, so I couldn't just throw it away. When I went back to the patio, Tee saw what I was holding and immediately launched into an explanation.

"I was going to give that card to you girls tonight—your mom's birthday seemed like a good time for it . . ."

And that's when I remembered: it's February 2. Mom's birthday.

The Chowders didn't stay long after that. Once we'd weathered their goodbye hugs, Tee promised to give Saff and me some space to process Mom's message.

I know I'm supposed to be touched, but honestly, I feel something more complicated. A heavy dread has settled into my chest and is turning everything below it into concrete. Trying my best to shake it off, I turn the key in the ignition and coax Gertrude out of the driveway.

"Put your seat belt on, will you?" Saff snaps, smoothing her hair back into a ponytail. "That warning light is there for a reason."

Ugh. I hate the way seat belts restrict my movement. "Thank you, *Mother*."

Annnnnd silence. Because those words sting both of us. Saffron pulls the edges of her sleeves over her wrist and onto her hands, like she's cold.

I feel instantly regretful. "Sorry. That wasn't cool."

Saffron looks out the window in silence, but after a moment she twists toward me. "If you don't snap your seat belt soon," she says, her voice tight, "I'm going to get out at the next stoplight and walk home. Want to do this on your own?"

"Fine, fine," I sigh as I click the belt. But in retaliation I turn up the music so loud that I can feel the bass vibrating against the steering wheel.

We drive past the cookie-cutter houses, past the outlet mall, and out toward the farmlands. I pull onto a long dirt driveway that lies behind the strawberry fields. Alicia, Mark, and their son Micah live on a legit farm, complete with a cow and chickens. It's not big enough to sell produce to local vendors, but they mostly live off what they grow.

"We haven't been here since that time we brought the Minions over to milk the cow. Was that almost a year ago?" I say.

"Something like that," Saff says tersely, clearly still irritated at me.

I flip open the vanity mirror and check myself out. I lined my eyes at home, but my lip gloss deserves a second coat. I apply and press my smackers together for maximum coverage.

"Saff—you want some lip gloss?"

"My lips are just fine without the gloss, thank you."

I'm guessing all sisters compare. And if I'm comparing, Saffy is prettier and more petite, with these ginormous doe-eyes, but she has zero fashion sense. My face is plain, but mascara and lipstick do wonders, and I know how to cinch, layer, and accessorize to make the most of what I've got. Whenever I try to convince Saff to fix herself up, she shoots me down, saying there's a whole beauty industry getting rich off women's insecurities and she refuses to be a part of it. Sounds like a convenient excuse to be lazy, but whatever.

We climb out of the car, dust swirling around our feet. I'm betting Saff is regretting her choice of flip flops.

"Truce?" I hold out my hand like she's a little kid. "Can we at least pretend to like each other in front of Alicia?"

"Deal." She accepts my hand, and we walk up to ring the doorbell.

The front door swings open. "Girls!" Alicia spreads open her arms and gathers us both in, doing the double hug and forcing the two of us closer than we want to be. There's a softness in Alicia's hug that feels motherly. I smell Saffron's shampoo, and the oil paints staining Alicia's shirt. "It feels like it's been forever since I've seen you two."

Alicia Johnson was my mother's best friend. They survived middle and high school together, and then attended the same university. They even got pregnant within a few months of each other. After Mom died, Alicia offered to take us in, since she was settled and equipped to raise us. But Aunt Tee said that she could do it, that she *wanted* to do it, even though she was only nineteen at the time and was working at FroYo Heaven for minimum wage. (I blame this for my yogurt addiction.) I'm not sure if she ever regretted putting her life on hold for us, but I do remember being dropped off with Alicia so that Tee could go off on days-long road trips with friends. That was before Luke, though. He settled Tee down for sure, and by the time they got married she was working part-time as a case manager for a non-profit hospice. I don't know how she does it, working with dying people and their families all the time, but she says giving back is healing for her.

So it all worked out for us, stability-wise. Now we only visit Alicia once or twice a year. This is sort of silly; she lives one town over. It's a ten-minute drive, max. Plus she knows more about Mom's life than pretty much anyone else. Mom was twelve years older than Aunt Tee, so she was out of the house and off to college by the time Tee was six. Meaning Tee doesn't have any juicy stories from Mom's past. Or if she does, she doesn't tell.

I used to love hearing Alicia's stories about Mom, but I sort of lost interest by the time I was in fifth or sixth grade. That was then, this is now. Mom is not a part of our "now."

Which is why coming here feels stupid—what's the point? No gift will make her any less dead.

Alicia ushers us both inside. She's an intriguing mix of chic and hick. Her hair is all short and stylish, complimented by large hoop earrings, and she's in killer shape from all that farm upkeep, *but* she dresses like a farmer, wears zero makeup, and is pretty much always covered in paint.

We step through the front door. "Don't mind the mess," Alicia says, not as apologetically as she should. Her mess requires more than an apology. Like financial compensation. Her mess could scar a person for life. "Or the smell," she adds as we edge down the hallway, past piles of dusty books and magazines.

"Bet you've missed the aroma of fertilizer and oil paints," says Micah, who's standing behind the kitchen counter, dicing pineapple. He's wearing a snug "Mesa Medical Center Volunteer" T-shirt. His arms have firmed up, probably from all the yard work. His hair is just like when we were kids—no gel, just loose bouncy curls. "I keep telling Mom all these fumes are to blame for my calculus grade. They're killing off my brain cells."

"Ooh, okay, I just won't breathe while I'm here." I cover my mouth. "I need all my brain cells. Saffy, you can spare a few, so go on, breathe deep."

"For the record," Alicia says, "he only got one B in calculus, the rest are As. We should all be so lucky." Micah is a bona fide dork, but I've known him since his birth, so I put up with him.

Micah shrugs and smiles in a self-conscious way. He has what I like to call deep-dish dimples. If it's a small smile of mild amusement, they're subtle. But if he flashes an all-out grin, not holding back at all, his dimples indent like ditches. In fourth grade, I fit a mini M&M in each one, and he walked around with green candies stuck in his cheeks, both of us cracking up so hard I wet my pants.

"Happy belated birthday, Micah. It was a few weeks ago, right?" I rest my arms on the counter, which is surprisingly free of clutter.

"Yep." Micah slides the pineapple chunks into a bowl. "I can now vote, get a tattoo, and be drafted into the army. Yippee."

This reminds me of the sticker tattoos we used to apply to our arms, and that time I stuck one to his forehead while he slept. The heaviness in my chest lifts. "That's how I feel too." I've been eighteen for six months, but honestly nothing has changed. "Big deal, right? Only it's nice that no one can tell us what to do anymore."

Alicia chuckles and says pointedly, "Micah—don't forget to slice the strawberries."

Micah pauses, knife still poised in midair. "Well," he says, looking a little sheepish, "I do still live in her house."

"Wuss," I mouth, so Alicia won't hear.

Alicia opens a cupboard, giving me a glimpse of mismatched glasses. Luke wouldn't be able to survive in the disarray of this house for ten minutes. "Do you girls want something to drink? When Micah's done chopping up the fruit, we can eat it on the back porch."

"Just water's great, thanks." Saffron scoots out a stool and sits down. I can tell by the way Saff is fidgeting that she's eager to get to the gift. I'm just as eager to avoid it.

We chat as we slice, catching up. Micah's already been accepted to Cal (he applied early action), although he's still hoping for some scholarship or grant money. He's been volunteering at the medical clinic two nights a week. His dad is still flying airplanes out of LAX. I see the look that passes between Alicia and Micah and I figure it's related to his dad's gambling. Micah and I used to hide in the coat closet and listen to his parents argue about it.

"What're your top three choices?" Micah asks.

"For what? Dinner?" I joke, dodging the question. "Pizza, tacos or chow mein." They don't need to know that I accidentally-on-purpose missed the application deadline for the UC and Cal State schools, which means college may not be in the cards for me. Both Micah and Alicia could tell you that I started reading at age three, and that I could add two-digit numbers in my head by age five. But they'd also tell you that I've always been pretty immature. That's why I got "the gift of an extra year" and started kindergarten when I'd just turned six. (Saff has never been immature, but Tee didn't want us in the same grade, so she got an extra year "to grow" too.) You'd think the extra lead time would've put me ahead of the curve, but college applications take planning, forethought, and effort—not my favorite activities.

I keep rambling. "Axel and I just hit our year anniversary. And Saff is still with Fletch." I hot potato the conversation over to Saffron. She's a tortoise. Once the questions shift to her, she sinks into her shell. She and her boyfriend are both that way. He always looks like he's thinking of a joke but he's too shy to say it out loud. Even though I give Saff a hard time about Fletcher, secretly I'm glad she's with him. Because I'll have to kill any asshole who ever hurts her, and Fletcher being her boyfriend significantly reduces the chances I'll be charged with manslaughter.

We pause, realizing all the fruit has been sliced and we've run out of small talk. Alicia's eyes soften. "I've missed you girls. No excuse for that. We've got to make an effort to catch up more often." I notice that the light lines around her mouth have deepened, and I wonder what my mother would look like if she was alive today. "Come, let's go on out to the back porch. I have something for you."

"How cloak-and-dagger." I pick up the fruit bowl and consider pelting Micah with a couple of strawberries for fun, but I decide it's better just to get this gift thing over with.

Alicia leads us to the screened porch. She brings in a red-wrapped package, about the size of a box of chocolate.

A healthy dose of humor smooths out most uncomfortableness, so when in doubt, I always fall back on a good joke. "Oh yay, fourteen-year-old chocolate," I say. "Saff, I volunteer you to taste each piece for me. Mold is protein."

"Cayenne." Saff's voice sounds tight, warning me.

"Okay, okay. Maybe it's fiber."

Micah chuckles and clears a spot for Saffron and me, which really amounts to shoving a bunch of decorative pillows onto the floor. I sink down on the couch, which gives under my weight. "Remember watching Disney movies out here?" I ask Micah, picturing us as toddlers, climbing all over each other. "Good times."

Alicia hands me the package and puts her hand on my shoulder.

I hold the gift gingerly. I guess I feel a little creeped out. My mom touched this before she died. The congealed cake in my throat threatens to come back up.

I force myself to unfold the handwritten note on top. *For Cayenne and Saffron, the spice in my life. I love you both forever.* The wrapping paper has softened over the years, and it peels away with the lightest scrape of a fingernail. I open the box. No moldy chocolates, thank god. Inside is a journal.

"Okay, girls." Suddenly Alicia's all business. "You're also going to need this." She sets a small laptop on the coffee table. "You'll open a desktop folder titled 'For Cayenne and Saffron.' Your mom requested that you begin here on this porch, because this is where you spent most of her last days together."

She steps back, looking almost relieved. Like her job is done. "Micah and I will give you some privacy. You can have as long as you like. And you can come back any time you want to access the files on our laptop again."

"You don't have to go." The cake crawls farther up into my throat and I feel a little desperate for them to stay, so that I can keep joking around and not have to feel anything.

"You need privacy." Alicia's voice turns firm, and for a moment I feel like she's scolding me. "Remember, girls, your mom loved you very much. This may not be exactly how you wanted to spend the day, but doing this is a gift to your mother."

Micah lingers for a moment before he turns and follows Alicia back inside.

"I don't even remember Mom," Saff says softly. "When I think of a parent, I think of Aunt Tina."

"Look, we don't need this kind of closure. Reading her journal would be like going backwards." I stand up, only to sit back down. "Not that I'm over her death, because I could never be over it, but I've moved past it."

"Alicia's right though. This is not just for *us*," Saff points out. "It's also for *her*. I think we have to do it."

"I hate it when you're reasonable. Which is, like, always," I say with a dramatic sigh. The good news is that the hard cake lump is no longer stuck in my throat. The bad news is that it's working itself upward. I glance around for a trash can in case I need to puke.

This suddenly strikes me as ridiculous. What, I can dodge a freaking locomotive, but I can't tolerate thinking about my own mother? I'm an expert at trash compacting all of those icky emotions. Now there's a tiny square of squashed reality that lies in the center of my gut. I despise crying. And puking. Or anything else coming out of my face—snot isn't all that pleasant either. So . . . the solution is simple. *I won't*. Mind over matter.

I swallow that cake pellet down as far as it'll go and pick up the journal. "All right. Let's do this."

Chapter 4

When I open the journal, a note on flowery paper falls out. The handwriting looks different from the handwriting on the other note. I realize that Mom may have had help writing, depending on how sick she was at the time. I take a deep breath and read.

To my sweet and spicy Cayenne and Saffron,

I have a thousand things I want to say to you both, but I know you won't remember. You're too little. So I'm recording them here in this diary and on some videos.

Why now, you ask? Because you're both about to launch into the world. I've asked your Aunt Tina and Alicia to make sure you get this gift during your last semester together before Cayenne goes off to college. I want you to get them when you're old enough to understand, and I want you to experience this together. It's your shared history.

Before you begin, here are my three rules. You

must follow them. Why? Because I'm your mom, that's why. (I love saying that.)
   Watch and read every entry together.
   Play the game. It'll be fun.
   Retain a sense of humor at all costs.
   For your next step, play Video #1.

Saff and I sit in silence.

Finally I say, "I guess she'd be disappointed that I missed the college application deadlines." I reach for a smudged unicorn figurine on the coffee table and turn it over in my hands.

"Yeah, and maybe that you've taken the easiest course load possible."

"Phsh." I poke my finger with the unicorn horn. "I'm developing my creative side." Yoga, photography and ceramics probably wouldn't have gotten me into Cal, but I refuse to be embarrassed by a dead woman's hypothetical disapproval.

Saff takes the unicorn out of my hand and gives me a pointed look.

I start up the laptop and easily find the folder titled "For Cayenne and Saffron." Inside there are six video files.

Deep breath. I open the first one and hit play. An image of my mother, Jenny Silk, materializes. The trash compactor in my gut squeezes.

Mom sits on the couch, a baseball cap covering her head. I remember her like this—fragile-thin, bald as an egg, clothes that swim on her. All the photos we have around Tee's house of her are before this time, before she got sick, back when she had hair so long that I could've wrapped it around myself. She adjusts the computer screen so she can get herself at a more flattering angle and clears her throat.

"Hey there, sweets! You ready to play? It's going to be fun, I promise." She pauses, smiling at the screen. Seeing the way her smile starts with her eyes crinkling, and then the twitching of the corners of her mouth, instantly brings back tickle attacks and pillow fights, Easter egg hunts and swimming sessions in the community pool. Saffron grabs my arm. I place my hand on Saff's like I'm comforting her, but in truth, I just want to hold her there.

"Okay, first off, let me prep you. I'll be filming videos for your clues. Clues to what, you might ask. And I'd say, clues to all sorts of things. Who you are, who I am, the gifts I'm about to bestow—be patient and I'll surprise you. I know I'm beautiful"—she makes a model pose with her hand behind her head—*"but don't worry, I won't make myself center screen each time."*

"That's totally something I'd say," I say, and my gut squeezes again.

"I know," Saff whispers. "Now I know where you get it. You're a thousand times more irritating though."

"I'll take that as a compliment."

Mom picks up the laptop or the camera—whatever's filming her—and leans it to the right, so the image shifts. On the couch beside her, snuggled in a patchwork blanket, are three-year-old Saff and four-year-old me, totally asleep. Saff has one thumb in her mouth, and the other wrapped around my shoulders. I rest my head on hers, my hair spilling onto her cheeks.

"Aren't you adorable?" Mom shifts the screen back. *"I could watch you sleep for hours. In fact, I was. Only then I got this brilliant idea to create a game for you. So you can remember how fun I am. And so I can tell you all the things you're too young to understand now. I mean, it would be wildly inappropriate for me to give you dating advice at this age. But who will tell you those things if I don't?*

I can't rely on Tina—her high school boyfriend sure isn't a winner." Mom leans toward the screen and whispers, *"Wait! If Tee's still with Brett when you're watching this, don't tell her I said that. If she dumped him years ago, go right ahead."*

I can't help but chuckle. I remember Brett. He had a huge head. I think I called him SpongeBob.

"Making this game is the first thing I've been excited about since my last doctor appointment, and the best part is imagining how much fun you'll have with it."

Saffron unlinks her arm from mine and reaches for a tissue from the box on the table. She offers me one, but I've been swallowing and compacting so diligently that I don't need it. Although I do have a homicidal urge to squash this fly that buzzes in, circling the bowl of fruit like a helicopter trying to land. For all that chopping work Micah put in, we haven't touched the fruit. Apparently, the fly intends to have its share.

"Here's how the game works. There will be seven gifts—one in each video. Why seven? Because if I add up your ages, I've had seven amazing years with you."

"Wait." Saff freezes, her tissue unused. "There are only six videos in the folder on the laptop. Why is she saying seven?"

"Who knows?" Maybe it's that fly buzzing around my head, but I'm irritable. "It's not like we can ask her."

"Sometimes I'll make you work hard to figure out the gift, sometimes I'll make it easy on you. Your first one was just handed to you. It's the journal that was in this package. I've been writing in it since I got diagnosed. I'm leaving blank pages in between my entries so that you can write back to me if you choose."

I flip through the journal. She'd written on every other page.

"My entries will focus on the things I want to tell you that I didn't get a chance to. The advice you never got to ignore, my thoughts on

how to live in this crazy world, random facts about me that you probably don't know . . ."

"Do you think she'll tell us who our fathers are?" I murmur. Neither of our birth certificates list a father's name, and Saff and I are so different, I doubt we have the same dad. "If she knows who they are, that is."

"I don't know if I can handle this," Saffron whispers, her lower lip quivering.

"We don't have to do it," I whisper back. "It's not like she'd ever know."

"Why are we whispering?" Saffron asks.

We both stare at the image of our mother on our screen. Because as impossible as it sounds, it feels like she's in the room with us, like she can hear what we're saying.

"There's a pretty good chance at least one of you is rolling your eyes just about now. But here's the thing. You literally cannot argue with me. I'm dead, you're alive, there's just no opportunity for negotiation. I know you'll play this game and I know you'll follow these guidelines, because this is all you have left of me."

"She's right," Saffron says, dabbing at her eyes. "We have to."

"We don't *have* to do anything." A spark of defiance ignites in my gut. How dare she barge into our lives and guilt trip us? I stare at the fly, which has now landed on a piece of pineapple and appears to be preening itself.

"We do. We have to." Saff is almost pleading.

"Okay. That sounded sad. No more of that! I promise this will be fun. It's way too shitty that I'm leaving you so soon, but I'm past cursing at the sky and beating the walls. It is what it is. There's nothing I can do about it. And now, all these years later, hopefully you've accepted it too."

"I *had* accepted it," I snap at the laptop. "Three hours ago

I was just fine." Of course, five hours ago I was dodging Betty-the-locomotive, but that's beside the point.

Saffron elbows me sharply. "Shhhh."

"What? It's not like she can hear me."

The fly must have had its fill of pineapple because it flies around in a circle again and dives back in toward a strawberry.

"Of course I know a sense of loss will stay with you forever— but hopefully the wound isn't raw anymore. Hopefully it's all in perspective. With this game . . . I want you to celebrate me. And more important, I want you to celebrate yourselves. You are the only living part of me left on this earth. You must enjoy it. That is an order!"

The fly grooms itself on the strawberry, and I swear it turns to look at me.

The fly must die. I slip off my shoe and hold it at the ready.

"And with that, here are your instructions. Over the next week, start reading the diary I've left you. You can write back to me if you want. Give yourself a week or two to let this all sink in. Then you can move on to video number two." Mom brings her hands to her lips and kisses them with a big smacking sound that I remember instantly. Mom always kissed with a juicy noise. *"I love you two so much."*

I smash my shoe into the strawberry, knocking the fruit bowl off the table. Pieces of fruit roll around the floor. The unsuspecting fly is flattened. His death is surprisingly satisfying.

On the screen, there's movement from behind Mom's body. A sleepy four-year-old me sits up, confused.

"Who are you talking to, Mama?" four-year-old me mumbles.

"Somebody very special."

Mom blows another kiss at the camera . . . and the image freezes.

"Well holy shit." Seeing my mini self, sweet and innocent,

deflates me. I stare at the fly smushed onto the table amidst pulverized strawberry and feel suddenly sorry.

"Tell me about it." Saff focuses on the frozen image of Mom.

I focus on the mess I can manage. The Mom stuff is way too complicated. "We're not going to be able to find all the pieces of fruit. A strawberry is going to get all rotten in the corner and no one will know it's there until they have an ant infestation."

I kneel down on the rug, which sort of bristles into my knees, as though many a drink has been spilled right there, then wiped up but not properly cleaned. I start crawling around on my hands and knees, collecting slimy bits of strawberries in my hands.

Saff touches my shoulder. "Cayenne, be serious for a minute."

"I am being serious. We *seriously* can't offend our hosts." The odor of fertilizer and oil paints is suffocating, like a heavy blanket over my head. "Listen. Let's clean up this fruit and get out of here. I say we take the diary with us and we can read it . . . or not. We have some time until we have to decide whether to watch the next video."

"What if one of us wants to and the other doesn't?" A red tint crawls over the tip of Saff's nose, something that always happens when she gets teary.

"No one can make us," I point out, piling all the dirty fruit on a paper plate and covering it with a napkin. What I really mean is no one can make *me*.

"Yeah but she said we have to do it together."

"She won't know." I shut down the laptop. "I'm done. I need to leave."

Chapter 5

My bare feet connect with the dirt by the shore. I step gingerly, anticipating a sharp rock underfoot. With the sun sinking in the sky, I can scarcely see my toes. Anticipation jacks my heart rate up a few beats. With Axel's fingers intertwined with mine, the thumping of my heart feels just right.

I texted him right after I dropped Saff off at home. She's staying in tonight, which is strangely comforting. I have no idea why I worry about her being out at night—maybe just because we don't have a mom to do that worrying, and the anxiety needs to land somewhere.

Me, on the other hand, I need a distraction. Preferably the Axel kind. Axel makes me feel important and exciting, so just being next to him is intoxicating. The wind whisks past, flipping my hair behind me and inviting a layer of goose bumps to bubble up along my arms.

I peek over the edge. The Bluffs are a series of high and treacherous cliffs that hang over the lake, accessible by a variety of trails. The smallest cliff, Baby Bluff, is twenty feet off the ground, and if you jump it'll make your skin sting and then go numb when you smack into the water. Mesa Ridge (middle cliff) and Pinnacle

Peak (largest cliff) have WARNING and DANGER signs plastered all over them. We don't know exactly how high they are, but based on their appearance we're thinking maybe forty and sixty. Axel and I aim to tackle them both eventually.

We're not the only ones. Each year people jump both. Mostly nothing bad happens. But every few years someone dies. They hit the water funny, or they're too drunk or high to swim, or they slam into a rock, and if they sink down far enough, they drown before someone can haul them out.

Axel and I do not have a death wish. We're shooting for the ultimate adrenaline high. We've been brainstorming a bucket list ever since we met. We've already completed two-thirds of it. This is what we've got left:

Baby Bluff—in the dark
Mesa Ridge—in daylight
Mesa Ridge—in the dark
Pinnacle Peak—in daylight
Train Dodging (Axel crossed this one off his list after the first try)
Car racing
Skydiving (expensive)
Parasailing (expensive)

Like I said, no death wish. That's why we aren't doing Pinnacle Peak in pitch black. The purpose is to defy Death, to take control of that lurking monster and harness it.

Axel's dad overdosed when he was a toddler, so he's grown up without a parent too. We totally get the fragility of life. We want to *live*. Like really live. We want to experience everything, be spontaneous, and create memories that stay palpable. We calculate the risks. We push ourselves just far enough, but not too far. Axel insists we steer clear of drugs and even alcohol. We always go for the natural high. The one thing that scares Axel is morphing into an addict like his dad. He says he's "genetically loaded" and doesn't want to play those odds.

Axel's mature in ways most guys our age aren't—just the fact that he stays sober speaks to that. Plus, he got emancipated last year and lives on his own with a roommate. He doesn't want to be dependent on anyone else. "People let you down," he says. I plan to be the first person to never let him down. The first person he can allow himself to be *inter*dependent with.

"You ready?" He turns to face me, inches from the edge of Baby Bluff. The darkening sky sharpens his features—his ski-jump nose, his eyes that are such a dark brown they're nearly black, and those chapped lips I always want pressed to mine.

"I'm ready." Maybe it's the anticipatory adrenaline kicking in, but I can hardly keep from wrapping my arms around him. "Only I can still see you. It's not dark enough yet."

"Guess we'll have to stall." He pulls me toward him and those chapped lips are all mine.

I close my eyes and lose myself. As if all the cells in my being consolidate for one purpose, to meld with his. That's why I love him so much. I don't have to think when I'm around him. Same with this jump. We did all our thinking ahead of time. Tonight, all I have to do is propel my body off that cliff. The rest will be instinct. Survival. There'll be no space to think about my dead mom trying to reconnect.

By the time Axel pulls away from me, the sun has retreated further, leaving just the slightest sliver against the hills, like the last bite of an over-easy egg. "Remember to jump *out*," he warns. He steps back, leaping out, over . . . down.

My vision hasn't adjusted to the dimmer light yet. I hear

the faint splash of his body connecting with the water. I hold my breath listening, listening, for the sounds of him surging back up through the water for a deep breath, the sounds of his arms connecting with the water to move him back to shore.

I wait forever. The three or four seconds stretch themselves like taffy. I hear the sounds of night in the mountains—bugs singing, water lapping, wind rustling the leaves, the faraway howl of a coyote . . . I can almost hear my own heart, probably because it's beating so hard it rattles my ribcage. A tiny thread of worry catches like a hangnail on loose fabric.

Until finally . . . "Wahoo!" This comes out almost like a battle cry, and I nearly jump out of my skin. In fact, I nearly fall off the cliff. I've been standing so close that any movement could've sent me tumbling.

I imagine Axel's arms slicing the water as he climbs out, heaves himself onto the bank, probably grabs hold of some rocks for leverage. "Your turn. It's a killer high!"

Don't-think-don't-think-don't-think-don't-think—I'm airborne.

Control and surrender swirl together as I hang in the air, as my stomach drops out beneath me then floats up above me, as my heart puts the brakes on, as I'm enveloped by that feeling of falling-falling-falling.

I plunge deep. Deeper, deeper, deeper, the coldness of the water shocking me.

My heart gets its act together, and I slowly remember to move my arms and legs, to swim up. The lack of light means I have no sense of how far away the surface is. I haven't timed my breath right—wasn't able to get enough oxygen before I went under—so my lungs burn. Aching-aching-swelling . . . until my head breaks the surface. I waste precious seconds realizing I can now breathe, before I actually inhale.

Breathe.

Breathe.

Breathe.

The world rushes in along with a surge of adrenaline, setting my body on fire. Axel wasn't kidding. Because the falling takes longer than the jump from the train, this high is more intense. I whoop in my head long before I can muster the lung power to make any actual noise.

Axel's cheering on my right, and I swim in that direction, powering through the water as easily as if it's air. When I bump into a rock I grab hold of a ledge to haul myself out. I lie on my side, shaking, all my muscles vibrating.

"What'd I tell you?" Axel asks from above.

I have no words.

He reaches down to help me up, then pulls me to his chest and covers my mouth with his. I haven't regained enough breath for a long kiss, but it doesn't matter. No kiss could feel as good as my body feels right now, as if every cell has downed a triple shot of espresso.

"I love you," he whispers in my ear, and his breath against my skin multiplies my goose bumps to the thousands. I love him back, more than I could ever put into words.

I tighten my arms around his neck and wind my wet legs around his waist, so that he stands holding me in his arms. We drip lake water from our hair and our ears and our noses. I can feel his muscles tighten as he moves, and the firmness of his body makes me feel safe.

He walks with me in his arms for a full minute before he lowers me to the ground. "This way," he says, lacing his fingers in mine and pulling me along.

"How do you know you're going the right way?"

"The location of the moon. Just trust me."

"I do. I trust you with my life," I say, and I mean it. Axel is the only one I can trust in this way. He can take me right to the edge of the world and look over it with me. He can tempt fate and deny her.

We don't have much trouble finding the truck—named Churro, at my suggestion, after Axel's favorite dessert. Axel left the keys hidden in some bushes nearby. He reaches behind the seats and brings out two plush towels. I wrap myself in one, climb into the truck bed, and pull my dry sweatshirt and pants out of my duffel bag.

I slip off my suit and slide into my sweats, grateful for the darkness. I know it's ridiculous to be shy in front of Axel, but I can never seem to shake that middle school self-consciousness that took hold before I grew breasts. Mine came in later than most—I truly didn't need a bra until eighth grade (although of course I wore one anyway), and I remember how I tried to hide myself behind my locker door when I had to change for PE. Now of course, there's no doubt I have boobs. I'm petite, so even though my breasts are average sized, by some optical illusion they appear large on my frame.

Axel's great for my self-confidence. Still, I like the lights off when I change in front of him. He prefers the lights on, for obvious reasons.

Axel groans when he grabs me. "Sweats? Seriously? Way to kill my rush."

"Oh, please," I scold him . . . nicely. "You can't even see me, and I knew it would be cold out here. You'll have to find a way to warm me up if you want something different."

He chuckles, and the laughter rumbles deep in his chest. "Oh, I think I can manage that." I think he can, too.

Chapter 6

Saff is waiting up for me on the couch, sipping tea. Her hair is pulled into a tight ponytail, and I wonder if that gives her a headache. I bet her chill quotient would multiply if she could just let her hair down now and then. "Where have you been? I want to read the journal. And I know we have to do it together."

I've seriously forgotten about the journal. The jump from the Bluffs wiped my memory clean. And now I feel detached from it, almost, like it's a balloon floating away from me and I don't care enough to grab it. I sit down next to Saff on the couch, folding one leg in so I can face her. "It's okay, Saff. Go ahead and read on your own."

"But she said—"

"Listen." I'm tempted to reach around her head and loosen her hair tie. "Mom had all kinds of ideas about what she wanted, but she hasn't been around for fourteen years. The world is a different place. We're different people. She wrote that journal and filmed the videos because *she* needed to do it. And it's fine if *you* need to read it." I leave her hair alone but pat her leg. "But I don't. I'm at peace with my life. I don't need to read her journal to feel complete."

A flash of anger strikes me. I could've used this from Mom in the third grade, the year Tee married Luke, the year I felt displaced. Back when I fantasized about my father riding in on a pony or a motorcycle and whisking me off to a better life. But not now. I'm settled now. "Listen. I'll take the blame for bowing out. You're off the hook."

Saff does not appear convinced.

I want to smooth things out for her, so I offer her a kind lie. "Would it make you feel better if I say that maybe I'll read some tomorrow?"

"It would if I believed you." Saff has the most readable face ever. She could never get away with a fib. It's her eyes. They're a crystal ball into her soul. And right now, they're pools of sadness. A deep sadness that makes me want to carry her around in my arms, something I did for months after Mom died. Saff stopped talking for a while and I pretended she was my own baby. I guess we both needed that connection back then.

I soften my voice and do my best to soften my expression too. "I promise I'll watch the videos with you. Go ahead and read on your own. Okay?"

I leave Saff on the couch, looking like she's trying to give herself permission to break a rule. We've always been different that way. As a kid, I just snagged an extra cookie or a dropped dollar, figuring someone would stop me if it wasn't okay. Saff, on the other hand, waited for permission, and if it never came, she missed out. Sometimes I wonder how we're even sisters.

* * *

I name a lot of things. My car Gertrude for instance. Axel's car, Churro. Betty, the latest train I dodged. So naming Death

Lorelei seems appropriate. Lorelei existed in my dreamstate long before I had a name for her. I realize this makes me sound a tiny bit batty. But I do not hear voices. I'm not depressed or manic or anxious. The only things I can be accused of are being impulsive, the consumer of way too many horror movies, and possibly over-therapized by well-meaning shrinks. After Mom died, Tee signed Saff and me up for therapy, as if that would somehow ensure we'd wind up well-adjusted. I'm not sure it worked on me, but I loved the one-on-one attention—not to mention playing with the toys, sand trays, and art materials stocked in the office—so it wasn't a complete waste of time.

When I was in sixth grade, one therapist suggested I journal my dreams. The entries and the sketches that followed birthed Lorelei. I was knee-deep in a mythology phase and came across a mythological siren called the lorelei who lured sailors to their deaths.

Once my personal version of Death had a name, she became even more real to me. Not only did she appear in my dreams, but she began visiting me in that halfway spot between sleep and waking, a space-time reality called hypnagogia. (It exists. I looked it up to confirm my sanity.) Sometimes I linger there, wanting to hold on to her, to confront her or challenge her. Sometimes I wrench myself from sleep to escape her, even when it feels like my eyelids are weighted with lead x-ray blankets.

In my dreamstate, she's frightening. Bald and so skinny the blue veins pop through her temples, the skin curving tautly around her bones. And yet she's chic and seductive—like a model—wearing dangly earrings and loose flowing silks. There's something about her that seems birdlike, and I worry that someday she'll peck out my eyeballs. The edges of her essence blur, as if she can walk through walls and disintegrate.

During my waking hours, Lorelei exists on the perimeter of my awareness, and I mold her into someone I can master. In these moments, I am brave. I taunt her. I place my life in her hands, only to yank it away. Over and over. I imagine my conversations with her. How I am besting her. How I am keeping her at bay.

Lorelei. I've been thinking.

Great. Just what I was hoping for. Lorelei is always sarcastic.

You're wrong. In a game of cat and mouse, the mouse always wins. Defies all odds. That's the whole point.

Show me, she sneers.

I will. Truth is, there's a double game going on here, only Lorelei doesn't know it. I'm distracting her. If she's focused on me, then maybe she won't think about the other women burdened with the Silk curse. As long as she's chasing me, I'm keeping her away from Aunt Tee, from Saff, even from the Minions.

Once sleep sinks its claws into my mind, though, Lorelei has the upper hand, transforming into a cackling witch, a trickster and schemer. She slithers into my dreams, reminding me this night could be my last. She wants me. She hungers for me. The more I dodge her, the hungrier she becomes. Taunting me, reminding me that in the end everyone dies, so there's no escaping, only evading.

It is simply a matter of time.

Chapter 7

Wanna ditch third period? I hide in the dingy Mesa High bathroom to text Axel. We're not supposed to use our phones during class, a rule as useful and well-followed as the ones that forbid gum-chewing and wearing short-shorts. *My house is empty. Luke's working, the Minions are at school, and Tee has a doctor's appointment in LA.*

It takes Axel about five minutes to respond, during which time I read all the Sharpie on the restroom walls. I dig deep in my backpack to find my own Sharpie and scribble over the word "SLUT" under Kelly Stevens's name. Not that I even like the girl, I just hate that word—one thing Saff and I agree about. Seems like we ladies should team up and ban it from the English language.

I redo my screensaver to an adorable photo of the Minions building sandcastles at the beach. I'm just about to get hurt feelings when my phone buzzes. *Meet you in the parking lot after second. Love your Valentine's Day spirit.*

We can barely contain ourselves during the ride to the house. He drives, and I entertain him with my tongue. We kiss our way through the front door, and his hands slide under my shirt as we stumble through the living room, toward the bedrooms at the back of the house.

His hands are magic, awakening a throbbing in every cell they touch. They graze each rib, circle my belly button, and skate upward to unlatch my bra.

When we're making out, I typically take charge. I like to direct his hands and how far we go. But today there's something about the heat of his skin on mine, the roughness of his lips, and his tongue deep in my mouth, that makes me float, unable to direct anything. My mind is fully absorbed in the moment, incapable of rational thought. He slips off his own shirt and helps me remove mine.

I close my eyes and let go, trusting him to guide me, trying my best to reciprocate. He's so good at what he does that I can scarcely find the brain power to instruct my hands as to what to do. But perhaps they have a mind of their own, because they're certainly moving.

We tumble down onto the softness of a bed, and I fully relax, allowing myself to be carried away by the moment. This might be the first time I've fully released control, and I kind of like it. I breathe in the soft scent of lilac.

Wait.

My eyes fly open. We're in Saffron's room. She's a fiend for lilac candles, incense, and potpourri. I extricate myself from Axel's lips, or try to. "We're in my sister's room!"

Axel lifts his head. "Who cares?"

"Me." And most definitely my sister. Saff would be horrified if she knew we were making out on her bed. She'd probably assume we were having sex, which we are not, but she'd be grossed out nonetheless. Fletcher and Saff probably have to google how to kiss without tangling tongues. "This feels wrong."

"Wrong can be exciting, you know that." Axel's back to exploring my body, and there's no room for words.

The moment is ruined though. Saff's flowered wallpaper and packed bookshelf distract me. Plus I keep rolling onto something hard, probably a book, because Saffron literally sleeps with them.

Axel's working his way lower and lower, and now all I can do is think. Thoughts are running through my mind haphazardly. "Stay up here," I urge.

He obliges and comes back up to my ear. His breath is hot against my skin, his words sending electricity down to my core. "It's Valentine's Day," he reminds me. "We have the house to ourselves. This can be that special moment you've been waiting for."

I hate to turn him down, but there's something that blocks me. I can't quite explain it.

He sighs. "Cayenne. We've been together for over a year. I've never been with someone this long without moving forward."

"I must be pretty special then." I blow a kiss in the air. "Worth the wait."

"You are." He sweeps my hair away from my face, kisses my forehead, and rolls onto his back. "I don't want to pressure you, I really don't. But I can't help wanting more." This gives me the urge to apologize or explain it away, and I really don't know how. "Your body wants this," he informs me, running his fingers down the length of me. He's absolutely right, because my body instantly responds. "It's your head that's stopping you."

I nod. I can feel that physical want, almost an aching in my core, craving more. And a few moments ago, I would've let him do anything he wanted. I probably would've wanted it too. It *is* my mind that's stopping me.

"Is it me?" he asks the ceiling. I notice Saff still has glow-in-the-dark stars glued there. "Is there something wrong with me?"

"It's not you," I manage this, because it's not. And I don't want to hurt him.

"You cross every line there is." He rolls back over onto his side and props his head up with his hand. "Even something as insane as train dodging. *I* won't even do that. But *you* do. So this is hard for me to understand."

"I am a mystery, even to myself. That's why you love me." I stretch for some humor. Some way to diffuse this situation. Because if I break down and say "okay," then he *is* pressuring me. Then I'm doing it for him and not for me.

I think of the word SLUT written on the bathroom wall at school. Why do I feel like I'm somehow disappointing him if I don't have sex with him? Do other girls feel like this?

Who am I supposed to talk to about this shit? I'm friendly with a lot of people but I don't really have super-close friends who are girls. At this moment I wish for a bestie—someone to tell me it's okay not to have sex even if it frustrates my boyfriend, that it's okay to do what I want even if I can't verbalize why.

I wonder if I'd be talking about this if Mom was alive. I wonder if I'd be dating Axel or dodging trains if Mom was alive. I wonder if I'd be accepting a scholarship to Cal if Mom was alive. All of a sudden, a wave of sadness seeps in and my throat winds up tight.

Axel must notice my mood, because although he runs his fingers down my body one more time, there's dejection in his movement. I've hurt his feelings. He climbs off the bed. "I'm gonna hit the shower."

I press my face into Saff's pillow, squashing my emotions. Sobbing would be losing control too, and I refuse to do that. Even though I want to.

That stupid book is pressing into my rib, and I wrench it free. Only it's not a novel. It's Mom's journal.

Something about finding the journal only moments after thinking of Mom makes it feel important. I find myself flipping through it, skimming random comments, and glancing at bookmarks Saff must have inserted.

LITTLE-KNOWN FACTS ABOUT ME:

I have a nasty habit of picking at my toenails.

There's never been a pimple I haven't popped. In fact, I probably would've popped yours too.

I hate the smell of mustard.

I like cooked tomatoes but not raw tomatoes.

I used to have an abnormally perfect belly button, but I didn't fully appreciate it until I'd stretched it out during pregnancy. Now I have stretch marks fanning out from my belly button, and I love them because they remind me of you both.

I curse like a sailor. By the time you read this, I'm sure you'll have a full #@$%&#@ appreciation of the breadth of the #@$%&#@ English language.

The idea of my mother cursing makes me smile. And now I know I inherited my zit-popping compulsion from her.

Wait. A large half-page sticky note is pasted to the opposite side of the page. Different handwriting—Saff's—is scrawled across it.

Saff wrote back to Mom. And I know immediately why she used the sticky note. So she could rip out her personal thoughts if I ever wanted to read the journal. I consider closing it—not perusing what she's written—but I can't make myself. So shoot me, I'm flawed. That's no secret to anyone. I can live with it.

LITTLE-KNOWN FACTS ABOUT ME —SAFFRON
I like raw carrots but not cooked carrots.

I pray every night. Which is weird because I don't go to church. But if I forget to pray, I wake up in the middle of the night and my sheets are drenched.

I think I love Fletch but maybe that's because he's the one who knows me best. Vanessa is a good friend too, but Fletch is my soulmate.

Axel is still showering, the epic water-waster that he is. I flip ahead in the journal. Is Mom ever going to tell me about my father? Clearly the guy was a jerk since he didn't stick around. But still. It feels weird to be eighteen years old and not know anything about him.

One of the bookmarked sections catches my attention.

HERE'S THE THING. I DON'T KNOW YOU.
I only know what I imagine you to be. I know how I think you'll grow and change. I know what I believe to be your strengths (and yes, your flaws), but by this point I will have missed at least 70 percent of your lives. So forgive me if I'm wrong. Forgive me if I sound like I don't have a clue.

On the plus side, I know the people you are pre-peer pressure, pre-self-doubt, pre-dating. So maybe I DO know you. Maybe I know the REAL you. Anyway, here goes.

Cayenne—I see you as completely driven. Call it stubborn, maybe, but once you put your mind to it, you can do anything. I remember how you cried when you made the smallest mistake, so I want to give you permission to make mistakes. Mistakes are how we learn. So give yourself a break here and there.

My heart catches, reading that. Because that's *not* me. Stuff my mistakes with feathers and call them a pillow—I'm comfortable enough to sleep on them. And I'm the opposite of driven—the gifted kid who smarted her way out of doing any work. The chronic underachiever. The waste of potential. But maybe that's not who I always was. Maybe that slacker quality is not an inborn trait, but something that evolved over time. If anything, Mom's description sounds more like Saff. She's the rule follower, the one who never allows herself to make a mistake. The good girl.

And Saffy-Taffy with your big heart . . . Don't forget to protect yourself a little. Even from toddlerhood, you'd give your last cookie to Cayenne, you'd pat MY hair and MY arm when I was trying to put you to bed. When we played a board game, you made sure your sister won. You're a natural born caregiver. Just don't burn out on me. You'll learn over time when to give and when to conserve. If you only give, give, give, you'll be left depleted.

A memory flashes in. Learning to play checkers. Bursting into tears when I lost against Mom. Saff trying to console me, draping her hot arm around my shoulders, patting my tear-streaked face, offering me the stale Halloween candy she'd stashed under her bed.

WHO AM I? —SAFFRON
Our three-year-old selves
Are not our forever selves.
Our real selves are molded and morphed
(And sometimes carved, creamed or crushed)
By the forces that touch us in our lives.
But maybe some people are more morphable than others.
I don't recognize the Cayenne that Mom described.
Maybe I never knew her.
There are shadows of the Saffron Mom spoke of.
I've learned to conserve, though—
View my heart as a resource,
Like water in a drought.
To be used sparingly.
That's why Fletch is so perfect for me—
He fills me up
Reminds me how to laugh,
Replenishes me.
He's my life preserver.

A discomfort settles deep in my stomach, like I drank some expired milk. Saff never knew me? *Please.*

I snap the book closed before I can get too pissed off. Honestly, it feels a tiny bit wrong to dissect Saff's thoughts without her knowledge. Maybe I should stop. But that doesn't mean I have to stop reading Mom's. She left the journal for both of us, after all. And it doesn't mean I have to tell Saff I'm reading Mom's entries. Maybe I can just avoid Saff's sticky notes. Too bad she picked such a bright color. It's like trying not to notice the marks of a highlighter.

The sound of running water stops, and the shower door slams. My moment of privacy is ending, so I return the diary to its safe spot under Saff's covers. Axel pads into the room, wearing a towel around his waist, seemingly over his disappointment, which settles me. He playfully shakes his hair at me like a dog, spraying water my direction. "If we hurry, we can get back to school before fourth period."

I agree, dressing quickly, smoothing Saffron's bed, and scanning the room for any evidence that we'd been there. I silently apologize to Saffron's old ragged teddy, perched on top of her bookshelf. It was a gift from Mom, and Saffron never wanted to part with it. *What can I say, Teddy? I'm complicated. This should come as no surprise to either of us.*

Chapter 8

Watch the kids for us tonight? Need some alone time with Luke. The message from Tee buzzes in on my phone. I see that both Saff and I are on this thread. I groan. I was hoping to hang out with Axel again tonight, but we can't turn Tee down—we owe her fourteen years' worth of favors.

Sure. We can stream a movie and eat popcorn. Saff beats me in responding. I'm guessing she didn't have the same knee-jerk groan reaction.

How about taking the kids out to the movies? Tee chimes in quickly. *I'll pay.*

I message Saff in a separate thread, without Tee. *Gross. They want the house empty.* I see no hypocrisy in this statement. I took advantage of the empty house earlier today but Axel and I are teenagers, not an old married couple in their thirties.

Saff sends me an "eek" emoji.

I message Axel. *Have to watch Minions tonight. Going to a movie. Wanna come?*

While I wait for him to respond I message Saff again. *Bring Fletch. I'll bring Axel. We can't let Tee have all the fun. Especially on Valentine's.*

Saff sends me a thumb's up.

Axel doesn't text me back for an hour. *Can't make it tonight. Sorry.* I am disappointed but not entirely surprised. Axel's not a big fan of the Minions and their dirty hands. He claims it comes from working at Donut Diva, serving grimy kid after grimy kid. I'm glad he's moved on from that job—though the boss was a crook and refused to pay him for his last week's work. Axel actually had to go back in and take what he was owed. At least he enjoys working at the sporting goods store, although his opinion of small children hasn't improved.

Fletch meets us at the theater with a box of chocolates for Saff. As soon as the Minions catch sight of him, they run over and leap into his arms. They love Fletch—he performs these cheesy magic tricks for them, and every time they see him, he's prepped a new one. It's sweet in a dorky way, I guess. This time he fans out a deck of cards, shuffling and cutting the deck. Somehow each of the Minions picks a card with her own name written on it in Sharpie. They squeal and run in circles with their cards.

After handing the chocolates to Saff, Fletch puckers up and pecks her on the forehead. I seriously have to bite my lip so that I don't laugh out loud. They're like a retired couple, I swear. Still, he makes her happy, so whatever.

I hate feeling like a third wheel, so I suggest Fletch and Saff see a "grownup" movie while the Minions and I watch the latest Disney release. The Minions sit on either side of me in the dark theater, hiding their faces on my shoulders during the scary parts. Their hands are soft and buttered, their breath popcorn salty, and I love every moment of it.

Truthfully, I might prefer this—having the Minions all to myself instead of being distracted by Axel. I spend more time watching their expressions than the movie itself. Their reactions are so pure: I see the fear, the humor, the excitement and the joy painted in an ever-changing canvas on their faces. It reminds me of what I might have been like at their age. Four. Young enough to believe in tooth fairies and storybook endings. For most of that year I still had a mother. Viewing the world through their eyes gives me a taste of how it might be to grow up in a typical family, with two parents who'd practically safety-proof the world to spare their children from pain.

The girls fall asleep on the ride home. I carry Maggie inside, and Saff's got Missy. Their bodies are heavy and their heads loll from side to side. Aunt Tee and Luke are sitting in the semi-dark living room, holding hands and talking in whispers. We tiptoe past, to the girls' bedroom.

I lower Maggie into her bed, deciding not to worry about potential tooth decay from the popcorn she consumed. Brushing her teeth would surely wake her up. I pull the covers up to her chin. "Cay?" She says sleepily. "I wuv surprises."

"I know you do." I brush back her hair.

"Maybe a surprise in the morning?"

"Maybe." I kiss her forehead. I've set myself up for this. Last summer I created Fairy Godmother Rosetta, who leaves little trinkets, notes, or treasure hunt clues under their pillows. They had so much fun with this game that I couldn't stop, even when I'd spent half of my babysitting money. Finally I told them that Fairy Godmother Rosetta would be taking a vacation, but that she'd pop by for a surprise visit every once in a while. I collect tiny treasures and save them in a shoebox on my top shelf for just these occasions. I'm pretty sure I've got some stickers, a few polished stones, and some little hair bows.

"Thank you for tonight." Saff touches my arm. "That was sweet of you."

"I can, on occasion, be considerate," I joke. "It's a stretch for me, but possible."

"I think Tee was crying."

"What?" My heart misses a beat.

"I'm pretty sure. Let's go check." Before I can respond, Saff adds, "I hope they're not getting a divorce."

When we pad back into the living room, they both straighten up, Aunt Tee swiping at her eyes and flashing one of those fake smiles.

"Everything is okay." But her nose is puffed up like a pastry and Luke's cheeks are wet. Clearly everything is not okay.

"Then why are you both crying? Luke never cries—except when the Lakers lose a game," I say, hoping for a laugh to break the tension.

No laugh.

"You do need to know," Tee says, and Luke nods slightly, as though he's giving her his blessing. "Okay, come sit down. I wasn't going to discuss this with you just yet, but I guess at this point, it doesn't make sense to wait."

My heart plunges to my belly. Is she sick? This is going to be bad news for sure. I edge over to the couch as though Tee has something contagious, and who knows, maybe she does. I sit as far away from her as I possibly can, forcing Saff to squeeze in between us.

Tee takes a deep breath.

"Please don't tell me you're dying," I blurt accidentally.

Tee shakes her head. "Cayenne. No. Let me talk."

Saffron reaches her hand for mine, and my throat twists up like it belongs to a cartoon character. I imagine smug Lorelei

49

crossing her bony arms and tapping her decrepit toes impatiently, ready to collect another life, and I want to scream. *Not fair! I'm the one tempting you. I'm the one you're trying to take. Not Tee!*

"I'm healthy. And I intend to stay healthy," she says.

I try hard to hear her through my inner panic. So she's *not* dying. So she's *not* leaving me. I breathe and try to focus.

"But none of us can ignore our family history. It's real. I went in to see a genetic counselor. They have this blood test that can identify certain types of cancer risk. One of them is the BRCA gene mutation, which is linked to breast and ovarian cancer."

"What language are you speaking? BRCA?" I heard her say she was healthy, but there's a delay in my processing. I can't quite catch my breath and my heart is double-timing it.

"Wait. You had a genetic test?" Saff asks.

"Yes." Tee clutches Luke's hand.

"Do you have it? The bad gene?" Saff is clearly processing this info more efficiently than I am. I still feel confused.

"I do. It's inherited, of course. If my mother had the gene mutation, which I'm guessing she did, then I had a fifty-percent chance of inheriting it, and so did my sister. Your mom was never tested, but it's likely she had it too."

All three of us are quiet, digesting.

"Listen, I'm not going to just wait around to get breast cancer. I know it's treatable, but cancer has a wicked track record with the women in our family. No offense to Luke, but I don't want him raising my kids alone." Tee gestures with Luke's hand still attached to hers. He wraps one of his long arms around her shoulders. "I'm going to have a double mastectomy. Elective."

"Whaaat?" A fresh gut-punch of shock hits me. I imagine her boobless, with Frankenstein-like stiches across her chest. This image makes me feel ill.

"I'll be in the hospital for a few days and I'll be off work for two months, but it's worth it."

I try to stay calm, and I find myself studying her chest. She has nice boobs. "Are they going to make you new ones?" I have to ask.

"Yes. I'll have reconstructive surgery."

I mull this over, imagining her with different breasts. I picture an eighty-year-old Tee with perky plastic boobs. Although I guess that's the point. Without this, she doesn't think she'll make it to forty, let alone eighty.

"I know it's a lot to digest," Tee says. "Normally when women get implants, they're keeping their own breast tissue and putting the implant underneath. In this case, all my own tissue will be removed. The skin will remain and they'll be inserting an implant under the skin flap."

"Gross." I visualize peeled-back skin and an oversized ice cream scoop full of fatty tissue. I nearly gag.

"Cayenne!" Luke's tone is scolding. "Try to be a tiny bit sensitive here."

"With all due respect," I say, for Luke's benefit, "don't you think this is kind of drastic? Can't you just get mammograms?"

"Are you seriously asking her that?" Saff interrupts me, with a kind of intensity I don't normally see from her. "Two minutes ago you thought she was going to tell us she was dying. Of course she should do this!"

"But why now?"

"Because I'm thirty-two. Your mom was diagnosed when she was thirty. I've been getting breast MRIs since forever, but honestly I don't think it's a matter of *if*, it's more like *when*. And I'm tired of waiting for that shoe to drop. I want to know I'll be here to raise my kids. If your mom had a chance to prevent her cancer, she would've done anything to be here for you two."

The lining of Tee's eyes is red. She must've been crying for a long time. "You know how we always joke about the Silk curse? For a long time I was thinking that all us Silk women are weaker, more fragile, somehow. But I actually just read this article about silk—spider silk to be exact. It's one of the strongest substances on earth. Even stronger than steel, although I'm not sure how that's possible. We Silk women are strong. And we're smart. This is the right thing to do. This is the strong thing to do."

"But what about ovarian cancer?" Saff presses. "You said the BRCA thing is a risk for that too. A mastectomy wouldn't change that, would it?"

"Nope. The surgery to deal with *that* risk is called a salpingo-oophorectomy. Ovary and fallopian tube removal."

I swear she's speaking a whole new language. "Are you planning to do the oopha loopha too?" I ask, pretending I don't see Luke's dirty look. Hasn't the man heard that humor is a coping mechanism? One of my therapists told me this more than once.

"Yes, but it'll put me into immediate menopause, so I'd like to wait a few years for that one. But I definitely plan to. By the time they find ovarian cancer, it's usually pretty bad."

"But—will this *guarantee* you won't get cancer?" I ask.

Tee gives me a small, almost apologetic smile. "There's never a guarantee. There are lots of other risk factors for cancer. But surgery reduces the risk, so I'm going for it. And honestly, you girls will have to face this someday, too. You'll have to decide whether to get tested for this mutation."

I can't exactly tell her that I've already accepted I'll die in my thirties. It's an unpleasant future, but it gives me a roadmap. Plus my thirties are *forever* from now. I need to focus on Tee, on her health and her decision. She's still talking, and I try to concentrate on her words. "You should be doing self exams right now. It's never too early to start."

I glance at Luke, considering making a joke about how Axel examines my boobs enough for the both of us! I hold myself back though, thinking that comment might push him over the edge. Instead I quip, "Exactly when do you plan on hacking off your body parts?" I'm not trying to be insensitive. I'm trying to survive my inner roller coaster, and joking around is my anchor.

Luke removes his hand from Tee's. His mouth has flattened into a thin line. "The surgery will be at the end of March. I need to be with her at the hospital. We want you two to watch the girls. If you can handle it."

"Of course we can," Saff reassures them. "Anything you need."

We're all quiet, and I'm not one for downers, so I try to think of something to alter the mood. "Well . . . I think we should have a party."

"What for?" Luke asks. He does not seem in a mood for confetti and balloons. And truthfully, he does not seem in the mood for me.

"A booby party," I assert. "A celebration of all things booby."

Tee smiles, this time not a small sad smile, but a genuine one that reveals a flash of teeth. "How about this—a goodbye to boobies party?"

Saff scoots to the edge of the couch. "Ooh. We can invite all your friends."

"We can have booby shaped cupcakes and a booby shaped piñata." I'm getting into this. "Maybe booby ice cream sundaes. If we place the cherry just so . . ."

"I like that idea." Tee leans back into Luke's arms, her smile nearly offsetting her swollen nose and red-rimmed eyes.

* * *

I can't sleep. Thank god it's not a school night. Images of skin flaps and hacked boobies invade my dreams, along with lighter visuals of whipped cream mounds and cherry-topped nipples. Lorelei swoops in and out of my awareness, taunting me. Despite my games of distraction, she's caught us all in her wicked grasp—me, Aunt Tee, Saffron, even the Minions. Her claws sink halfway into my chest, reminding me that our lives are vulnerable to her every whim.

Why are you after us? I scream, flailing my arms, hoping to distract her so that the others can escape. *Get a life!*

I'm sadly misunderstood. She raises me up in one hand, looking almost wistful.

How exactly am I supposed to interpret your claws piercing my chest?

Claws? She huffs like she's offended, but my distraction is working. The others scramble away and hide.

If this is a love squeeze, you seriously need to invest in a nail clipper.

You're so negative. She clicks her tongue. *It's all about perspective.* She doesn't notice that her four other captives have escaped.

So you're saying, with a different perspective, my impending doom would be all butterflies and lollipops? I flip around like a gymnast on the uneven bars, unhooking myself from her grasp.

Very funny. She wiggles her fingers, ready to impale me once again, but I dodge her and open my eyes.

Half-awake, I place my hands gingerly on my chest, where Lorelei's claws clutched me in my dream. Just above my boobs.

Will Tee miss hers? I didn't even think to ask her earlier. Arguably, the breast is the ultimate symbol of womanhood. What does it mean to be a woman without these parts?

I can't imagine losing my breasts. Without them I'd feel undesirable, I'd feel sorry for myself, and maybe other people would feel sorry for me too. That thought edges under my skin and makes me cringe. Saff would say I've been brainwashed by societal norms and maybe she'd be right, but I can't help it.

Tee would probably say that not having breasts is better than dying, and it's not like I can argue with that logic, but it still pisses me off that our best chance for survival requires self-mutilation. And she admitted there's no guarantee she won't still get cancer!

My neurons are working overtime, my thoughts spinning like a hamster stuck on an endless wheel. I have to get up. *Move around*, I tell myself. *Think about something else.*

I tiptoe into Saff's lilac-scented room and grab the journal from her nightstand.

I pad back to my room and flip to the spot with Saff's bookmark. The words immediately shift my thoughts, almost as if Mom's putting her arm around me, the way she did that time when a car hit our neighbor's dog. I was three, I think.

I remember something drawing me closer. A need to check on the dog. A need to try to fix it. I remember Mom's arm solidly around me, leading me home. "Don't look, sweetheart. Come this way."

Me being me, I couldn't help but look. But only for a moment. Then I turned back into her arms, to the smell of cinnamon and cloves from the pumpkin bread she'd baked earlier, and the soft warmth of her skin.

THINGS NOBODY TELLS YOU WHEN YOU BECOME A MOM

Nobody tells you that it's nothing like babysitting. Because when it's your own kids, it's #@$%&#@ personal! You pour your heart and soul into your kids and there's nothing that matters more.

Nobody tells you how much you'll worry. It started the moment I found out I was pregnant. First . . . if you'd grow okay and be healthy, and then when you were born . . . if you were nursing enough and pooping enough (seriously), and how you were growing and when you learned to crawl, and if you were safe . . . And now of course I worry about how you'll be without me.

Nobody tells you that you'll be a different kind of mom, a different version of yourself, at each stage of your kids' lives. You can't really predict which version will pop up.

Here's something I won't ever get to find out. Would I have been the wanna-be-cool been-there-done-that kind of mom, who'd host the keggers at her own house so no one would drive drunk? Or would I have been the super strict you-won't-repeat-my-mistakes and not-under-my-roof kind of mom?

The one perk about being dead is that I don't have a chance to mess up your teenage years. Hopefully you'll always remember me as that fun jumping-on-the-trampoline and playing-hide-and-seek-in-our-pajamas kind of mom.

Unless you hate me for being dead. Which is entirely possible. And for that I apologize. It wasn't in my plans either.

I'm not sure I ever hated her for being dead, but maybe I resented her. Maybe I thought that if she'd really loved me, she'd have been able to fight off the cancer. I know she didn't leave me on purpose, but somehow it still feels like it's her fault—even though that makes zero sense.

Maybe it's the late hour or my scrambled brain, but I close my eyes to blink and *bam!* I'm right back there on the trampoline with Mom. She always played with us, like it was actually fun for her. She pretended we were her kangaroo babies, holding us tight to her front while we jumped together. We played "rocket," where she timed her bounce so that she could use her weight to propel us up high into the sky.

I shift my focus, and before I know it, I'm skimming Saff's entry. I force myself to stop—I promised myself I wouldn't. Unless maybe Saff *wants* me to read them. Maybe she knows I'm taking the journal and she's leaving them for me specifically. Might be a stretch. But possible.

I peek again. Impulse control has never been my strong point.

THINGS NOBODY TELLS YOU WHEN YOU LOSE
A MOM —SAFFRON
How you'll forget her face.
And her voice.
And her smell.
How not having her will become your normal,
And how you won't even miss her
(As awful as that sounds)
Because you don't know what to miss.
How you'll find yourself looking
For replacement mother figures.
Without realizing it.
Your teachers at school, your auntie,
Even your big sister.

But no one will measure up
To what you think you want.
Which is, you know, ridiculous.
Because you don't know
What you want in the first place.
Which sort of works out just fine . . .
Unless something jogs your memory,
Making you remember what you lost on some visceral level,
Which, obviously, sucks.

Saff is such a trip. Here she is, totally embracing this whole reconnect-to-Mom game, making me feel like I'm a bad daughter because I'm not all gangbusters about this journal. But when I read what she wrote, she sounds every bit as conflicted as I am. Like, sure it's great to have these fragments of our mother, but they're stirring everything up again. We're both caught like fish on a hook, and we're getting reeled in.

We're going to keep watching these videos. And probably keep reading these entries. We feel compelled to. How can I both hate it and love it in the same moment?

Chapter 9

"Just what is going on in here?" I say in a pseudo-parent voice. I've come to investigate a suspicious cascade of laughter from Saffron's room. "You sound like hyenas. Could you be any louder?"

"Oh we could. Much louder," Saff's best friend, Vanessa, deadpans. She can only hold it for a moment before both she and Saffron start cracking up again. They're staring at Saff's phone.

Vanessa happens to be my favorite of Saffron's friends because she gets my humor. Some of Saff's other friends are so polite that I can't tell with they're thinking. Plus I think I scare them.

Vanessa goes on, "My mission for tonight is to get your sister to relax. We've got a physics exam tomorrow and we're totally ready! So what does this girl want to do? Study more! I mean, I'm all for setting the curve—and you know we will"— she high fives my sister—"but a few cute animal videos are the only thing I'm interested in studying right now."

"Ah, in that case, don't let me interrupt you."

"Too late," says Saff. She sticks out her tongue.

I whip out my phone and aim it at her. "Oo, hold still. That'll make a great photo. Really captures your cheery personality."

"Leave, Cayenne," Saff says, swatting in my direction, even though she's too far away to even come close to reaching me. "You're crushing our endorphins."

"Begging your pardon, milady." I bob a fake curtsey. "I just came in here to ask if you wanted to stop by Alicia's tomorrow." I think I do a convincing job of dropping this casually. It's been two weeks since we watched Mom's first video and I'm kind of surprised that Saff hasn't brought it up yet.

"Oh. Sure." She looks like she wants to ask me a follow-up question, but Vanessa is shooing me away, so I flash a thumbs up and leave—the considerate sister that I am.

I can still hear them talking from out in the hallway, though.

"No, seriously, I think it's sweet the way she teases you," Vanessa says. "Chris used to be like that with me, and you know what a jerk he can be these days."

"Yeah, your sibling situation officially sucks more than mine," Saff admits. I choose to take this as a compliment.

*　*　*

Saff and I are sitting on the porch, smelling Micah's burnt popcorn, hearing the rumblings of his conversation with Alicia in the other room, and watching our second video from Mom.

"*So, sweets . . . do you know where I am?*" She must be standing behind the camera, because I can't see her. "*It's our secret garden. Do you remember?*"

With some visible effort, she shifts the camera upward, and I glimpse a tree trunk. Four jean legs hang down, bare feet dangling, the soles of our feet dirty. The camera inches upward, and I can hear Mom breathing more heavily. I wonder how sick she's gotten by this point. Not bad enough to be housebound apparently. And then I see us, perched on a branch, staring at the sky.

"Wow. We're up pretty high," I say.

"I'd never let Missy and Maggie climb up to that branch," Saff says, pressing pause.

"I would," I retort, but truthfully I'm not sure. If one of them came home with a broken bone, Luke would never forgive me. "Why are you stopping the video?"

"Let's pause it when we want to talk."

"Works for me." I wait. "So what do you want to talk about?"

"Nothing. Just didn't want to miss anything." Saff smiles and un-pauses it. Clearly the "pause" button is her way of keeping me from interrupting.

"This was my thinking spot. I came here at first when I was pregnant. The world around me was getting louder and louder—not literally, just, there were so many interruptions to my ability to think. So I came here and found quiet. After you were born, Cay, I brought you here to nurse and sometimes to sleep. I'd stash my journal or my book in the diaper bag, set you up on a blanket so you could gaze at the leaves rustling in the sky . . . and I'd just sit here and be. Just BE. I hope you both haven't lost the ability to be alone with your thoughts."

Neither Saff nor I say anything. I guess I think the best when I'm driving alone. Sometimes I've gotten halfway to Axel's house before I realize I forgot to turn on any music.

"Today's gift is my secret garden. I come here to connect to nature when I can. Not so often anymore." Her voice tightens. *"Do you remember this spot? Can you find it? Let me show you a few landmarks you can use to rediscover this place."*

The camera tips forward, slamming me with a falling sensation. The lens narrows in on a patch of dandelions. All of a sudden, a memory hits me, of a time before I knew that dandelions were weeds. I remember plucking them from the ground, talking to them like they were little people, with skinny green bodies and wispy heads, dancing in the wind. I remember watching how their fuzzy heads shifted shape with the breeze, how I pursed my lips and blew. How I made a wish and watched the hairs break free and sail away.

I press pause on the video. "Do you remember blowing dandelions?" I whisper to Saff.

"I do. I think we blew hundreds of them at once."

"We're probably responsible for half the weeds in the county."

I start the video again. I hear shuffling, and the camera shakes as she moves around. "Earthquake!" I joke, but Saff doesn't laugh. She stares at the screen, mesmerized. There's a gray blob in the top right-hand corner. It comes into focus slowly. "What is that? A UFO? Maybe we were abducted by aliens."

"It's the water tower. But that's a terrible clue, because you can see it for miles."

The camera moves again. Mom's voice, hoarse: *Cayenne, here, take my camera. Can you point it toward the swings?*

My four-year-old face, smudged with dirt along the length of my nose, and serious eyes poke over the branch. *"Okie, Mama."*

Something catches in my throat. I pause the video for a moment and study myself. "Look at me, Saff."

"I know."

"It makes me want to cry, but I don't know why."

"It's your expression, Cay. There's something about your expression that's so sad."

"It's my eyes." They seem old and tired. "And my mouth, I think." My lips lie flat, like someone has ironed them. "I must have known."

"That she was dying?"

"Yeah. I must've known. Why else would I look so sad?" I stand up and peer into one of Alicia's decorative mirrors. "That's not how I look now, is it?" I square off and stare straight ahead at myself.

"No, now you just look pissed."

"Shut up."

Un-pause.

The camera shifts again, rapidly, and I have to turn away. All that movement makes me dizzy. "How bizarre is it that I'm watching myself and I have no memory of this at all?" The camera zooms in toward a swing set, but beyond that I glimpse a webbed climbing structure. "Wait! Look at that! We called it the Spider Web Park."

"Oh yeah!" Saff grabs onto my arm. "Remember how I couldn't climb to the top and you helped me? You kept saying 'Don't look down, one foot at a time.' You were a good sister to me, Cay."

I can't help but notice that she speaks in past tense.

Suddenly, a little kid screams, and the screen blurs as if it's falling, and then *thud* it hits the ground camera-up. All we can see is an umbrella of leaves with bits of sun and sky poking through.

"*Hold on, Cay! I'll grab you.*" Mom's voice, stronger now.

"*I'm okay, Mama.*" My voice trembling. "*I can fall, it's not that far. I don't want to hurt you.*"

"*I can reach you, baby.*"

"*But I don't want to break you!*"

"*Cayenne, don't break Mama!*" Saff's tinny voice, full of lisps and slurs.

"Wow. Did I really talk like that?"

"What do you think you got all that speech therapy for?"

Sobbing. Little kid sobbing.

"Oh my god. I remember this, Saff. I remember hanging on to that branch and crying." I remember the way the tree branch splintered into my hands, the way my arms ached, and the uncontrollable sobs that kept bursting from my body. "I won't be able to hold on for long."

"*Ma-ma . . . m-move . . . b-ba-ack!*"

"*Watch out, Mama!*" Saff yells.

Even though we can't see anything but the canopy of leaves above, I remember what happened next. How I held on as long as I possibly could, how my fingers loosened, how I dropped what felt like a mile, but was probably only about six feet. How my mother stepped back, respecting my wishes, allowing me to crash onto the leaves below. How I sprained my ankle in the fall, and how Mom cried harder during the x-ray than I did.

We hear the crash as I slam down, the crackling of leaves, and the sound of whimpering.

"*Are you hurt?*"

"*I'm o-kay.*" My speech is halting, like I'm trying hard to hold it together.

"*You didn't break Mama,*" Saff says. "*Good job, Cay.*"

And Mom's shaky voice. "*You sure are a tough cookie. Spicy and tough and sharp as a tack. Watch out, world, here come the Silk sisters!*"

She must notice the camera there in the leaves then, because she peers down into the lens, her cheeks thin and her bald head exposed. There's something beautiful in her fragility. Before she got sick, my mom was a head-turner—but in this moment, with her eyes full of emotion, she seems lovelier than ever. Even without her hair and with a conspicuously flat chest. From what Tee says, she never got breast reconstruction because she was too sick for any additional physical stress.

She takes a deep breath and speaks directly into the camera: *"It breaks my heart that I can't be there to catch you when you fall. Today"*—she wipes a tear—*"or in the future. I hope you can keep landing on your feet."* Click.

Chapter 10

Saff convinces me to spend the afternoon at the secret garden, lounging on a blanket and eating salted almonds. We sit in silence, except for the almonds crunching and the shrieks of nearby children. She's been entirely too serious since Tee's announcement about the surgery, and I decide it's my sisterly duty to break her out of her somber shell.

On the way home, I drag her to the grocery store to do some shopping for the *boob-voyage* party, since Tee has put us in charge of the tit-tacular festivities.

I yank a cart from the stack. "What kind of budget do we have to work with?"

"Luke gave me four hundred smackeroos," Saff replies.

Luke's usually tighter with cash. "I guess he wants us to go all out, huh?" I push off and hop onto the cart with both feet, taking a little ride.

Saff quickens her pace to keep up with me, shooting me a *how-old-are-you?* look. "Yeah. I think he's messed up over this whole mastectomy thing. God, that's an ugly word. Mastectomy. Ugh."

"Yup." I know Luke wants Tee to do it from a practical

standpoint, but I wonder how he *feels* about it. They've been married for ten years, but assuming she escapes the Silk die-young curse, they could have like sixty more years together. "Not only is she losing her breasts, but *he's* losing her breasts too."

"They're not *his*! He doesn't own them," Saff snaps at me.

"God, Saff. I'm not suggesting that. But I'm guessing he's enjoyed them over the years."

"That is way too gross to even think about." Saff gags. "Plus, you realize you're objectifying her by talking about her breasts like that, right?"

Guess it's time for another round of Saffron-Criticizes-Everything-I-Say. "Well, you can't deny that this decision is impacting him too."

"The only reason it should is because his wife will be in pain."

"I don't think it's that simple." But secretly I wonder if she's right. Maybe whatever Luke feels shouldn't be an issue. Like Saff said, it's not his body. This reminds me of how I felt when I turned Axel down the other day. Like somehow it was my responsibility to make sure he was satisfied. What is that about?

The cart is fast approaching a curb, so I step off. "Listen, Saff, I'm not trying to argue here. Let's have fun with this—both with the party prep and the actual event. Maybe we can hire a manicurist for the party, and we can all get chi-chi's on our toenails? Luke included."

Saffron sighs. "How about the breast cancer ribbon? That might be less alarming."

"We could give people a choice. Honkers or ribbons."

"Let's make a list of what we'll need," Saff says as the automatic doors slide open to welcome us. "We should only buy nonperishable stuff today. We can do another shopping trip the week of the party."

I shiver involuntarily as we enter. Damn, they keep this place cold. "Do you think they carry a BOOBY piñata?"

Saffron looks around as if to see if anyone is staring. "I'm going to start counting the number of times you say that word. The twins are more mature than you."

"*That* word?" I pick up two oranges and flip them around so the navels face outward in my hand. Oranges are quite bosom-esque. "What's wrong with it?"

"I think you just like saying it for the shock factor. I prefer *breast*."

"Oh, don't be such a boob!"

"Can I point out that you just used a symbol of woman-hood to insult me?"

"Sheesh! I can't even have a conversation without you ana-lyzing my every word!"

I set my orange back down on the pile—carefully, of course, so I don't set off a cascade of rolling produce. I turn away from her and walk backward, letting her push the cart while I pull out my phone. "I'm going to google it. 'Goodbye to boobies party ideas.' Oh oops, I misspelled booby." Every time I say "booby," I speak it extra loud. An older gentleman glances up from examining apples for bruises. "Ooh, pin the tail on the honker?"

Saff sighs, shifting her gaze to the old guy and then back to me. "You're too much."

"What's the alternative?"

"Oh, I don't know, taking life seriously?" Saff snaps, but a moment later she softens. "I guess I should be grateful for your enthusiasm."

Satisfied with my victory, I steer the cart away from the produce section. Saff follows me. "I saw this stupid video online," she says, "where these ladies had balloons taped to their butts and people had to run up and try to pop the balloons without using their hands . . . and it wound up looking really *wrong*." She cups her hand over her mouth as if she wants to hold back her idea but then releases it. "What if we gave everyone balloon breasts and they have to pop them without using hands? They'd have to hug and squeeze."

"Creative! And we could come up with some fun way to use Tee's old bras. We could make them into slingshots or a hat, or pin them up on her walls."

"Yeah but she's going to have fake breasts. She'll still need bras."

"Maybe not, maybe they'll be rock solid."

Saff rolls her eyes. "Honestly the reconstructive surgery seems almost more of a hassle than the mastectomy. Aunt Tee told me it'll take hours. Plus the implants have to be replaced at some point, it's not like she can just put them in once and be done."

So they've been talking about this without me. That's fine. I guess. "Why would anyone *not* do the reconstruction, though? Unless they were super sick and weak like Mom was. They'd have to walk around boobless."

"I mean . . . lots of reasons," says Saff, looking at me like she's not sure whether I'm being serious. "It's cosmetic, not health-related, so I'm sure some women prefer not to spend the extra money on it. And I'm sure there are ways they could, you know, pad themselves out when they're in public if they don't want to get *judged*."

She puts a subtle emphasis on the last word, like I'm the

one who would judge these hypothetical boobless women for their flat chests. I'm still trying to think of a clever enough retort when she moves on.

"Besides, it's not like we have to have breasts. Except for breastfeeding, what's the point of them, really? They make running harder, they're sore when we're on our periods. Sure they look nice, but we only think that because society has made us believe it. What if we'd never been subjected to that message?"

"They're also erogenous zones," I note with a smirk. "That makes them important."

Saff flushes but nods. "I know," she says in a businesslike way. "But I'm pretty sure women lose their sensitivity when they have a mastectomy, so that's a moot point."

We're in the paper goods aisle now. She starts examining various celebratory-themed napkins.

"So are you saying you don't support Aunt Tee's booby-replacement plan?"

"I support whatever she wants to do. I just don't know if I'd bother with it if it were me."

Ugh. I don't like the thought of Saff going through any of this. Having to decide how much of herself to chop off and scoop out just to improve her odds of making it to forty.

She compares the prices of two sets of compostable plates. "I mean, no one suggests we should get fake tonsils if we have our tonsils removed."

"Bad example. No one can tell if your tonsils are removed because they're inside you."

Saff rolls her eyes. "Exactly my point. Who cares what anyone else thinks? If a woman wants reconstruction because it makes her feel more whole, that's great. But she should do it for herself, not for other people."

This conversation is making me feel more uncomfortable than I want to admit. "New topic. What type of appetizer is the most like a honker?"

Saff puts one package back on the shelf and tosses the other one into the cart. "Meatballs?"

"Ugh. But they're so bumpy. Maybe we can make a pastry that's boob-like."

"Remind me again why we're symbolizing the *ingestion* of breasts?"

"Because the whole point of this party is to have fun. To lighten something awful. Okay?" I soften my voice. I know this is hard on her. It's hard on all of us.

"Fine," Saff says. "Only I don't think *everything* we serve has to be boob-like."

"Ooh, you said boob!" I practically shout.

"So what if I did?" Saff slips into a sheepish half grin—like she's sort of proud of herself but also mortified by me. "I can say it if I want to. It's context and intention that matter."

"Or maybe I'm wearing off on you." I can't help but hug her. I'm surprised by how good it feels. I guess I haven't hugged her in a long time.

Saff laughs, and her half grin shapeshifts into a real smile with teeth and everything. When she stops laughing, she reaches for her comeback. "God help us."

* * *

For the first couple weeks after Mom died, I brought cinnamon graham crackers into bed with me and ate them under the covers at night. Not great for my teeth, and hard to hide the crumbs from Aunt Tee, but there was something so private and comforting about filling myself up with a sweet and crumbly treat. I needed filling up back then. I felt like my insides had been hollowed out.

My thighs are grateful that Tee caught me and put an end to my binging, but every night there's a moment before sleep sucks me in, when I crave something for myself. Something to fill up my insides. I used to drag a stuffed animal into bed with me, even when I was way too old for such nonsense, but now I pack my bed with extra pillows and wrap my arms around them while I sleep.

I'm lying in bed, listening to the sounds of night. Lorelei is at bay, since I'm not remotely close to dozing off. My brain is just spinning and spinning, twitching at the slightest sounds—even a low cough or the squishy noise when someone flips over. Gradually those sounds settle and all that's left is the overhead fan and the ticking of clocks. A moment of emptiness hits me, and I consider foraging through the pantry for something.

I stumble out of my room, pausing by Saff's door. I spy the journal on her nightstand. She's submerged underneath the comforter. I tiptoe in and gently edge the comforter down, away from her nose. I wait until her chest rises and falls a few times before I snag that journal.

I ease my door shut, climb under the covers and read. Something about it fills my empty core, settles my spinning mind, making sleep seem possible.

DATING ADVICE

You might be thinking to yourself, what exactly makes Mom qualified to hand out dating advice? I concede. My relationships clearly didn't last.

Although I have the best daughters in the world, so I must've done something right.

I did learn something from my mistakes though. Perhaps you can learn from mine.

Here goes:

Dating takes practice. You have to practice who you are within a relationship. And you have to practice picking the kind of person you want to be with. There are some qualities you'll think you want but that turn out to not be that important, and there are some qualities you don't know you want that really ARE important.

When you're all gaga over someone it may not seem to matter if they're doing all the talking, but if you're looking for someone for the long term, they've got to value what you have to say.

No matter how much you think you agree with your partner, they've got to be able to compromise—because I guarantee you will someday disagree about something, and they've got to be able to see your side too. They have to care enough about your opinion that they're willing to put their own aside at least some of the time.

Look for someone who's hardworking (this trumps intelligence any day).

Look for someone who knows when to say when. People who party a lot may seem fun and exciting, but that gets old fast. Nothing kills a relationship more than when one person grows up and the other doesn't.

Find someone who makes it easy to love

yourself. If your partner's critical of how you look, for instance, that's a red flag. I hope you'll be with people who see you as beautiful (and encourage you to see yourself as beautiful), whatever your body type or shape or size might be.

Similar interests are important, so that you don't get bored of each other when you're no longer in that lust phase. But you can also appreciate and support your partner's interests even if you don't share them all.

I know people often have to make their own mistakes to learn, but some mistakes cannot be fixed. Even if you do learn from them, they may leave your life forever altered. So keep your eyes open, girls. Be mindful of every choice you make.

For a moment, I wonder if she was referencing Saff and me when she said, "some mistakes cannot be fixed." I'm guessing we were both "accidents." If so, she made the same mistake twice in a very short period of time.

I shove that thought aside and think about Axel instead. He pretty much meets her criteria.

Listens and compromises—as much as any other guy.

Hardworking—when he wants something.

Makes it easy to love myself—definitely. And he's super into me.

When to say when—that boy doesn't drink a drop, so yeah.

Similar interests—a big fat yes! We love all the same things.

This sparks a warm feeling in my chest, because Mom would've liked Axel. I probably would've dated him regardless, but this is a definite plus. I turn to Saff's entry.

FLETCH —SAFFRON
Fletcher fits me like a wetsuit.
His hand molds to mine,
His glasses hug his nose.
Even his name ... stretches around him
Compact and strong.
Smart and thoughtful
And I feel something for him
That I think might be love.
It's warm and comforting.
It's a hot chai latte,
Warming my insides with a tiny spark of caffeine
To bubble up my heart.
Is that love?

These entries transport my mind into some distant, foggy, contemplative place that makes me want to curl up. I quietly close the journal and stumble back to Saff's room to return it to its place.

I gaze at her sleeping self. She looks so peaceful and pure. I know I shouldn't be reading how she feels about Fletch, but it reassures me. I'm glad she's at least thinking about whether he's right for her. Aside from the fact that he's boring and they have no chemistry, they seem happy together. She's so innocent, really.

I fall back into my own bed, and sleep wraps around me. Warm, comforting, like the chai latte in Saff's entry.

For the rest of the week, sneak-reading Mom's journal becomes my new late-night snack. I devour it after everyone's asleep. My brain has gotten used to this. It fills me up, just like the graham crackers did, but without crumbs or cavities. After reading, I'm primed for sleep, so my brain bypasses that half-way point where Lorelei lurks.

My mind digests the entries, and the feelings they've awakened, over the course of the night. I know my wheels are still turning, because I dream all night long. I wake during the night sometimes, my throat tight, but by the morning everything in my psyche feels neatly organized.

I don't feel empty. I feel full. I know now that I haven't just been hungry for something, I've been starving.

Chapter 11

Micah messages me Friday during fourth period. I play it cool for about ten minutes, but I'm just dying to read the text, so I ask to use the restroom and sneak the phone in there with me.

You coming to watch another video diary entry this weekend?

Saff's been bugging me to go back on Saturday. *Possibly.*

We'll leave the key under the door for you.

I close myself into a stall and text back, *What? We won't get to enjoy your sunny personality?*

Not this time. We're driving up for a meet and greet at Cal. One of those early action picnics.

Oh, I see. So your future is more important than your oldest friends in the world? I add a smiley emoji so he knows I'm joking.

If my oldest friends in the world want to hang out with me, they know I live ten minutes away.

Low blow to use logic against me.

And they have my cell number. And they drive.

Okay, okay. You made your point.

After a few seconds, Micah adds, *Stay as long as you like. Make yourself at home.*

An idea sparks. *Can we use your hot tub?*

As long as you don't drown. Don't swim alone. Smiley emoji.

Thank you, O wise one.

Je t'en prie.

Your autocorrect just went wacko.

It's French. It means that it's my pleasure.

I'm reminded why I don't hang out with Micah. He's way too academic for me. *Now you're just showing off.*

That's also my pleasure.

* * *

I entice Axel to join me at Micah's for the hot tub. Saff will meet me here in an hour, and Axel will take off when we're ready to watch our video. I give him the grand tour first, leading him throughout the house, showing him the laptop on the porch where we watch our videos, and winding our way out to the hot tub.

"This place is epic. It's like they stole a farmhouse from the Midwest and plopped it down in the middle of California." Axel takes off his shirt and helps me with mine. I'm wearing his favorite purple bikini under my clothes, and I can tell he's very happy about that. God, he smells good. Some combination of hair gel, cologne and salt.

He pulls me into the water. It's intensely hot but strangely refreshing. The water laps at my skin, the bubbles popping up all around me. He slips his hands around my waist, sliding me directly up against him. I wrap my legs around him. His bare skin glistens, his body firm against mine. He kisses my collar bone from one end to the other, then pulls back to admire. "You are hella hot, you know that?"

"Glad you think so." My cheeks feel warm, maybe from

his compliment or maybe from the heat of the spa. My purple push-up bikini top does wonders for my boobs.

He kisses me, tasting of strawberry and lemonade . . . and everything melts out of my reality. I could do this all day. And all night.

After what seems like moments, but probably is more like twenty minutes, Axel whispers in my ear. "You know what I want to do right now?"

I can imagine. He's like a little kid in a toy store—he sees no harm in asking for what he wants. Maybe someday I'll say yes.

Between kisses, he whispers, "Tightrope across the roof."

"What?" Oh. Okay. I try not to feel insulted.

He peers into the backyard. A ladder rests against one side of the house, where perhaps someone has been repairing the roof. I consider this. "Can't we just stay right here forever? Please?"

He trails his finger along my cheek, stroking the slight cleft in my chin. "Ten more minutes. Then we'll take a walk."

The ten minutes pass quickly. If there's an award for kissing, Axel would win it. He's somehow both delicate and strong simultaneously.

He scoops my hand into his, and we walk to the ladder. He tests it to make sure it's secure, and we climb, dripping. The wetness makes the ladder slippery. I grasp each rung firmly before moving my feet. Each time my foot slides, I feel a tiny surge of adrenaline. And once we make it to the roof, we stand, gazing at the view. I can see for miles, because the land is so flat here.

"Beautiful, huh?" he whispers.

"Totally."

I realize he was one hundred percent right to want to climb up. This moment doesn't detract from the ones before, it accentuates them. He kisses my neck, and goose bumps layer my skin. God, I love him.

"What the hell?" Saff's voice is so scalding it practically blisters. I'm surprised I didn't hear her drive up; Aunt Tee's hatchback, which Saff uses on the days Tee doesn't work, is a heartbeat away from the junkyard.

"Want to join us?" I call down to her, knowing she never will. I balance on one foot and extend my other leg behind me, dancer-like.

"What is wrong with you? Come down!"

I don't appreciate being told what to do, thank you very much. I'm going to walk across before I get down.

"If you break your neck, I'm not changing your diapers!"

I call back, laughing, "If I break my neck on this roof, I'll sue for a million dollars and hire a live-in diaper changer."

Saffron storms into the house. Sometimes I feel sorry for her.

* * *

My suit is still wet when I peel it off. I change, kiss Axel goodbye, and dash off a message to Micah. *Hey Brainiac, thank you for the hot tub. You having fun at the picnic?*

He must be bored because he immediately texts me back. *Meh. I hate this get-to-know-you crap.*

It's called being social.

More like being fake. Everyone's trying to impress each other. I'm not impressed.

YOU MUST BE SOCIAL. THAT'S AN ORDER. PUT YOUR PHONE AWAY.

Aye, aye, captain.

I mean it. Stop!

I'm a polite texter. If you text me, I respond. It's called etiquette.

I send a smiley emoji.

See, you have etiquette too.

I send another smiley.

Okay, fine. Goodbye.

I resist the urge to say goodbye back. About sixty seconds later, he messages again. *Okay, maybe you don't have etiquette.*

Goodbye, asshole!

This time he sends a smiley, and I put my phone away.

Chapter 12

"Hey there, my sweets!" The screen focuses on Mom. *"I think it's about time for me to tell you more about your names. And your history."* Saff and I have hijacked Alicia's porch to watch the next video. She hasn't said a word to me since her diaper comment, and she's sitting as far away from me as possible. We could fit four people in between us.

"So when I was preggo with Cayenne, I craved everything savory—pickles, chana masala, salsa, even hot Cheetos. Who knows why? I started calling Cayenne my Hot Lil Peppa, just to be silly."

Saff scoots closer to see the screen, and I'm grateful for Mom's distraction. Maybe Saff will forget she's mad at me.

Mom is filming herself in the kitchen, stirring a big bowl with a wooden spoon. She wipes her forehead with her arm, setting her blue beanie askew. She's more angular than before.

"I remembered an old folk tale. It's about this princess who compares her love for her father to her love for salt. At first he's offended to be compared to something so common, and he banishes her. Many years later when they reconnect, she serves him unseasoned food, and he realizes how salt and spices make life flavorful. During my

pregnancy that story kept appearing in my dreams, and I figured it meant something."

Mom's voice is starting to sound familiar. I've gotten used to hearing it. I can even hear her voice in my head now. Not in a hallucinatory way, just like I can imagine what she'd say to me, and how she'd say it. This is new.

"Now technically salt is a mineral, not a spice, but that story made me want to name my kid after something spicy. I played around with different options—like Pepper for example—but Cayenne was the best one. Saff's pregnancy was much more mellow, so I named her after a spice with a subtle taste. By now you two probably either love your names or hate your names. I'll take credit, but I won't take blame, how's that?"

I elbow Saff. "You like your name?" I realize she might still be giving me the silent treatment, but I ask anyway.

"Sometimes I love it. Sometimes I hate it. You?"

"Yeah. I'm used to it, I guess." I relax. I know it's ridiculous to care whether Saff is mad, especially when I go out of my way to piss her off, but her silence gets under my skin. I'm glad she's talking. "Thank god Mom didn't get more creative and pick a name like Paprika or Cumin or Turmeric."

"I'm proud of your names, and I'm proud of how hard I've worked to cultivate curiosity and a love of learning in you two. Every night we read for an hour before you go to sleep."

Pause.

"Do you remember that?" I ask.

"Kind of. I remember lying in Mom's bed, the three of us, one on each side, all cozy."

Play.

"We went to the library twice a week for story time, and each time I checked out the full twenty books allowed. Okay, some of them

were for me. But most of them were for you two. I'll admit we lost a few over the years, but I figured the fees were a small price to pay for raising two ravenous readers."

Pause.

"Didn't she make us pay for one once?"

"We had to work it off, I think." Saff nods. "We lost a book and then we had to do chores to pay her back. Is that right?"

"Yeah. We scrubbed the floor. Do you remember how we tried to skate around the kitchen on wet rags?"

"Yeah. I think we got that idea from an old movie." Saff laughs, remembering. "It didn't work as well as we thought it would."

Play.

"One time, Cay, you kidnapped a book on purpose. You knew I returned books whenever we checked out new ones, but it always upset you. You still didn't quite understand that we were just 'borrowing' them. So you hid a favorite library book under your mattress, and I found you and Saff, your co-conspirator, flipping through the pages in secret after bed. You couldn't read yet, but you'd practically memorized it."

"Somehow that doesn't surprise me," I say, smiling.

"Yeah, okay, it's coming back to me now. Maybe that's why she made us work it off. One of those life-lesson kind of things."

"I didn't catch you with your stolen property until long after I'd paid the lost-book fee . . . so I kept it. I couldn't give it back to you because what kind of a message would that be? But fourteen years later, I'm returning that book you sticky-fingered. Do you remember which one it was? If so, all you have to do is find it. I've asked Alicia to put it somewhere on her shelves. Your gift today is that special book. Look inside it, and on page nine you'll find a bonus gift."

Apparently Alicia felt compelled to save sixty-seven picture books to commemorate Micah's childhood. Luckily, she's stacked them all on one baby-blue bookshelf in the guest room. None of them have a library emblem on the spine, so we lay the books out all over the room, flipping to page nine in each one.

Saff gasps and grabs an old favorite about a llama. Stuck between pages eight and nine is a folded piece of paper with a heart on one side.

"We loved this book," I say, touching the smooth pages. "I wanted it to be mine forever."

"I remember it now. You did have it memorized. You read it to me in our closet, on top of pillows and blankets."

Saff opens the paper. Inside is a thick envelope. I reach into it and pull out a stack of photos. Pictures of each of us as infants, being held by Mom, by a very young Tee (sporting braces and edgy purple hair), plus lanky Luke along with a skinny version of Ryan-the-Reject, and youthful-looking Chowders. An athletic Alicia, in leggings and a T-shirt, holding a shrunken baby Saff. A plump boy toddler with brown ringlets hugging toddler-me. "Aw. That must be Micah, right?"

Saff frowns. "Why are the Chowders in all these?"

"Who knows." I shrug. "Tee and Luke have been together for practically ever."

"But she's like fourteen or fifteen in these pictures, and Luke's gotta be nineteen, right? They didn't start dating till we were in elementary school, when they were both in their twenties."

I'm only half-listening. I've moved on to photos of each of our birthdays (well—the first four for me and the first three for Saff). In the background are the same crew—Alicia, Mark, Micah (at various stages of development), Tee, Mom, Luke, Ryan-the-Reject, and the Chowders.

Toward the bottom of the pile we find some photos of Mom in her late teens and early twenties. Loose hair, bare midriff and bare feet, tanned face shining like the sun was smiling directly down on her. Holding hands with a boy, kissing him, laughing with him. I stare at him, taking in all the periphery details.

"Wait a second . . ."

"No way." Saffron cuts me off, her face reddening in splotches. "I know what you're thinking but NO WAY."

"I'm breaking the rule—we're watching the next video now. We can't wait."

Surprisingly, Saff concedes. An old image materializes, one of Saff and me, both very little, holding hands. This is a video of a video. Mom's pointing her camera at a laptop screen, which is playing this ancient video. Saff has wispy duck-fluff hair and walks in that off-kilter, wobbly new-walker way, with me holding on to her. My own hair hangs to my shoulders, still a little fine, but much thicker than hers. I'd guess we were two and one in this video. Saff plops down on her butt, as little kids do, and bursts into tears. The camera zooms in. I help her up, pat her head and mumble in nearly unintelligible toddler-ish, "Is okay, Saffy, is okay."

The image freezes. "*Aww, wasn't that precious? Makes my heart melt every time I see it.*" I realize Mom plans on interspersing her commentary with the background video. "*So, my sweets, this is video number four, and I think you're ready for some important information. I ask that you withhold comment or judgment until I'm finished. I know it may be hard, but try.*"

"Uh. Oh." Saff groans. She's even splotchier than before, and I worry about the sudden onset of hives.

The screen shifts to an image of a very young, slim, and handsome Ryan-the-Reject. His nose lies straight and perfectly placed, unlike the current, almost curved, version. *"Your father is Ryan Channels."*

Saff and I suck in simultaneous breaths, the kind you take when someone shoves you in a pool unexpectedly. The kind where you try to inhale as much air as possible before you're submerged.

"I'm hoping he's doing well and is a part of your lives. Sadly, I don't know if he will be. His parents promised me that they'd do their best to keep him involved in your world, but they also promised me that they wouldn't tell you your dad's identity until you'd had a chance to form your own."

Saff exhales. I realize I've been holding my breath, still feeling the shock of submersion. I release the air in my lungs, and it seeps out, leaving me depleted.

The image changes to another photo of Ryan, this time in a bathing suit, dripping wet and lifeguard-buff. *"Please don't hate me for keeping this information from you. I never intended to keep it a secret forever. And when this all started, I certainly wasn't planning on dying. But at the time of your births—yes, both of your births—Ryan could barely function well enough to keep himself fed and showered. I told him I intended to keep him at arm's length. And he agreed. He knew he'd fallen into some kind of awful quicksand, and he needed to focus on his recovery without having dependents. Without worrying about child support or meeting your expectations."*

I realize Saff and I are clamped on to each other. She's hooked both her arms through my left one, holding on as if I'm a life preserver. If we were in the water we'd drown, gripping each other in a panic, neither of us trying to swim.

"Please know that I did not make this decision lightly. When I was pregnant with you, Cay, I confidentially consulted an attorney about the pros and cons of putting him on your birth certificate. One of my high school friends had a child with a raging alcoholic, and I

watched what happened when they divorced. The burden fell on her to prove everything, and the court wound up giving him partial custody. Any time my friend's kid was with him, she could be sure he wasn't sober. The idea of having no control over your safety . . . this haunted me. That's why I purposely did not acknowledge his identity on either of your birth certificates."

"I can't decide if I'm mad or sad," I whisper.

"I'm both," Saff says, her voice so soft I can barely hear it. "How could she do this to us?"

"I know that in many ways, it was wrong of me to keep your dad from you. But I did the 'wrong' thing for the right reasons. I hope you'll forgive me for this. Plus, I had high hopes that he'd still be an integral part of your lives, just not in the official role of a father."

I visualize Ryan-the-Reject standing behind the Chowders, shuffling along. "Depends on what you mean by integral."

"Okay, let me backtrack, so you can understand how this all evolved."

The photo changes to one of a shaggy-haired Ryan wearing a football uniform. And Mom in short-shorts with killer legs, perky boobs, and long hair pulled back in a ponytail. They both squint at the camera, the sun clearly in their eyes.

"Ryan and I met in high school. We had a ton in common—both athletes with enough energy to be bottled. We took honors classes, on the way to good colleges. Ryan had a gentleness that I loved. He never argued, never insisted on being right, was willing to compromise and always wanted to do the right thing. And that smile, combined with those sensitive eyes—man, those won me over every time."

"He does have a nice smile," Saff acknowledges.

"Yeah. He looks so different with his old nose, and when he was, you know, fit." Ryan-the-Reject now has a gut that's halfway to Santa status.

The photo shifts to one of an accident scene. A car, scrunched like an empty soda can, somehow curling around the base of a tree. *"Midway through senior year, after we'd already applied to colleges, Ryan had a massive car accident. He'd been partying—in fact we'd both been partying at my friend Rachel's house. I spent the night and slept it off. He drove home, and on the way, he slammed into three parked cars and wrapped his around a tree. That accident shattered several things. It shattered most of the bones in his body, it shattered the skull of a homeless guy who was sleeping in one of the parked cars he hit, and it shattered his belief that he was a good person. The man's name was Tom Brown. He'd been living in his station wagon for a few months while he tried to get back on his feet. He died at the scene, and your dad was charged with vehicular manslaughter."*

We both inhale in unison again, as if we've been sucker punched.

The screen displays a newspaper article, with an image of Ryan in a courtroom, and although the trial must have taken place long after his bones healed, he still looks broken.

"Sorry, girls. I know it's a lot to swallow. Ryan served four years in prison. Four years is nothing compared to the life that was lost. But it was an eternity for Ryan. He changed in there. He suffered from chronic pain due to his injuries, and chronic depression because of his regret and self-hatred about what he did. The doctors in prison over-prescribed him pain medications, and he got hooked, as many chronic pain sufferers do."

"How sad," Saff whispers.

Something twists in my chest, and I hold my hand there as if that will somehow help.

"I went off to college and met new friends, dated, had my own life, but I visited him in prison over summer break. In my mind,

we were no longer together. I'd moved on. But I still loved him. And I guess I had some survivor's guilt. It could've been me. I could've driven home that night. I might've, if Rachel hadn't asked me to stay. Part of me felt responsible for him and wanted to fix him."

We see a photo of a slightly older Mom, wearing a pencil skirt and a silky top with dangly earrings, her hair twisted up on top of her head. Ryan sits next to her in crumpled shorts and a T-shirt, his post-break nose curved. His hair is gelled back, and he's half-smiling, but the somber puppy-dog eyes grab me.

"It wasn't until his parents called me, a little over three years after he'd been released, that we really reconnected. They were worried about him, they told me. Thought he was depressed. Thought it would be good for him to spend time with old friends. I was in between boyfriends, and I might have been a bit lonely myself. It was the year after my father died of a heart attack—he'd been my only parent for most of my life. Your aunt Tina moved in with extended family, and I missed her. Financially, I'd been doing well—bought my own condo, had a great job, had a ton of friends, but all it took was one look from those eyes to suck me back in."

Saff pauses the video and stares at the image of our parents.

"That photo!" Saff points to it. "Mom and Ryan don't match at all."

"True. But he's still kind of cute there."

"I guess," Saff shakes her head. "I just can't believe that our father was under our noses all this time and we didn't know it!"

"He's not a bad man, girls. He's a good man who hit trouble, and didn't know how to grow from it. Some people trip over adversity and it makes them stronger. Some people get stuck, and that's your dad. I always tried to see the best in him, to give him the benefit of the doubt. We wound up dating casually. I told him I no longer wanted exclusivity, but that I enjoyed his company. That was true."

"So basically they just hooked up," I say.

"Sounds like it."

"Cayenne, you were a surprise. A lovely, lovely surprise. I hadn't planned to get pregnant, but once I was, I adored you immediately, even though you were the size of a raisin inside me. Ryan tried really hard to pull it together. He went to rehab, swore off prescription meds, got a job. I accepted his involvement, because I wanted a two-parent family for you."

Photos slide past more quickly now: Ryan painting a baby room, assembling a crib, hugging a very pregnant Mom.

"But every small stumble set him back. He arrived late to work and was written up—he relapsed. He forgot to pay a bill—he relapsed. We got in an argument, he felt like a failure, he relapsed. Pain killers were his go-to. The second things got rough, he knew just where to find them. Then he'd feel guilty and try to start fresh again, but it was clear he couldn't stay clean for long. By the time I was six months pregnant, we both knew I could not rely on him to step up to the plate as your father. So he agreed to this arrangement."

There's a tender image of Ryan holding newborn me, and the screen stays on it for a long time. So long that I feel pressure building along the bridge of my nose and against the corners of my eyes. I won't cry. I refuse to cry. I glance at Saff. Her face is wet.

"Clearly I am not a quick learner. After you were born, Cay, single motherhood was harder than I thought. The sleepless nights, the funky hormones, and exhaustion from nursing. Anyway, he moved in for two months, helping me around the house and taking care of me and you."

The screen displays images of newborn me, smiling in that lopsided new baby way, one cheek higher than the other, blowing spit bubbles, in one of those portable infant bath tubs, and with some kind of green pureed vegetable all over my cheeks.

"I blame my vulnerability, my post-baby body and feeling so inse-cure and alone in the world. So when Cay was only five weeks old, I got pregnant with Saffron. At first I freaked out. I'd been nursing. I didn't think I could get pregnant while nursing. But clearly I could and I did. After a little while, I realized what a blessing this would be. That you'd have each other, no matter what happened between me and Ryan. And I decided this was meant to be."

"So we were both accidents," I say, my voice hoarse.

"Surprise sounds nicer."

"Same difference."

Baby-me is kissing Mom's swollen belly. *"I gave Ryan those nine months to pull his act together. He'd been so helpful to me when you were born, Cay, and I thought maybe . . . plus I did love him. I'd always loved him. We really tried, girls—we went to counseling together for months. But he was still a mess, so we stuck with the same arrangement when Saff came along. I have high hopes that he's made a lot more progress by now, that at this point you can connect with him and feel blessed to have his company. If he's kept his word, he should still be part of your lives, so you'll be good judges of how he's grown and changed."*

Saff and I turn to each other, and I read her hesitation. We don't know what he was like when we were little, but he isn't exactly a role model now.

"I beg your forgiveness, girls. I know I've robbed you of time with him. I hope you'll understand why I did this and why I'm telling you now. My biggest motivator was safety—I couldn't bear the idea of Ryan supervising you in the pool or driving you around while under the influence. Now that you're grown, I know you can keep yourselves safe. Your own identities have been formed and you're mature enough

to view Ryan with the understanding and compassion he deserves. He's a good man, and I wanted you to be able to fully appreciate that. I want you to be proud of where you come from, and to recognize that our decisions were made with love."

Once again the screen shifts, showing multiple images of toddler-me with baby-Saff. Kissing her head, holding her (with grownup arms supporting), playing with squishy multicolored baby blocks.

"Life is messy, girls. It's messy and complicated and our job is to do the best we can with the lot we've been handed. To grow from adversity and not crumble from it."

The screen freezes with an image of the four of us. Ryan holding me, Mom cradling Saff. Both of them gazing down on our heads as if they've just been handed solid gold. Mom's hair is loose around her shoulders, like a shawl.

"Okay, so that's a lot. I dumped a ton on you. Please do me a favor, and don't watch the next video until you've come to grips with this. These are all meant to be gifts, and you'll benefit most from them if you watch with open hearts."

I shut down the laptop. Neither Saff nor I speak for a long time. In fact, we drive home in silence. No music, just the empty sound of air rushing past.

Chapter 13

It's pitch black. I checked the train schedule before I left the house, and I know the 8:55 train from Norwalk should be along soon. I've never dodged at night before, but the moment the thought entered my brain, I felt compelled to do it, to quiet my mind.

It's all too much. My dad being Ryan-the-Reject, Tee's upcoming surgery, these journal entries and videos dredging up the past. I can't handle it. I feel the slight tremor on the tracks before I hear it. Train is coming.

"Screw you, Lorelei!" I send daggers in my mind. She stole my mother. In a way, she stole my father too—if he hadn't killed that man, he might never have struggled with addiction and he could have been my dad from the beginning. And now Lorelei's lurking in the shadows, threatening Tee—intimidating her enough that she's willing to surgically remove parts of her body. I understand why she's doing it but I hate that she has to. I despise Lorelei for having so much power over my life and the people I love.

I'm not like Tee, running scared. I confront Lorelei every chance I get. I must control her, battle her. I imagine hopping around an arena in an elaborate swordfight. Me sweating bullets, and her seeming disinterested.

For a smart girl, your lack of creativity surprises me. She's holding her sword between two fingers, as if it's as light as a smoothie straw.

Why, you bored? I'm holding my sword with two hands, and it's so heavy I can hardly keep it upright.

Out of my skull. How many go-rounds is this going to take?

Only there's no time to answer, because my insides buzz, my heart hammers, my skin prickles. In a strange way, I feel myself relax. *Whir-whir-whir-whir.* My mind begins to quiet, my thoughts begin to settle. Survival is all I know. I bend my legs, I revel in the adrenaline.

Only, something is off.

I jump too soon. Like ten seconds too soon. I miss the secondary blast of air from the train as it passes.

The chug of the train flying by sounds like hysterical laughter. Lorelei is getting her jollies from my failure. There's an emptiness in the pit of my stomach, a rancid dissatisfaction. I roll away from the tracks, lying there in the sand, and stare at the stars, wondering why.

* * *

By some strange unspoken agreement, neither Saff nor I bring up the Ryan bomb for over a week. Like if we don't talk about it, maybe it won't be true. Neither of us mentions watching the next installment of Mom's video diary. I avoid the journal too, as if picking it up will infect me with cholera.

But on Sunday, when the Chowders invite us to come over and cook soup, Saff and I accept the invitation. The Chowders live in the nice part of Pendrum Park, where even modest homes cost as much as an acre would cost in our neighborhood. Their house has a purposely rustic feel. As we walk up the red brick walkway, I play my childhood game of stepping separately on each brick.

"Are you mad at Mom for not telling us?" Saff's next to me, matching my steps. This is the first real conversation we've had in days.

"Are you?" I shoot back. I know she is. Or I think I know she is.

"I asked you first."

"Fine." I stop walking. "Yes. And no. I'm so mad that my blood boils every time I think about her leaving us with Tee, who was practically *my age* at the time . . . while we had an actual father . . . a grown man, who could've helped out . . ."

"I wonder what Ryan would've been like if he had to step up to the plate. Like if Tee hadn't wanted to take care of us. Would he have gotten his act together?" Saff lowers her voice as she climbs onto the porch. I follow her.

"Maybe. I think he would have if he could have, you know?"

"Yeah. I guess Mom didn't think he was capable."

"Okay—and that's what kind of pisses me off." I sit down on the porch steps. I speak softly now. Not a whisper, but quietly enough that no one inside will hear. "Like who was *she* to make that decision? How could she possibly know?"

"Would you trust him to raise Missy and Maggie on his own?" Saff matches my volume.

This gives me pause. "No. Good point. He could watch them for a few hours, sure, but long-term, honestly I think you and I could do a better job than Ryan. We're way more responsible than he is. At least *you* are. Jury's still out on me." I'm kind of joking about the last part, but Saff takes me seriously.

"Maybe." Saff twists to face me. "But if you had to make a choice, you could *choose* to be responsible. Make sense? I don't think Ryan was in a position to choose after that accident. Sounds like he really got stuck for a while."

"God. I hope I don't turn into him." The thought settles like a glob of uncooked bread in my gut. Now it's real. Too real.

"You won't. But that's part of why she waited all this time to tell us. We're at a crossroads, you know. We're entering adulthood."

"Ahem." I clear my throat. "I am already an adult."

"Technically." Now Saff's using that I-know-better tone that makes me want to pinch her.

Before I can act on the impulse, she adds, "Let's go in already."

Inside, the smell of sautéing onions greets us. The kitchen is just off the entryway, and I can hear the sizzling on the pan. Nonna Chowder traps me in a bear hug, like always, squeezing her massive arms around me, as if the goal is to get me to pop. But now it feels different. Maybe less intrusive. More like she's trying to absorb me and less like she's trying to squish me.

She pulls back and says her usual "More beautiful every day." For the first time, I sense the pride in those words. That my beauty is part hers. Something that connects us, in some small way.

When she moves on to squash Saff, I wonder if she also interprets this embrace in a new way. Papa Chowder calls out from his spot on the couch, "Hold the press. The Spice Sisters are here to help season the day."

Out of habit, I roll my eyes at the excessive dorkiness. But this, too, takes on new meaning. Now this is my dorkiness too, since he's part of me and I'm part of him.

Nonna ushers us into the kitchen, where she's spread out the cookbook. "It's corn chowder today, ladies. Out of respect for all the vegans in the world."

"Um. Nonna," I say, "chowder has butter and cream. I think you mean vegetarians."

"Details, details." She waves her hand dismissively. "All right. Let's set you to chopping. I saved you from the onions."

"Thank you." Saff and I speak in unison.

We chop and season, boil and simmer, all from a somewhat distant place. This is our *grandma*. The only grandma we'll ever know. All these times she's invited us to cook with her—these were her attempts to connect with us. And Papa Chowder, parked there on that leather couch, turning the pages of his magazine, but soaking up our conversations. Suddenly I feel so guilty for all the chowder sessions we've missed in recent years. Neither of us understood the significance of them.

And that does make me mad. Because although maybe Mom was right to keep us from our dad, was she right to keep us from our grandparents?

After the soup is fully prepped, simmering on the stove, I get up the nerve to ask my question. "Is Ryan housesitting? Or is he here today?" I seriously almost said "Ryan-the-Reject."

Nonna freezes momentarily, her back turned to mine, as she stirs the soup. "Ryan?"

"Yeah. Just wondering."

"You girls never ask to see him."

Saff and I share a glance. That's because in our minds he's always been such a nonentity. "Yeah, well," Saff says, clearly at a loss for an excuse. "We thought maybe he'd want to hang out."

When Nonna turns to us, her eyes glisten with tears. There's emotion written into every line in her creased face— some mixture of relief and concern. But still, as the wooden spoon drips chowder onto the tile floor, she doesn't put her knowledge into words. She waits for us to say more. Papa Chowder stands up in the adjoining room, watching us.

Saff and I rush in for a hug simultaneously, and this time it's us squeezing her. Papa comes over and folds into the hug behind us, and we stand there for a long time.

Papa speaks first. "We knew you'd find out soon. Your mother promised us that she'd tell you in one of the messages she left. We just didn't know exactly when you'd get that particular message."

"It was so hard not to tell you," Nonna adds. "All these years. But it was Jenny's wish, and we loved her."

"And we understood why," Papa adds. "We had concerns about that choice, and it was painful, but we understood that she was doing what she thought was best."

Nonna pulls herself away, with effort. "I'll go check if Ryan's up." I glance at the clock. It's nearly noon.

A minute later Nonna bustles back, all business, saying he'll be showering and out in a few minutes, and why doesn't everyone sample the soup, even though it'll be much tastier once it sits for a while. She moves about the kitchen with purpose, pulling out crackers, pita chips and hummus, and arranging all the food on the table. Saff and I eat out of politeness, asking an array of questions that never mattered before this: about their own family histories, about how they met and got together, about their careers. We own all this now too, as our personal history. It's something we can share with them.

Ryan the Re—oops—Ryan-my-dad ducks his wet hair into the kitchen, avoiding eye contact. Not that he's ever been the most social, but right now his discomfort spills all over the place. I think we all feel it, because we shift the conversation from intimate to superficial. Ryan samples the food on the table and drinks a tall glass of water. Finally, he meets my gaze. "How's about a walk? Just me and the girls?"

We fall over each other agreeing what a fabulous idea this is. Nonna and Papa busy themselves cleaning up and staying out of our way. Saff and I slip on our shoes and pull back our hair.

But once we're out on the trail that winds through their neighborhood, we focus on sidestepping clumps of manure.

"Why exactly are there laws about picking up dog poo, but not horse poo?" I ask, just to break the awkwardness.

Ryan laughs. "Think of the bags people would have to carry for their horses."

"They'd be huge," I agree. "And the shovels!"

"One of us should invent a horse pack to carry pooper scoopers and bags." Saff steps around a large dump of poo.

"Or we should change the poop laws. It's discriminatory to force dog owners to pick up poo and not horse owners," I point out.

"Yes! It's classist. Because it's mostly rich people who own horses," Saff says.

"Maybe there *is* a horse poo law and we just don't know." Ryan dodges another clump.

"Well, if there is, it's not enforced, and I for one resent it." I'm having fun being silly, and thinking about anything other than the real issue at hand. "It affects my wellbeing."

"Maybe you can sue for damages."

"I like the way you're thinking," I say. "We must be related."

And there! It's out. Ryan stops and turns to us. It's painful to watch him try to find the right words.

Saff must feel the same way, because she speaks first. "It's okay . . . Dad." The word "dad" doesn't sound natural, but she smiles anyway. "We understand. We just want to get to know you better."

Ryan/Dad just stares at her, still fumbling. He rubs his crooked nose as if the answer's in there.

I want to rescue him. I can't stand to watch him struggling. It makes me want to turn my head away. So I say, "It's so strange that we've known you forever, but I don't feel like I really *know* you."

"You and the rest of the world," he mumbles, his head down. He jerks it back up with visible effort. His hair is still damp. I notice he shaved today. "But I *want* you to know me. So I'll try harder."

Saff and I both accept this, and we begin to ramble forward again, slowly.

"Walks are good," he says slowly. "Let's try to take a walk every week. Makes the quiet less awkward, if we don't know what to say, you know?"

We both agree, not for ourselves so much as for him. He must need that—to be doing something besides just talking. Maybe Nonna does too, maybe that's why she's been trying to get us to cook all these years. Walking seems like a good way to connect with Ryan. Nature can soak up the silence, make it comfortable, and Ryan needs that. If we want to get to know our dad, we need that too.

* * *

When we get home, Saff immediately escapes to meet Fletch, leaving me to help Tee fold laundry. She always sorts in her bedroom, making her mattress a mini folding station. "How'd it go?" Tee asks, pulling a tiny Minion shirt out of the pile and smoothing it.

I grunt. "About as well as it could've, considering the circumstances."

Tee considers me. "Ryan's okay, Cayenne. Give him a chance. I've been telling you that for the last fourteen years."

"Yeah, but for the last fourteen years I didn't know who he was!" I yank a pair of jeans out of the massive pile. "You were all conspiring against us!"

"Cayenne." Tee places a neatly folded shirt onto her bed. "To be fair, your grandparents and your father have been in your life all along. They just didn't have the label."

I groan. "That matters!"

"You're saying you'd have been more receptive to them if you knew?" Tee grabs a floral skirt and shakes it out to minimize wrinkles. "You'd have invited them into your life and embraced them with open arms?"

"YES!" I fold the jeans into a tight rectangle. "I should've at least had the option!"

She sighs. "I'm not disagreeing with you, Cayenne. I never fully agreed with your mom's decision. But I was also pretty young at the time, and it wasn't my secret to tell. Besides . . ."

Tee sets the skirt on the bed, unfolded, and pulls me close. She pats the bed, and we both sink down onto it. "To be totally honest—I *wanted* to raise you girls. I loved Jenny so much. She was my idol—she was my lifeline when our own mom passed away, and again when our dad did. Losing her left me in a lot of pain, and honestly, having you and your sister . . . I feel like you saved me. I had to be strong for you both. I had to grow up real fast. If I hadn't poured my energy into you, I think I'd have allowed myself to hate the world."

I've never thought of it this way. I've always figured Saff and I were an inconvenience and that she had to put her life on hold for us. I never thought about *her* needing *us*.

"So yeah, maybe I could've tried harder to change her mind about Ryan. Maybe I could've gone against her wishes and made him a more official part of your lives. But I was desperate to hold onto anything that reminded me of my sister."

"Do I remind you of her?" I ask.

"You do." She pauses, staring down at the stack of tiny clothes she's created on the bed. "I've been thinking about her even more than usual lately. I wish every single day that she could've had the choice to avoid her cancer. It's unfair—I get that chance and she didn't. But I know she'd want me to do this surgery. This is my chance to tip the odds in my favor. She would be cheering me on." Tee wipes her eyes.

"I'm sure she would, Tee. I think you're doing the right thing." This is the first time I've said this, and maybe the first time I really believe it. As painful and unsettling as the surgery sounds, it's her way of taking control of the Silk Curse.

"Thank you for saying that." She sniffles. "Because believing it's right doesn't stop me from feeling scared, or worrying about what might go wrong with the procedure, or wondering whether new cancer prevention techniques will pop up that are less invasive."

I just hug her. Tee and I don't get the chance to have heart-to-hearts very often, and this feels good. Maybe I should fold laundry with her more often. "That's precisely why I'm going to throw you the best booby party ever."

I can't sleep. My chest feels constricted and heavy, as if a fifteen-ton boa is winding his way around and around and around me. Lorelei doesn't visit my dreams, because I can't relax enough to get anywhere near sleep.

One moment I hate Mom. HATE her, hate her. Like seething fury, a volcano in my belly. And I hate Ryan/Dad—both for being who he is and for not revealing himself to us. Just because Mom told him not to reveal his identity doesn't mean he had to listen. He could have told us at any time, but instead he hung in the background for *years*. Years when we needed him or wanted him. I wouldn't have judged him when I was seven. I wouldn't have known how to judge him. Now I can't extricate my judgment from my image of him.

And the next moment . . . I totally get it. I get her wanting to keep him at a distance. I get her being worried about safety. And I get him feeling incapable. But getting it or not getting it . . . it still feels the same. The weight is so heavy it's suffocating.

At about two in the morning, I find myself with the journal in my hands. I consider ripping it into tiny shreds.

I resist. Barely.

And I read.

CHOICES

You know that poem by Robert Frost? "Two roads diverged in a yellow wood?" Life is all about choices.

Only in my life it hasn't been two roads diverging, it's been ten, maybe twenty. I could've taken so many different turns that would've led me down different paths.

In life there is no rule book. There's no game plan. There's just you. Trying. Trying your goddamn best in the face of all odds. Anyone else can judge. Think they know better. Think they'd have done better.

But just know this. I made the best decisions I could with the information I had at each moment. I might have made other decisions at other moments with different info.

I am sure I made mistakes. I am human. Practice forgiving me. Maybe it will help you forgive yourselves the next time you hit a crossroads.

My heart is hungry, ravenous even. I gobble up Saff's entry as well.

THE BIG NEWS —SAFFRON
DNA, twisted together like pretzels.
Genes making up every cell in our bodies.
I cannot believe that HE is part of me.
That I'm part of HIM.
I don't get mad very often.
Sure, I feel it bubbling down below,
Simmering maybe.
But mostly it lurks outside of my awareness.
This Dad thing though.
This goddamn conspiracy to keep him at a distance.
It SUCKS!
It makes me so teeth-gritting ANGRY.

But that feeling, it doesn't fit my skin.
Like it's two sizes too small,
Uncomfortable and itchy.
Nearly unbearable.
I don't know what to do with this feeling.
I don't know how to make it go away.

I fall asleep imagining Saffron wearing a skintight suit of anger, trying to bust out of it any way she can.

I wake up with a jolt. Shit. I forgot to take the journal back to her room. I scramble up, journal in hand.

Saff's still curled into a ball, on her left side. I slip the journal back onto her desk and tiptoe back to my room.

And I don't feel guilty this time. Reading Saff's journal entries is bringing me closer to her. She's too private to tell me what she's really feeling, but it helps me to know. It's strange, but knowing she's pissed off releases some pressure in me.

Chapter 14

The sun devours the sky, making me wish I'd doubled up on my sunscreen. Axel holds my hand as we hike up to Mesa Ridge— our second jump from the Bluffs. School let out early today, for the kind of teacher in-service/student play day we all love. "I wish I could've met your dad before that accident, before he got all messed up."

"Yeah. You and me both." I've briefed Axel on every detail from the video and from our walk with Ryan/Dad.

"He has like, coolness potential, if he wasn't such a total loser." We're nearing the last loop up.

"That should make me sad, what you just said." I match his steps. "Or angry. But you're totally right."

"We're good like that. I can say anything without offend- ing you." Axel drops my hand so that he can step up onto a rock, his bare back glistening. When I first met him I thought he played football or water polo, because of the muscles in his back and arms, but then I figured out he just does a lot of heavy lifting at the sporting goods store where he works. He's the kind of guy who's good at every sport but doesn't want to be tied down to one.

"Almost anything," I tease, stepping up behind him. "But I agree with you about Ryan. I've always thought of him as my step-uncle, and that's how he still feels to me."

"He's a poster child for 'say no to drugs and alcohol.'"

"Yeah," I say, swiping the sweat off my nose, "it's interesting that we both have a family history of drug addiction. I didn't know it before, but now that I do, it makes a certain kind of sense. Do you think there's something inside us both, something we were born with, that craves the high?"

"Maybe. The counselor I saw after my dad died said that family history and personal use patterns are big factors in addiction. We can't change our family history." The ground flattens at the cliff, and Axel stops for a moment, gazing at the view. "That's why I stay away from substances and only go for the natural highs. They're still addictive, but they don't mess with your brain."

It might be the heat from the day or the altitude, but I feel suddenly nauseous. The main reason I don't drink is because Axel steers clear of all that. "Thank god I didn't fall in love with a partier. I would've totally gotten sucked in." Axel has probably saved me from myself.

"Yep. I'm a good influence on you. You should stay with me forever." He drops down onto his knee in the dirt. "Marry me. Have a busload of kids."

"Oh shut up." I swat his head. "I'm never getting married or having kids."

"I know," he says, grinning. "That's why I said it. I'm not getting married or having kids either. Independence . . . that's what I want."

I boost him up off his knee. "We *are* perfect for each other."

Axel pulls me in for a quick kiss, his arms resting on my shoulders.

Leaping the lower cliff in the dark was much scarier than this. There's no one in the blue-green water below me, and the rocks have broken off below, meaning there's no chance of hitting one on the way down.

"Let's do this." I turn in his arms and kiss him square on the lips, closed-mouthed and quick. I slip out from under him, pivot, and say, "Me first this time."

As I leap, my senses kick into overdrive, one at a time. The rushing of wind against my ears and the faraway whoop of Axel's voice. The earthy smell of air as I suck it in, the salty taste of my lips. The blurred scenery smearing as I plunge. The sense of emptiness as my stomach drops out from under me. Followed by the sensory overload.

I imagine Lorelei watching me, salivating. Clasping and unclasping her bony fingers. I lift my middle finger to the sky, flipping her off.

This is the best feeling in the world.

Chapter 15

"You two come out here much?" Ryan/Dad asks, readjusting his backpack. On Friday he messaged Saff and me, suggesting we hike from the beach up to the Bluffs this weekend.

His current housesitting gig includes the care, exercise, and entertainment of three dogs—a chocolate Lab, an English cocker spaniel, and a dachshund—one for each of us to walk. The owner travels extensively and pays extra when Ryan takes them on day trips. We've been walking for an hour, and Ryan's already taken several photos of the dogs and texted them to the owner. Seems silly to me, but whatever.

Saff shoots me a look. Once, in a misguided attempt at sisterly bonding, I told her about Axel's and my bucket list—big mistake. Instead of considering it uber cool, she marked it as more evidence of my irresponsibility.

I'm in no hurry to mention that Axel and I jump off these cliffs. I probably wouldn't hesitate if Ryan was still my stepuncle, but now that he's something else, I'd prefer not to tell him. "We like to swim here," I answer, settling on a half-truth. "I'm not, uh, normally up for cardiovascular activity." More accurately, I only tolerate cardiovascular activity for a goal.

Like climbing the cliffs to jump. Not walking for the sake of walking.

"Cayenne makes laziness an art form," Saff explains. She's wrapped the dachshund's leash around her wrist several times, and her hand is turning a deep shade of pink. "Although you probably already know that."

"Sounds familiar. I think you inherited that from me," Ryan says. I can hardly keep from gagging—resembling Ryan is the last thing I want. He tugs on the Lab's leash and adds under his breath, "Your mom was not that way."

"Can we talk about her?" Saff asks, tugging at her dog. He's buried his nose deep into some bushes, investigating. "Or does that make you uncomfortable?"

Ryan turns to Saff, studying her, maybe thinking about how he wants to respond. "Yes . . . and yes." He whistles, low, and Saff's dog scampers toward him, yanking on Saff's wrist. "I don't like talking about her, or thinking about her, really." He kneels and ruffles the dog's fur. "But we *can*," he says, straightening up. "We probably should."

"It's just . . . that I don't really remember her." Saff carefully unwinds the leash from around her wrist and shakes her hand out. "I've got the video diary, and the journal, and photos around the house, but I don't have clear memories of her."

Ryan looks up from the dog. "Jenny was great."

"Can you be more descriptive?" Saff asks, flexing and unflexing her fingers. She doesn't seem angry, though I know she wrote that she was in her journal entry. She seems more curious than anything. Maybe she's over it. Or maybe she's ambivalent, like me.

"Really great. Stupendous. Best woman I ever met."

Saff considers this and then says, "Maybe more specific?"

"I'm no good with words. I don't know . . . She was a rock star. Super smart, motivated, fun. Beautiful. That woman did more in her thirty-one years than most people do in sixty." Ryan finds a large smooth rock and hauls his backpack on top of it. He unzips it, and I peek inside. He's crammed the backpack with water bottles and small containers of nuts, granola, and dried fruit. "Hungry?" Ryan asks, maybe to change the topic.

"Starving," I respond, definitely to change the topic. "Anyone mind if I steal all the dried apricots? I'll leave the raisins as compensation."

Saff ignores me. "You must have loved her."

Ryan kind of freezes, his hand in midair, going for the granola. He scoops a handful of it into his mouth, and then mumbles with his mouth half-full, "I'm no good at this kind of conversation."

"But we have to have it. *Dad*." Now I do hear the anger in her voice. Doesn't she know when to lay off? Clearly Ryan's struggling with this.

"We actually don't have to talk about this stuff. We can just hike and ingest granola. It's okay," I tell him.

"No. Saffron's right. It's just—I'm not used to—" Ryan breaks off, his words garbled because of the handful of granola between his cheek and teeth. "Shit. This is hard for me."

I silently second that.

Saff is not so silent. "We could talk about horse crap every time we walk, there sure is a lot of it up here. But I've missed almost eighteen years of having a father. I don't want to wait any longer."

Ryan swallows his mouthful of granola, grimacing, as though he hasn't chewed it enough first and it hurts going down. "Yes. I loved her." He runs a hand through his hair, leaving tiny speckles of granola. "But I didn't deserve her."

Saff finds a seat on a rock and I perch on another one. Ryan stands, facing us, but up on the rock, we're taller than him. Neither of us speak, just wait for Ryan to go on. "She hung out with me, but it was more like a gift, like charity, and I knew it. She didn't want anything more."

Hearing this makes me sad.

Ryan twists away from us to stare at the horizon, and both Saff and I reposition ourselves so that we can hear him. "The less she needed me, the more I adored her. And it's not like I had many other people in my life."

A stream of ants crawl along the rock, searching for sustenance. Ants have a purpose. They know their path instinctively. Ants don't bother with college apps, soul searching or reconnecting with long-lost parents.

"I let her down over and over again." Ryan turns back toward us, and his eyes are full. I absolutely one hundred percent do not want to see this man cry. "And I let you both down over and over again."

"Okay, so I get why she didn't want you on the birth certificate. But once she found out she was dying, wasn't that like a game changer?" Saff presses.

"Not for her." Ryan's eyes dry up, the liquid evaporating so quickly that I wonder if it was ever really there. There's low-grade frustration in his tone. Suddenly I wonder if he resents Mom for limiting him in this way. For not trusting him. For not thinking that an imperfect father was better than no father at all.

"What about for *you*?" Saff shifts impatiently on the rock. "What about for *us*?"

"Listen. I've never been a guy who could get anything done without directions. Not putting something together, not finding a restaurant, nothing. There were no directions for being a dad." The emotion retreats. "The idea of that, of being alone and in charge, it terrified me. Plus I couldn't stay clean. I tried." He tosses more granola into his mouth, as if giving up on himself.

"How hard?"

"It's more complicated than just willpower. It's a disease." Ryan crunches the granola and stands his ground. "And you were in good hands."

"Tee was *nineteen*!" Saff's eyes catch hold of me like a fish hook, and some of the accusation pierces me, as if I should be jumping in to help her. But I only want to run away from this conversation. Why is she pushing him so hard?

"I did try, you know. I was depressed and mad at myself for being incapable. I told myself that once I got clean for good, I'd request a paternity test and then I could take you back." He pauses and swallows. "But by the time I got my act together, Luke had stepped in to help Tee, and I thought maybe you were better off."

"That's a cop-out."

"Maybe." Ryan shrugs. "But it's also what your mom wanted."

"That's a cop-out too." Saff hops off the rock, like she can't stand to sit any longer.

"She was the kind of lady who never needed directions for anything," says Ryan. "She just knew. Irritatingly, she was always right."

"Says who?" Saff steps into Ryan's space. "I'm not buying this whole conspiracy *we know better than you* shit. Maybe

115

she *wasn't* right." Wow. If I wasn't so uncomfortable, I'd be impressed with Saffron's gumption. "You *could* have stepped up. You *should* have stepped up!"

Ryan studies her. This might be the first time he's looked her in the eye so far. "You may not remember, but early on I used to take you both out for lunch on Saturdays, but you were always missing Tee, and counting the minutes until you could go back. I guess I felt inadequate and so I . . . I just stopped trying so hard." He breaks eye contact and fiddles with the leash. "You don't have to accept me as your father now. But I'm offering." He backs away from her, his voice constricted. "I'm gonna take a break. I'll be back in a few." He and the Lab climb up toward Mesa Ridge, stepping out of earshot.

Saff turns to me, her cheeks roasting red, like she might burst open any second. "Why didn't you say something?"

"Why didn't you chill out?" I shoot right back at her. "What are you trying to do, push him into a relapse?"

"That's not fair, Cay. You're suggesting that if I call the guy out on his shit, I'm going to make him fall apart?"

"Basically."

"That's exactly the kind of thinking that got him in this mess. He's capable of owning his decisions. Mom clearly thought he was a total loser. The Chowders expect nothing from him. And we've bought into the idea of Ryan-the-Reject for years. I refuse to believe that anymore."

"Believe what you want. But I don't get the point of getting so carried away. I say we just see what happens. Either he'll pull it together or he won't. It doesn't matter what he *says* right now with you screaming in his face, it matters what he *does*." I climb down off the rock. "Sheesh, Saffron. I'm supposed to be the hot tempered one, not you."

She shakes it off, walking around the landing, rubbing the dachshund behind the ears. Ryan wanders over to us after about twenty minutes. He's quiet. On the way back to the beach, we don't say much, and when we do, it's all horse-poo caliber small talk.

Chapter 16

"Looks like someone coated this place in Pepto Bismol," Saff comments as we put the final touches on the living room.

"Not bad, considering." I check the clock. Booby party guests should be arriving soon. We've got a playlist jamming in the background, all women's empowerment themed. Saff and I have channeled our energy into prepping for the party. We've been walking with Ryan/Dad once a week, but keeping all conversations in safely neutral territory. Neither of us have suggested watching another Mom video.

Nonna's clinking around in the kitchen, probably checking on her cream of beet soup, also a lovely shade of pink. We'll serve it in bread bowls with a floating round crouton placed strategically in the center. We haven't spelled out for Nonna that the bread bowl will be yet another image of a breast, assuming the floating crouton doesn't migrate to the side, but I have to assume she knows.

Saff and I return to the kitchen. Nonna's holding a bottle of light pink wine, which she's clearly been sampling. "Breasts are a nuisance once you get to my age," she babbles. "They're heavy, they sag to your belly button. Maybe I can sign up for this."

"Not the image I want," Saff whispers to me. Nonna's saggy jugs pop into my brain too, uninvited.

"I can't go without a bra anymore, girls. Not even at bedtime. And who sleeps with a bra?" Nonna gestures with a wooden spoon for emphasis, and little splatters of pink beet soup fling outward. Ugh. Another unwanted image.

"How're we going to sober her up before everyone else gets here?" Saff whispers again.

I move the pink chardonnay out to the living room, away from her tiny "sampling" cup. We sit her down with a glass of water.

"I liked my breasts until I was about forty." Yep, she's definitely drunk. "You know, in the sixties, when I was just a young teenager, I followed all the news coverage about burning bras and protesting against the Miss America Pageant. Some of that was media hype—don't know that women were really burning bras all over the place . . ."

Saff and I exchange a look.

"Anyway, the point was that bras were viewed as symbolically oppressive. Women wanted to be seen for who they were as people and for their contributions to the world, not for how they looked. But I think plenty of women are still just as obsessed with breasts as men." Saff and I exchange glances. "We're obsessed with size and shape, and we're even harder on ourselves than men are."

"Here, Nonna. Drink some more water." Maybe we need to hide her in the back room until after the party.

But as soon as the guests arrive, it's clear we shouldn't have wasted any time worrying. Maybe because there are no men or small children, maybe because of the giggles that start with our booby party games, maybe because of what Tee is about to do, or maybe the pink chardonnay has morphed into a truth serum—no one seems to have a filter.

Truthfully I can't follow all the conversations, but I hear plenty of fascinating snippets.

"You're gonna lose ten pounds overnight. Bam! The newest diet."

"You think they weigh ten pounds?" Tee cups her hands underneath her breasts as if she can weigh them.

"At least."

"We could try weighing them. Do you have a food scale?" Luckily no one can find the meat scale—probably because I slip back into the kitchen and hide it in the fridge. No way do I want to watch Tee weigh her breasts.

"Okay, question. Does anyone here get hair growth on their boobs?"

"What?" Laughter.

"*No*, seriously. I have to pluck this one hair that keeps sprouting up on my left breast."

"Oh, that's normal. I get those too."

"It's a mini forest for me." Followed by jokes related to hair removal methods.

"I think you're a trooper to have the reconstruction, Tee," says Vanessa's mom, Lucy, one of the few women here I know by name. "I looked it up—forty-four percent of women choose *not* to reconstruct after mastectomy."

"More power to them! I think that's brave."

"Why is that any braver than going for reconstruction? It's actually less surgery."

"Besides—you'd never have to wear an itchy bra again!"

"Well, Tee"—Lucy again—"if you get cold feet about the reconstruction, Vanessa swears by these bras she's been wearing since she transitioned. I think the same company makes mastectomy bras. I can send you the info."

"Isn't it the best when you find a bra that's comfortable?"

"Totally. A comfortable bra is more important than comfortable shoes."

"Just think—your nipples won't get sore during your period."

"Will you even have nipples?"

"Yes. They're doing a nipple-sparing procedure."

"My nipples don't get sore on my period. Just when I was breastfeeding."

"Oh, breastfeeding!" General murmurs of empathy. "Mine got all cracked and even bled a little. No one warned me about that."

"I loved breastfeeding. Especially when little Max would reach up and touch my chin. It was the coziest thing ever."

"I probably would have loved it if I wasn't nursing twins. I tried to do them at the same time, you know, for efficiency, but I swear I felt like a cow."

"It was pumping that made me feel like a cow. All hooked up to that machine and everything. Ugh."

"Breast milk is liquid gold, ladies. People are selling it these days."

"Yeah, but I'd never give my baby someone else's breast milk. That's just weird to me."

"You would if it was a choice between that or formula."

"They make formula out to be this evil thing, but please."

"Easy, ladies, we're scaring the children." Suddenly all eyes are on Saff and me. We probably do look a little overwhelmed. We busy ourselves getting the cake ready to bring out, and by the time we set it on the table, they've toned it down. Kind of.

"You know what we need to do?"

"What?"

"A lingerie photo shoot. So you and Luke can remember your pre-surgery body."

"Yeah, but ladies? My surgery is tomorrow."

"Then we'll just have to make it happen today."

* * *

Apparently a friend of a friend of a friend's cousin is a professional photographer who has a studio in town, and since it's midday Sunday, she has no photo shoots scheduled. After an appeal to a sense of solidarity with her fellow women, and an offer to double her traditional fee, she agrees to do what the ladies call a boudoir photo shoot.

Saff and I watch Tee's friends wet and blow-dry her hair, using a round brush to create extra volume. They ransack her undies drawer, selecting a lacy black bra and matching panties. They pick out a silky deep-blue nightie. They redo her makeup, adding thick black liner, fake lashes, a layer of powder, and ruby red lipstick.

"She could be a model," I whisper to Saff. "I hope I look that good when I hit thirty."

Nonna stumbles into the Minions' bedroom to lie down, claiming fatigue, but I'm betting it's just too much pink wine. The rest of us carpool over to the studio, stuffed in the back of some soccer mom's car, next to a duffle bag that smells of sweaty cleats, Icy Hot, and wilted grass.

We sit quietly in the darkened edges of the studio, watching Tee try not to get the giggles while arranging herself seductively for the cameras. Truthfully, she laughs most of the time.

It's hard not to, what with all her friends watching, as she places her hand behind her head, tilts herself back, and bats her eyes at the camera. I'm sure some of the shots will come out with her laughing, but honestly I think she's prettiest that way. Her laugh lines crinkling, her lips spreading wide to expose gleaming white teeth.

Somehow the other ladies start posing for photos too, albeit without the heavy makeup and hair prep, and just in their regular clothes, or in sexy nighties they've borrowed from Tee.

"So you're not offended by this?" I tease Saffron. "Aren't we, like, objectifying their bodies here?"

"We're appreciating beauty. There's a difference."

"You're confusing. It's okay for us to appreciate beauty but not okay for men to do that same thing?"

"It's all about choice." Saffron speaks slowly, like I'm dense. "It's about doing what makes you feel good, not just going along with other people's standards or expectations."

"How about you two?" the photographer asks us, discovering our hiding spot in the corner. When we both hesitate, she adds, "No need for a lingerie shoot. Let's just take them as you are right now."

So Saff and I run our fingers through our hair, apply the lipstick I keep in my purse, and pose. The photographer arranges us. Places my arm around Saff's shoulders, leans my head against her, and snaps. Has us lie on our backs, facing in opposite directions, and snaps. Catches us laughing at the wild things the ladies are saying in the background, and snaps. Has Tee get dressed, then kneel behind us with her arms draped around our shoulders, and snaps.

We drive home in Tee's car. "Great party, girls," she says,

smiling at us in the rearview mirror with some mixture of appreciation and apprehension. "You did good. This was the perfect last day with my breasts."

"You ready for tomorrow?" Saff asks.

"As ready as I'll ever be."

Chapter 17

Tee's scheduled check-in time at the hospital is at the ungodly hour of 5:45 a.m.—on a Monday, no less. The sound of the shower at five nudges me awake. Shortly after, Tee peeks her head into my darkened room.

"Nervous?" I ask softly, so she knows I'm awake. I scoot back to make more room.

"A little," she admits, padding over to my bed and easing herself down. Her just-washed hair drips on my face.

"You can back out. Or postpone."

"No—it's the responsible thing to do." There's a mix of emotions in her voice. "For my girls. I want to be at every one of their school plays. I want to be the one to explain to them about periods and teach them how to drive. I want to be at their weddings. I have to do this." She shakes her hair, and little shampoo-scented droplets splatter on me. "Take care of my babies while I'm gone, okay?"

"No problem." I wipe the dampness off. "This is practically a vacation for you. You get to lie in a bed, someone will bring you food—"

"With a morphine drip," Tee adds, some humor creeping

in. "You're right. Now all I need is a massage."

"But seriously." I reach my hand out, searching for her fingers. "Good luck."

"Thank you," she says, accepting my hand. "And good luck surviving my kids." After a moment she adds, "Cayenne. I've been thinking. The mastectomy isn't a cakewalk, but timing the oophorectomy will be an even harder decision. I kind of wish I'd known about my mutation earlier. I might've started having kids younger, maybe had more of them—"

"The stress is causing you to lose your mind," I say. "More kids? The Minions are plenty of work as it is."

She forces a laugh. "Well, it's just—all of this might've been easier if I'd had more time to plan. I think you and Saff should seriously consider getting tested for the BRCA gene soon."

"Maybe. Someday."

"You can decide when. I just—I—information is power, you know?"

"Yeah, and ignorance is bliss."

"I understand not wanting to know. Especially because you're both so young. Just start thinking about it." She lets go of my hand, stands up, and moves softly toward the door.

"Wait, Tee?"

"What?" She half turns at the door frame.

"I love you."

She catches the words with some surprise. We're not really an "I love you" kind of family. I hear Luke say it to the Minions sometimes. But Tee uses those words sparingly. And I say them . . . uh . . . never. I mean who would I say them to? My sister? That'd be weird, wouldn't it? She'd probably laugh. I'm totally in love with Axel, but I don't use those words with him either.

Tee stands there in the doorway, the hallway light outlining her frame, and smiles. "I love you too, Miss Cayenne Pepper. Stay spicy."

I lie in bed for a while after she leaves, just savoring the warmth of my comforter, the silky sheets that mold to my skin, the sound of the overhead fan shushing, and the smell of flowery shampoo. Maybe her words leave warmth too, coating me with something sweet and good, perhaps a chocolate shell. I do like chocolate.

Sleep grabs hold of me, pulling me downward, and I see an image of Lorelei dancing with flowy scarves in both hands. She wraps a silky red scarf around a woman, like a constricting python, until she is trapped. I cannot see the woman's face.

I wake again at nearly seven, which means I'm already twenty minutes behind schedule. I've got a toy hunt to orchestrate. Saff and I decided it's our mission to make this surgery day filled with fun for the Minions. They don't really understand what's going on, but they'll definitely miss their mom, and we want to keep them distracted.

Before I even brush my teeth, I grab my hand-drawn treasure map and a box of trinkets. I zip around the house, planting toys in semi-hidden places, and finally I tape the treasure map onto their bathroom mirror, anticipating the squeals of excitement when they discover it. I might have even more fun with this than they will. And honestly, I'm probably benefitting from the distraction more too. I don't want to think about Tee, lying on a cold operating table, while they . . .

Ugh. Don't want to picture it. I don't even feel up to joking about it today—it's too real.

* * *

Nonna and Papa pick up the Minions before school and in the afternoon Saff and I will join them at the mall. After the longest school day ever, we arrive at the shopping center and Saff messages Nonna to ask where we should meet.

"Oh, how adorable!" she says when Nonna texts her back. "The girls are getting haircuts. They decided they want to donate their hair!"

"Aw, Luke's gonna be so bummed," I remark. "He loves their hair."

"Cayenne. Sometimes I can't stand listening to you, and I mean that in the most loving way possible." Saff half-shoves me, but not hard enough to make me stumble. We step onto the escalator. "Do you even hear yourself? It's their hair, not his. He doesn't own it. And it's replaceable."

"Sure, but he's their dad and they're little. Isn't he supposed to make decisions for them? Like how he makes them eat broccoli even though they gag?"

"Different, Cayenne, and you know it. Long hair isn't healthier for you than short hair. And I doubt Luke would care about his kids getting haircuts if they were boys."

I glance up. We still have a lot of escalator ahead of us. Sometimes I don't know how to navigate these conversations with Saff. I'm just talking about hair, but somehow, she's extending this way further.

Saff's revving up. "So if you asked Luke, he'd insist that he's a feminist, that women can do anything they want—he'd encourage his girls to be firefighters if they wanted, he'd say they can do whatever they put their minds to. But he'd have no problem telling his daughters not to cut their hair, even though that's inherently sexist."

I watch her out of the corner of my eye. My sister loves

lecturing me about my shallow mindset, but she's being even more intense than usual. "Are you . . . okay, Saff?'"

"I'm fine," she snaps. "It's just—Vanessa's brother is being shitty to her again and it pisses me off. Apparently last night when their mom got back from the party, he joked that if Aunt Tee didn't want her breasts anymore, maybe Vanessa could take them."

I wince. "God, that is shitty." My heart hurts for Vanessa.

I suddenly realize that all this talk of breasts and ovaries and womanhood probably feels way different for someone like Vanessa than it does for me. Maybe that should've occurred to me earlier, like before I yelled about boobs in a crowded grocery store. I wasn't trying to be insensitive—just funny. But sometimes those two things overlap in ways that don't occur to me. Typically I don't spend too much time worrying about offending or hurting anyone, because my humor is who I am, take it or leave it. But maybe I need to rethink that approach.

"And it's been *years* since she transitioned and he still says messed-up stuff like that. So the thought of a guy getting to dictate a woman's relationship with her body feels extra gross right now."

"I get it," I say cautiously. "But also—that's totally not the same. We're just talking about haircuts. What Vanessa's dealing with is on a whole other level."

"God, Cayenne. I wasn't trying to equate the two. I just think everyone should be in charge of their own bodies. That's all."

When we enter the hair salon, we both paste on cheerful expressions. Missy and Maggie are facing large mirrors. Their hair curls around their ears, and their little eyes are gleaming. "Cay! Saff! We're helping!"

"It was their idea," Nonna explains proudly. "We were talking about how Mommy's doing her surgery so that she won't get sick, and they had all these questions about what kind of sick, and we explained about cancer and hair loss, and before we knew it they were asking how they could help, and I told them some people donate their hair . . . and then they insisted on it." Nonna smiles at us. "I have some pretty impressive grandkids." It's so strange to be included in that statement, and I decide not to burst her bubble by telling her Luke will disapprove.

Nonna and Papa insist on treating us all to a snack at the food court, and none of us argue. Ryan/Dad meets us there, and I notice how he slurps his noodles extra loud to make the Minions laugh. I wonder if he did that kind of thing when I was little. Saff is still standoffish with him, but I'm finding it harder to resent him. He really does seem like someone doing his best, even if his best falls short.

We're on kid-duty for the rest of the day, so after the hand-off, Saff and I surprise the Minions with a trip to Mom's secret garden spot. We boost them up to climb trees, we lie on our backs and fly them in the air on our feet, we practice somersaults. When laughter from the park calls to them, we push them on the swings and send them soaring high. I've stuffed my pockets with candies, and I hide them throughout the park, sending them on their second treasure hunt of the day.

I follow them around, recording videos. I'll document this week, put it to music, and give it to Tee as a get-well gift. "I'm going to start taking videos of the girls," I tell Saff. "Maybe I'll make them a video compilation of every year of their life." I'm already thinking of what to title year four. Fabulous fours? Frustrating Fours?

"Mom's rubbing off on you," Saff teases, her mood vastly improved.

"Nah." I hold my hand to my heart in an overly dramatic way. "I just want to document these precious moments for posterity." I fake-swoon. "Because time flies." Saff just shakes her head and giggles. It's the truth though. I really do want to start videoing the girls so they have these memories when they're older.

Afterward we crash at home for a princess movie marathon. About ten minutes in, Saff and I escape to the kitchen to pop popcorn, sprinkling extra salt and drizzling melted butter.

Luke texts us. *Surgery's done. She's in recovery now. All went well.*

"Seriously?" I check the time on my phone. It's after five. "How long was that surgery?"

"Her check-in time was probably way before they actually started," says Saff. "Plus, Tee told me the reconstruction would take a lot longer. She had the option of doing it all at once, or doing the reconstruction in smaller procedures over time, and she opted to get it over with."

"Ooo, too bad I'll never find out what half-reconstructed boobs look like." I crunch a halfway popped kernel, deciding that now that it's all over, I'm allowed to joke again. I'm a little surprised at the intensity of the relief I feel. I didn't even realize I was holding in so much tension all day long. I'm so glad it's done and she's okay.

Saff looks unamused, so I change the subject. "Hey, now that the hard part is over, you want to tag team with the Minions for the rest of the night? I need a break. How about I go hang with Axel for a few hours, and then you get a turn to escape with Fletcher?"

"That sounds really nice, actually," Saff agrees. "I don't know how people do this parenting thing full time. It's exhausting."

That's not the only part of this day I'm finding exhausting, but I'm sure some time with Axel will be the distraction I need.

Chapter 18

"Let's head up. We've got two hours before we have to be back to relieve Saff." I double check my phone clock one more time before stowing it with my purse and my shoes under Axel's passenger seat.

"It's too early." Axel keeps one hand on the wheel while lifting his other to gesture at the sinking sun. We're going to jump Mesa Ridge tonight, and Axel thinks part of the fun is walking up in darkness. "I can keep us entertained down here." He leans in close, pressing his lips to mine.

"I know you can." I kiss him, but slowly pull back. Saff wants me home in time for her and Fletch to catch a nine o'clock movie. "But let's walk up now. We'll get situated up there, watch the sun set, have some alone time with only the sun as our witness, and then when the time is right . . . experience the rush of our lives."

"Well, when you say it like that . . ." Axel smooths my hair, his hands gentle.

"And arrive home in time for my wonderfully neurotic sister." I get of the car and start for the path, gesturing for him to follow me.

"So how's your aunt doing?" He catches up quickly and steps onto a huge rock. He reaches his hand down to me and I let him pull me up beside him.

"Surgery's over. It went well. But she was under anesthesia for most of the day. Intense." His legs are longer than mine, so I have to work to get up that rock. My quad muscles thank me with an appreciative ache.

"Extreme, if you ask me," Axel says, still holding my hand. "Letting the fear of death dictate how she lives her life."

For some reason his comment irritates me. "Would you think it was extreme if she had cancer?" The soles of my feet feel tender.

"Of course not. But she doesn't even have cancer! She just thinks she *might* get it."

I'm suddenly defensive. "Just think about my family history, Axel. We die. All the women die. And all in their thirties." The intensity in my own voice surprises me. "Why would anyone take that chance?"

Axel stops walking and studies me. "Is that what you're gonna do when you're thirty?" His voice is quiet.

"What?" I drop his hand and step back. A tiny rock pierces my foot, and I hold it, balancing on one foot, and rubbing it.

"You said all the women in your family die in their thirties. So it'll hit you too."

I sit down in the dirt to examine the sole of my foot. "I'm only a little more than halfway to thirty. I don't have to think about this yet."

"You're almost *two thirds* of the way to thirty." Axel kneels in front of me, bringing us back to eye level. "How old were you when you grew boobs, like thirteen?"

"This is a weird conversation," I point out.

He runs his finger along the edge my sore foot. "Maybe. But, Cayenne, I think it's a conversation you need to have."

A tiny dot of blood blooms on my foot, mixing with dirt. "For your information, growing breasts takes a long time. They don't just pop out, you know. I think I started when I was eleven maybe, at twelve I got my training bra, and I got a real bra at about thirteen."

"Okay so you've had boobs for somewhere between five and seven years." Axel uses the edge of his swim trunks to blot at my dot of blood. "And in another twelve, you'll have them surgically removed?"

"Hold on." I move his trunks away. "Why are you making this about *me*? I never said *I* was going to do this. We're talking about my aunt. I have no idea what I'll do when I'm thirty. Who knows? Maybe I don't even have the stupid gene. Or maybe by then they'll have a quick cure, and I can just get vaccinated or something."

I stand up, perching my injured foot on its toes. Frustration motivates me to push on ahead, leading the way.

Axel's close behind. "How much have you researched this gene? What percentage of people who have it actually get cancer? Have you looked into the numbers?"

"God, you're irritating. I don't know. I'd google it but I don't have my phone on me, because we're about to jump off a cliff." The path loops, and I follow it blindly. I move faster, favoring my injured foot. "Can we stop talking about this now?" We hardly ever argue. I wonder if he's as surprised by the frustration in my voice as I am.

Axel reaches for my hand and pulls me back, so that we're face to face. His forehead creases like an accordion. "Look, I love you, Cay. But I'm worried, because you've got all this craziness coming at you—your aunt's surgery, your dad, and these messages from your dead mom. Who's been dead since long before you grew boobs, by the way."

"Let's call them breasts." I shake him off. I have no idea why I'm saying this—I call them boobs all the time.

"You're the most amazing, most fun girl I've ever been with." His lips part for a tentative smile. "Don't lose that part of yourself. I don't want you to change."

"What the hell are you talking about? I'm not changing." I say this firmly, because it's true. "I'm up here, ready to leap off a cliff, same as you. Besides, it is possible to have a serious conversation and still be a fun person, you know." I feel myself softening. "I'll always be fun," I say, although at this moment I feel a million miles away from fun. I push ahead, walking until the rocks clear and the ground flattens toward the edge.

I glance down. The water sparkles below, alive under the dipping sun. Truthfully, I'm not in the mood to jump. This conversation has already hijacked my heart—I don't need a forty-foot leap to ramp it up. Plus, all this talk of life and death makes jumping seem a bit, I don't know, juvenile? That thought surprises me, and I shake it off.

Axel edges behind me and slips his arms around my waist. "You're not afraid, are you?" he asks, almost playfully.

"Of course not," I snap back.

"There's my badass girlfriend," he says approvingly. "You've got balls of steel. Are you afraid of anything? You afraid to die?" He reaches for me again.

I don't want to be. I visualize Lorelei visiting my dreams, and how badly I want to contain her. "A little," I admit. "But fear is human. I'd be lying if I said I wasn't afraid of *anything*."

Axel coaxes me right to the edge. We stand, curling our toes over, the wind flirting with our hair, and the edge of cool air bristling my skin. "How about you?"

"Sometimes I am and sometimes I'm not. It's weird. Most of the time I'm not. I want to live and play hard, and if I die young, oh well. But when I actually think about not breathing, about never taking another breath, or never having another thought, it kind of freaks me out." He puts his arms around my shoulders and they warm me.

"It *is* kind of weird to think about not existing anymore. I mean I guess there's heaven and all that, if you believe in it, but who knows what that's really like anyway? And not being here on this Earth, not eating and breathing and speaking— well, I guess it's kind of like imagining a time before we were born." I shiver. "That's a weird concept too."

"So . . . what are you most afraid of?" He asks.

"Loving someone and then losing them." I answer immediately. I don't even have to think about it. "That's my biggest fear."

"Where does jumping off this cliff rate?"

"Oh, it doesn't even register." And it doesn't. I'm not craving the rush, but the jump doesn't scare me. I move forward.

"Wait—" Axel's arms tighten around my shoulders. "The sun's still out . . . and I believe you said something like 'alone time with only the sun as our witness.'"

"Oh. That." I swivel in his arms so that I'm facing him, my back against the gaping drop.

He kisses me deeply, and I soften under his lips. He moves to my neck and my ears, and I tilt my head up toward the setting sun to expand the length of my neck. The wind blows suddenly, and the force of it—plus the fact that I'm already leaning backward—tips me.

Axel's arms absorb the movement. "Careful," he whispers in my ear. "Somehow I think a backwards jump off this cliff might trump our whole rush hierarchy. Maybe someday."

"A backwards jump might rearrange my entire face," I agree, imagining my nose and chin connecting with any of the rough rocks that line the side of the cliff.

One year, when Saff was ten and we were at the community swim camp, she and I had a backwards jumping contest into the pool. She didn't get the distance she needed, and she split her chin on the concrete. The lifeguard helped us manage the blood, and there was a lot of it, but he kept asking us, "What's your mom's number? I need to call your parents." Both Saff and I were crying too hard to say anything. Saff turned ghost white, more from her fear of blood than from the pain, but it scared me. I kept thinking, *What if she dies? Then I'll be all alone!*, which of course was completely ridiculous, but I was in panic mode, so I couldn't think straight. Finally I remembered Tee's phone number, and we called it from the lifeguard's cell. The ER doctor stitched Saff up so neatly that you can hardly see the scar.

I press back against Axel's bare skin, edging us away from the cliff a bit. "I can't concentrate on you when I'm this close to the edge," I explain. "And I want to concentrate on you."

"I like the way you're thinking." His arms relax, allowing us to shift away from the sheer drop. "I bet it's a rush though. It is for me."

"Me too." My heart rate has accelerated, making every cell in my body stand at attention. I feel wholly, completely alive.

Let's just say that Axel and I maintain that rush, that complete connection, until the sun dips in the sky and the moon replaces her watch. I lose myself, aware only of his lips, the light roughness of his skin against mine. He doesn't press for anything more than we've done before, and that reassures me. His touch absorbs me, zapping my brain of the ability to think, wiping away the thoughts of Tee, of toxic breasts, of troublemaking Minions, of my frozen-in-time-mother, of my complicated father . . . wipes it clean of everything. All that is left is this moment—many moments, dancing with each other, diving in and out of connectedness, simultaneously one and separate.

"And this is why I love you," announces Axel, nudging me out of my adrenaline-drunk state. "Let's end this night with a bang." He boosts me up, stabilizes me, and guides me toward the edge. "Together. We'll hold hands." I entwine my fingers in his, listen to his countdown: "On three . . . one, two, thr—"

We hang suspended in midair, connected, the wind circling around us, guiding us down. At some point, we're no longer falling in unison. I lose my grip, or he loses his, and we separate, plummeting downward in darkness. The rush of the wind against my ears makes me deaf, so I have no idea if he's hit the water yet. My adrenaline-saturated brain doesn't care. Maybe it's a millisecond, maybe a full second or two—

I land on top of him, my feet hitting something hard but fleshy. The impact fires through my leg, all the way up to my thigh, waking me from my trance as I suck in my breath.

The water consumes me, as it always does, but this time I try to open my eyes to see where Axel is. I swim upward, up-up-up toward oxygen. As I break through, I curse the darkness that bleeds over everything. I can't see. Not the shore, not Axel bobbing on the water. Panic spirals through my veins, paralyzing me. I can't get enough air, even though my head's well out of the water. I wonder if I might be hyperventilating, because no matter how fast I inhale my lungs don't fill. I tread water, trying to slow my breathing so that I can at least hear Axel's voice.

"Axel!" I call out, my voice hoarse and not loud enough to be heard "A-Axel!" I try again.

Nothing.

Shit. How hard did I hit him? What if I knocked him out? Or disoriented him? Or what if the force of my body's impact plummeted him too deep to reach the surface in time? If he doesn't get to the surface, how will I find him? Can I find him? And help is an eternity away. My phone is in the car—it'll take forever to get to it.

"Axel!" I shout, louder this time.

Nothing.

An ache spreads across my chest, racking me with tearless sobs. This does not make it easier to breathe. *Get it together*, I instruct myself. It feels like a lifetime, but it's probably only seconds. I close my eyes and focus on controlling the sobs, regulating my breaths, gathering the thoughts that threaten to spill into the water and be lost forever.

Once I've reined myself in, I listen. For breaths, for splashing, for any sign of life.

Nothing.

I focus hard, scanning for anything I can see in the moonlight.

Nothing.

I submerge myself to search in the dark water, as if I can find him in that nothingness. Maybe he's just gone farther down. Maybe I'll find him floating not too far under my feet.

I realize quickly that I'm wasting precious time, that the odds of connecting with him underwater are slim, even though we clearly broke the surface at the same place. My foot's impact might have rocketed him in a different direction.

Nothing.

Maybe I just killed him. The tearless sobs creep back up again, making it difficult to concentrate. I have to at least try to get help. I orient myself, swimming toward what I think is the shore.

"Cayenne!" I hear from a different angle.

"Axel?" I half-scream.

"Oh my god, you scared me," he calls back.

I burst into tears and swim toward his voice, the salt of my relief mixing with the water. Somehow I make it to the shore, where he stands dripping. He wraps his arms around me.

"I-called-to-you . . ." My words break through my hiccup sob-breaths.

"I had to get right to shore." He speaks into my hair, easing us both onto the ground. "Man, you really whacked me. I was afraid I'd pass out, so I swam right over. I didn't hear you calling. Probably the water in my ears."

"I-thought-I-killed-you."

"No. Just gave me a head bump. And the biggest rush of my life."

"I'm *never* doing that again." I press my hands against my forehead. "It's not worth it."

"Hey, take it easy." He pats my back.

I wipe my face.

"You never cry." This is not entirely true. I rarely cry, because I hate crying.

"I know. I just thought—"

Axel presses against me as though he's a human Band-Aid. When he speaks again, his voice is stronger. "Tomorrow we'll feel better. Before long we'll be ready for Pinnacle Peak. It's all about facing our fears, right? That's how we know we're really living."

"I want to go home," I tell him.

So we do.

On the drive, it occurs to me that both Tee and I are allowing Lorelei to control our lives, but in different ways. She's running away from Lorelei. I've been running toward her, in a never-ending game of chicken.

Chapter 19

"You're late!" Saff snaps before Axel and I are even through the front door. "We're gonna miss the previews." She stands up from the kitchen stool. Her completed homework is stacked neatly in front of her.

"Sorry, Saff." A twinge of guilt creeps in. "I owe you a latte."

"Your hair is wet," Saff says sharply. "And somehow I don't think you were lounging in a hot tub." She shakes her head at me, clearly disappointed, then grabs her keys, slinging her purse over her shoulder. "Kids are in their room, and they've been quiet for a good twenty minutes, so hopefully they're out for the night." She texts rapidly, probably coordinating details with Fletcher. "Luke is spending the night at the hospital with Tee."

"Okay." I dump my stuff on the counter. "Have fun." Maybe because tonight sucked so royally, I feel even worse about showing up late. I'm just as irresponsible as she thinks I am. "Sorry, again," I call after her.

Once Saff clicks the door closed, Axel beelines for the freezer and grabs a bag of frozen peas to place on his head. He quickly shifts his attention to the fridge.

"Hungry?" I ask him, trying to shake off my mood. He's practically drooling onto the floor.

"Starving."

"Okay. I am too." I'm considering tearing into leftover veggie lasagna and just picking off the mold. Everyone in our house tries to save leftovers, and Luke's been distracted enough lately that he's let his fridge-cleaning routine slide. "Wanna order pizza?"

The Minions must have not really been asleep, because as soon as Axel gets on the phone and says the word *pepperoni*, they creep out from their room and climb all over us with "I'm hungry too," and "I just wike cheese, no pepperoni" and "Can we have quarters for the games?"

I do a visual check in with Axel, who's still on the phone with Pizza Palace. "Let's take them out!" I can film a few more videos of the Minions for Tee.

He covers the phone and whispers, "It's nine-fifteen."

"The night is young," I protest, though I know it's way past their bedtime. Maybe I can redeem this crappy night by cementing my status as the fun cousin.

Axel grumbles a bit, but eventually he tells the Pizza Palace clerk "pickup" instead of "delivery."

The Minions smell like toothpaste and they're wearing footie pajamas. They're too little to be self-conscious about leaving the house in pjs, though. They run, squealing, to slip on their crocs and climb into Gertrude.

I buckle both girls into their car seats, catching a whiff of their sweet smell. Saff must've given baths tonight too. They both smell like lilac gardens and baby soap. Axel straps on his seat belt, unusually quiet. Maybe he's not too thrilled about being roped into this whole babysitting routine.

I'm backing out of the driveway when one of the Minions screams.

"What? What?" I hit the brakes and twist all around. I didn't hit a dog or a squirrel, did I? I would've felt something, a bump or a thump or something like that.

"You forgot your seat behwt!" Missy screeches.

I almost laugh. They take everything so seriously. If they see someone with a cigarette, they run away wailing, as if the secondhand smoke will hunt them down to poison their lungs.

"Oh, silly me." I click right in. "There. I'm safe now."

"Impressionable young kids," I explain to Axel, who's giving me the funniest look. "I don't want to set a bad example."

He shakes his head and laughs. "You are a trip, Cayenne."

"I'm okay with that. At least I'm not a bore." I drive more slowly than usual, aware of the Minions in the back seat, chattering with as much excitement as if I'm taking them to Disneyland. Yep, I definitely win the award for the Fun Cousin.

* * *

An hour, one large pizza, countless refillable sodas, a series of phone-filmed videos, and a mind-numbing quantity of quarter arcade games later, we strap the Minions back into their seats to head home.

"I can drive if you want," Axel offers.

"Sure." I toss him the keys, slip into the passenger seat, and cue up some music. "We can car dance."

Axel pulls out of the lot, shaking his head at my silliness, but I'm too hyped up on fountain soda sugar and caffeine to care. I bop my head to the beat, leaning back and belting the words out loud. I peek back at the Minions, who are doing their best to imitate me, but sleep is pulling at their eyelids, slowing each blink and waterlogging their movements. I capture this on video before I say, "It's okay if you fall asleep, girls. It's pretty late." Apparently that's all the permission they need, because I swear they're out before I even turn back around.

I tap my fingers on the windowsill, drumming out the beat, but it's been a long day, and a yawn creeps up on me. "How can I be both pumped and drained at the same time? My body wants to sleep and my brain wants to party."

Just then, some jerk in a red convertible cuts Axel off. "Asshole!" he snaps. I check to see if the Minions heard that. The last thing I need is them jabbering curse words to Luke. He'll never let me babysit again. I'll go from Fun Cousin to Bad Influence Cousin in a flash. But no, the girls are out, their heads flopping to the side in a way that looks painful. Little kids must have necks made of rubber.

Axel floors it, veering to the right and edging past the red convertible. "Stop it, Axel," I scold. I love the guy, but does he really have to go neck-to-neck with this loser? I twist backwards to get a better view of the Minions. They're still out cold, their little heads bouncing up and down with the movement of the car, like Bobble Head dolls. It's comical.

Bam! The sound of crunching metal, the thrust of Axel's car scraping and rebounding off other surfaces. My head whipping to the side, slamming back toward my chest, and my whole body smashing against the dashboard. We must be spinning, because the world blurs around me, and I lose my up and down, my left and right. I hit the inside of one of the doors with my shoulder, my ankle crunches like an accordion . . . and reality starts to melt away.

Am I dying? Darkness creeps into my line of vision, rapidly inching toward the center, but even as my vision goes, I can hear the Minions wailing. I try to hold on for them, I really do, but my reality slips away. I sense Lorelei's presence, watching over me. Lurking. Hanging her head and wringing her hands, in mock sorrow, as if she hasn't been hungering for this moment. *The game is over,* she whispers.

Hanging there in the empty space are two thoughts.

One: "The Minions! Are they okay? I promised Tee I'd take care of them."

Two: "I'm not ready to die."

Chapter 20

Except for some periodic beeping, the world feels unreasonably quiet. I focus on breathing for a long time, just centering myself in my skin. *Where am I? What happened?* My brain feels blank. It takes all my strength to hold on to consciousness . . . I feel myself slipping away again, but I try to hang on.

I breathe deeply, inhaling an antiseptic hospital smell. There's brightness behind my eyelids. What if I can't open them? What if I'm in a coma with my brain active and trapped in a slug shell of a body?

My heartbeat accelerates, and I try desperately to open my eyes. My lids weigh a thousand pounds, but they do open, thank god. I'm in a hospital room. It's empty, aside from a guest chair and an array of medical apparatuses. No roommate. No visitors. No flowers or balloons. How long have I been here? What if I've been in a coma for years? What if I'm old?

I scan the room, soaking up as much information as I can. An IV is taped to my hand. I'm strapped to monitors that appear to be tracking my heart rate, among other things. There's a device around one of my fingers, probably to track oxygen levels. I'm aware of a dull ache with each breath, which tempts me to stop breathing.

I wiggle my finger, and it moves. Good news. I feel like I can wiggle my toes too, but I've read somewhere that paralyzed people experience the sensation that they're moving their feet when they're really not. I try to move my leg but meet some kind of resistance. It feels heavy—am I even moving it? Shit. A bubble of panic bursts inside me. I find a square red button on the side of the bed and push it.

Nothing happens for a long time. Finally a nurse enters. She's young, but she moves with a confidence that makes me think she's been doing this a while.

"Glad to see you awake. I'm Jasmine." She examines the monitors behind me and checks to make sure the intravenous fluids are flowing. "How's your pain, on a scale of one to ten with ten being the most extreme you can imagine?"

"Maybe a five. Which makes me scared to ask . . ."

Her lips tilt up slightly, as if she'd like to smile reassuringly, but can't. "You're pretty medicated right now. What do you remember about the car accident?"

I start to say, "Nothing," but her words have jogged my memory. Fragments of images piece together. I visualize being flung around our spinning car. I hear the wailing Minions.

"I didn't have my seat belt on," I confess, remembering. "Are the Minions okay?"

Now Nurse Jasmine lets loose a real smile. "Sometimes the medication makes people confused. You might be a little confused right now. You're asking about Minions?"

"Oh, sorry. That's just what I call the little girls. My cousins."

She moves over next to my abdomen and pats the sheets. "They'll be okay. We ran a bunch of tests to be sure. One of them has a contusion where the seat belt pressed against her, and the other is complaining about some neck pain, which is probably whiplash. We're keeping them overnight for monitoring, but I think you lucked out."

I imagine their tiny bodies tucked into white hospital beds, and my heart cracks. I cannot believe we had a car accident while I was watching them. My one job was to keep them safe and I *failed*.

"So it's still the same night? I haven't been in a coma or anything?"

"You've been semi-conscious, in and out a bit, which you may or may not remember."

"I don't remember." My lips are suddenly dry, as if they've been baked in an oven. "How is my boyfriend?"

"He's being treated for contusions from the air bag. But otherwise he's fine."

I think of the red convertible. "What about the people in the other car?"

"Minor injuries." Nurse Jasmine unhooks something that leads to my IV.

"Am I going to be okay?"

"You've got a laundry list of injuries, all of which you should recover from. You're lucky you didn't get thrown from the car." Her forehead furrows. "You said you didn't have your seat belt on. How come?"

"I forgot." I swallow hard. "Can I have a drink of water?"

"You forgot why? Or you forgot to put it on?"

"Both. I think," I mumble. Maybe the pain meds are wearing off, because my head is beginning to ache, as if it's being compressed inward on both sides.

"How do you forget to put your belt on?" Nurse Jasmine asks, not unkindly. She moves over to a pitcher I hadn't noticed and pours a small amount of water into a Styrofoam cup. "Isn't it automatic, like brushing your teeth in the morning or pouring milk in your cereal bowl?" She places a straw inside and holds it to my lips. "Take a very small sip at first, and let's make sure it stays down."

"Yeah. Not for me. I mostly ride without one." I take a tiny sip, just enough to moisten my lips and mouth. The water soaks into the crevices immediately, so I steal another small sip before she can take it away. I consider explaining that I don't like confinement—whether it's from seat belts or tight pants—but that would sound batty.

"Consider yourself lucky then. Hopefully you'll change that habit." Nurse Jasmine lists off the damages I've sustained: a closed head injury (most likely a concussion—which explains the head-squeezing sensation), a fracture of my right ankle, two broken ribs (hence the ache from breathing), and multiple contusions (the most painful bruises I've ever had). She moves back over to the computer by my bed and types information in, checking the monitors periodically. "Would you like to have something more for the pain? It's important to stay on top of it during these first hours after an accident."

"Okay." A thought hits me. Are the Minions all by themselves? "Can I call my sister?"

"She's here. She's with the little girls." Nurse Jasmine flicks her finger against a syringe to rid it of bubbles, and then inserts it into the IV. "You might feel this a bit. Some people say it stings slightly." I nod. "But I'll tell your sister that you're awake and asking for her."

"Okay." I do feel the medication enter my veins, circulating quickly through my system. It weighs me down, pulling at my body, making me both sink into the bed and float at the same time . . . until my eyelids sag, and I hover in nothingness.

Chapter 21

When I wake again, I sense someone's presence. My vision is fuzzy at first, and I blink hard, thinking it's Axel. But as the room comes into haphazard focus, I see Micah's shaggy curls.

My instinct is to shrink away from him, to hide myself and my stupidity. Even the slightest twist makes me feel like my ribs will snap in half. I start to turn my head, but my compressed brain scolds me, so I stay still. I'm so embarrassed that he's seeing me this way.

"How ya doing?" He sets his hand on my arm, like that'll somehow help me feel better. The meds are probably making me hallucinate, but the sensation of his skin on mine seems to send radiating heat up toward my chest.

"I've been better. What're you doing here?"

"Saff called me. She thought someone should be with you, but she didn't want to leave your cousins."

Shame creeps into my skin, broiling my cheeks. It's my fault. I convinced Axel to take the girls out with us so late, and I let him drive, knowing he might take a risk with the kids in the car.

"I feel shitty." There's something about being friends with

someone since we were both in diapers—I can't lie to him. I can't even lie to *myself* in front of him.

"You look shitty too," he jokes. I haven't seen a mirror yet, and I feel a spark of panic, wondering if I've permanently disfigured my face. I touch my cheek. "Just kidding. You're just a little bruised." He smiles. I reach for the hand that he'd rested on my arm. "I'm sorry you feel shitty."

"Yeah. Luke and Tee are going to hate me forever."

He moves his hand off of my arm, but I don't move mine. It feels good to hold on to something familiar. In a flash I'm back to being seven years old, holding his hand to cross the creek. The creek rocks wobbled, and we figured holding on to each other would decrease the chances of falling in.

"I think Luke is pretty shaken up, yeah. But nobody's told Tee yet." Micah sets my hand back on my bed sheets, and for a second I worry that without his touch connecting me to this earth, I might float away into the sky like a wayward helium balloon.

"How do you know?"

"Saff told me. Your boyfriend called her from the accident and she texted Luke. They decided not to tell your aunt right away. Everyone's mostly okay, and there's no reason to stress her out. She needs to focus on her recovery."

"Mostly okay," I repeat.

"Yeah, except for you. You're cuckoo in the head, Cay." Hearing him say this makes me want to shrivel up like those plastic shrinky-dink toaster toys. "Not wearing your seat belt? Come on. It's not like we're living in the sixties or something."

I turn my head away. I don't need to hear it anymore. "How's the car?"

"Totaled. But I'll take pity on you and give you a lift now and then."

"You're sweet, Micah."

"So I'm told." He points to a meal tray that the nurse must've brought when I was sleeping. "Can I get you anything? Lukewarm mystery meat stew? Slimy canned peaches? Gloppy lemon Jell-O?"

"Sounds lovely. You can have it. I need a nap." It feels like my brain is nearing maximum swell. The lights are too bright. I need to shut my eyes.

"That sounds about right. You've been awake a total of five minutes. You should sleep."

"It's the pain meds, they make me loopy."

"You were born loopy, Cayenne," he teases.

I close my eyes, and my voice sounds miles away. "Do you remember that creek we used to play in?"

"How could I forget?"

"We always held hands so we wouldn't fall."

"Yeah, but we did fall. We fell a bunch of times, and we both got drenched."

"I forgot about that."

"But it was fun."

"Yeah." I'm drifting away. "Suuuuper fuuuuun." I try to open my eyes, but the lids are too heavy. "Caaan you staaay for a whiiile?"

"I'll be here," he promises.

My voice is too far away to use, and my lids are cemented shut, but I sense him stroking my hair, smoothing it, and his gentle touch soothes me. I feel a little like a puppy, but not in a bad way.

With him watching over me, guarding my mystery meat stew and slimy peaches, I relax and let myself float.

Chapter 22

Micah must've slept in my room. I spot him curled up on a hospital chair with a blanket, his sleeping face soft, when a nurse checks on me. A different nurse this time—they must've changed shifts. This one is grandmotherly, all cinnamon and brown sugar. She smiles, nodding her head toward Micah. "What a sweet boyfriend, sleeping here all night in that awful chair."

"Oh, he's not my—" I start to explain, but I stop. Too much work.

I can't believe Micah is missing school for me. When the doctor stops in during his rounds, Micah straightens up and wipes his eyes and his mouth, trying to act as though he's been awake all night. He listens while the doctor gives me the rundown. I'll be staying one more night, and assuming I'm stable, I'll go home tomorrow morning with medication for pain management. Due to the broken ribs, the doctor will be watching me for any signs of pneumonia and working to prevent lung collapse (which sounds harrowing). They'll be giving me breathing treatments to expand my lungs.

I'm just offering Micah some of my gloppy cream of wheat and stewed prunes when Saff storms in. She pauses in the doorway, bristling like a porcupine, her lips pressed tightly together as if she can just Ziploc-seal up all that anger inside.

My thoughts swim, drowning in a mess of muddy explanations. "I'm sorry," I finally squeak out, and I swear my throat nearly closes up before I can finish.

"*Why*, Cayenne?" Saff glares at me with eyes so scalding they could burn through metal. "You, of all people, know how precious life is, how we can lose someone we love at any moment. Why do you take these idiotic risks? Not wearing your seat belt? Letting your irresponsible boyfriend drive Maggie and Missy in the middle of the night? Don't you care about anything?"

I turn to Micah for help. He just sort of freezes, like he doesn't particularly want to be pulled into this family argument and maybe if he stays really, really still, we'll forget he's there.

"The girls thought you died, Cayenne. When I got here, they were hysterical. They thought you died in front of them."

My throat tightens even more. Maybe I've injured my windpipe or something. It could be swelling. If I go into anaphylactic shock right here and now, Saff will feel sorry for not at least offering a smidgen of sympathy.

"The girls thought it was their fault for not reminding you to put on your seat belt. What if you had died, Cayenne? They'd have to live with that guilt forever." Now that she's opened her mouth, the words stream out, unfiltered. She doesn't even give me time to respond. "Do you ever stop to think about the people who love you?"

I poke at the IV taped to my hand. I do care. It's just that my heart is swelling, pumping so full of blood, and aching so badly it might burst inside my chest. I imagine myself popped like a balloon, blood everywhere.

"People survive, Saff," I say, because I have to say something. "Mom died and we survived."

Saff looks stung, like I've Tasered her from across the room. "Is that what you want for the people who love you, Cay? Survival? Walking around every day feeling like they're missing a part of themselves? Think of how different our lives would've been if Mom hadn't died. I can't even believe you said that." Saff turns halfway toward the door, and Micah slides down low in his chair.

She has a point. I mean, yes, we survived, and I'd like to think we're mostly well-adjusted—although after witnessing this argument, Micah will probably beg to differ. Plus there are the small details of train dodging and cliff leaping. Still, I'd give almost anything to have my mother back. An arm, a leg, a lung, a kidney . . .

Saff whips back toward me, her need to tell me off overpowering her desire to walk away. "You're selfish, Cayenne. You think what you want and what you need trumps everything else."

I press my hands to my forehead, but this snags the IV, so I lower it. "I am not. Shut up."

"Do you ever think about me, Cay? How I'd feel if you were gone? You're all I have left." Saff steps closer.

"Not true. You have Aunt Tee. You've got the Minions." My words sound flat. Tired.

"Are you seriously saying that to my face? Whatever. You don't get it. You know what? I'm done. Clearly I care more than you do, and it's exhausting. Don't call me when they release you. Get another ride home. Or walk." On any other occasion the idea of me walking the four miles home in this condition would've struck me as funny.

Saff reaches into her bag and pulls out a box of chocolates. She drops it onto my bed near my feet, apparently not caring whether this will cause me any pain—which it really doesn't because of all the medication the nurses have given me. When she leaves, Micah finally shifts position.

"So that went well," I tell him, hoping that if I ignore the tears pressing against my ducts, they'll dry up and disappear.

"Could've been worse."

"Thanks for standing up for me there." I blink hard, my best crowd control for those pushy tears.

"She scared me," Micah confesses without the slightest hint of a smile. "I've never seen her so mad."

"Me neither."

Micah picks up the box of candy. "Want to drown your problems in chocolate-covered caramel?"

I shake my head. My throat is so tight that if I bite into a caramel I'll clog up my windpipe and suffocate . . . which at this moment does not sound too bad. I sigh. "Where is Axel, anyway?"

"Your sister banned him." Micah quietly opens the chocolates.

"Excuse me?"

"Does this surprise you? He caused an accident, totaled your car, and sent you and your cousins to the hospital." He pops a round chocolate into his mouth. "I'd like a few minutes alone with the asshole myself."

"Why does everyone try to control my life? I'm an adult."

"So I've been told." Micah flashes me an openmouthed, chocolatey grin. The jerk.

Chapter 23

When I finally check my phone, Axel has sent eleven separate apology texts. I guess he's more afraid of Saff than I would've thought, because he doesn't show his face even once. Micah's right that my sister is freakishly scary when she's mad. It looks like her eyeballs are going to detonate out of her head. Still, how would Saff know if he visited me? It's not like the nurses are acting as Saff's spies, on the lookout for banned boyfriends making a little sympathy visit.

Micah has taken off for a few hours, and I'm just twiddling my fingers (not literally, because of the IV hand, which is starting to ache as they dial down the pain meds) when Fletcher steps in, holding Maggie and Missy by the hands, one on each side. A deep purple bruise leeches onto Maggie's left cheek, and Missy wears a small bandage. They're both so miniature next to Fletch, who's not that big of a guy, really. Something about their pale faces and their serious eyes punctures me, a metaphorical fishhook piercing my heart.

I know those eyes. I remember them from my own expression in that video from the park. Before I fell from the tree. Where I stared at the camera and my eyes were old.

I straighten up as much as I can and try to ignore my screaming ribs. "Hey there, cuties. Come on over."

They're frozen, perhaps scared by the hospital apparatus. Fletcher leads them both forward and releases their hands. They clutch each other and shuffle toward me.

"I'm fine, girls." I reach for them both. "I promise I'm fine."

Maggie's face crumples first. Missy holds off another few seconds, but after she hears the first whimper from her sister, her mouth folds under and she wails. I edge myself off the bed, since it's clear they'll never make it close enough. Favoring my fractured ankle, I inch over until I can gather them in my arms. Fletch scoots up Micah's chair, and I sit down on it, gingerly pulling them as close as I can and smelling their little-girl hair. It's hard to believe that less than a day ago I was worried about Luke's reaction to their adorable matching haircuts. Now he's probably more concerned about physical and emotional scars.

"I'm sorry," I whisper, wishing Fletch would leave so I can be alone with them.

Maggie sniffles, her cheeks stained with tears and her nose running almost to her lip. "Don't ever die, Cayenne."

"I won't," I say, realizing the foolishness of that statement as soon as Fletch clears his throat.

"Promise, Cayenne?" Missy's hands are cold and gummy. She presses them to my cheeks. "Promise you won't ever die? Not ever ever?"

I take a moment. "I promise I'll do my best to live until I'm old and gray. Maybe even until you're old and gray."

These words settle them. That, along with some caramel chocolates. I search for little treasures to send home with them and settle for one of those stretchy gloves that can be blown up into a balloon with five fingers. Only I don't have the air in my lungs to blow it up, so I have Fletcher inflate it and tie it up for them. He entertains them with the disappearing penny trick for a while, and then he leans against the wall, quiet. For a moment I wish he'd come over and hug me or something. I need a hug—so badly that I'd accept one from some x-ray tech or a night custodian.

Once I set the girls up with a video on my phone, Fletch says quietly, "Don't say things you don't mean, Cayenne."

I just sit there, and as pathetic as it is, I still want a hug. I want someone to tell me it's okay.

"These girls adore you. Saff adores you. So don't speak lightly." His voice is gentle, but stern.

"When I make a promise, I make a promise," I tell him, and in this moment, I mean it.

* * *

Ryan/Dad shows up at discharge to take me home. He hardly speaks, just sits in the chair next to the bed, fiddling with his phone and picking at the skin around his fingers. His facial hair is overgrown. He seems bored, and frankly, I'm all lectured out, so this arrangement works just fine for me.

Even the ride home is mostly silent. He turns the music up and thumps his fingers on the wheel as he drives. The pain has officially moved in, settling into my muscles and bones like it plans to stay awhile. It's all I can do to survive the turns, which Ryan/Dad makes with wide and quick movements. We thump over the train tracks, not far from my secret dodging spot, and I visualize myself jumping, rolling, getting sand stuck in my teeth. A wave of nausea washes over me, and I weakly ask Ryan/Dad to pull over.

Given my current condition, it is very difficult to vomit on the side of the road without getting ick all over myself. I do my best.

We drive again and after a while I drift into a Vicodin-induced haze, but when he turns the music down and clears his throat, my eyes pop open. I catch him looking at me, and I sort of point to the road. I'm not in any hurry to have another accident.

"There's one thing I can promise you, Cay," he says, like we're mid-conversation instead of mid-nap. "I will never judge you."

The Vicodin has zapped my ability to think of snappy comebacks, so all I can muster is "Thanks."

"Pruning," he says next.

"Wha . . . ?"

"Definition of pruning—cutting something down so it can grow."

"I'm confused, Da—" I stop short, realizing I almost called him Dad.

"It's a good metaphor." He palms the wheel, hand over hand, to make a turn.

"Yeah. I'm really drugged out. I have no idea what you're saying."

"For life." He turns to look at me again, too long. I gesture wildly toward the road, but this is a mistake because my ribs are howling and my arm feels like it might fall off. Maybe he can prune my arm off and I can grow a new one. "We get cut down too," he goes on. "We can use those moments to redefine ourselves."

"Like you did?" My words trail out long and slow, and I imagine them in elongated cartoon word bubbles.

"No, like I didn't." Ryan pulls up to the curb by my house. "Like I wish I had. Like I'm trying to do now."

"You're smarter than you look." The Vicodin has switched off any filter I might have once had. I imagine myself reaching up and popping my cartoon word bubble. "No offense."

"None taken."

This time I'm sure it's the Vicodin, but I'd much rather sit in the car having an awkward conversation with Ryan/Dad than set foot in my own house.

* * *

The pain meds have blurred the lines between reality and fantasy. I lie in my bed in a haze, imagining conversations with Lorelei.

Stay away. I won't let you take me. I won't let you take my family. And I won't let you take me away from my family, I tell her, thinking how badly I want to be here to watch the Minions grow up. *Back off.*

She touches her hand to her heart. *Ouch. That hurts.*

Shut up. Don't mock me.

Who, me?

What do I have to do to get you to stay away from me and my family?

The game is over. I told you that already. Lorelei preens, smoothing her hair and re-wrapping her scarves. *But I'm not leaving yet. I'll go when my job here is done.*

Then you're gonna be waiting awhile, you old witch.

You're missing the point. Still.

But when I blink, she's gone, no longer willing to waste her time. Leaving me with my lingering questions.

Chapter 24

Tee's been released from the hospital, moving like she's turned part zombie and saying things like "Man, that was brutal" and "I'm so glad that's over." Between the two of us with our pain pills, we could start our own opioid distribution business. She's also got these drains the surgeon left attached to her body. They're tubes attached to plastic packets, which fill up with a yellowish fluid. Just looking at it gives me the urge to hurl. She dumps the fluid out several times a day and then it fills back up again.

I guess Luke gave Tee the watered-down version of what happened. Minor accident, small injuries, kids okay, car in shop. Tee doesn't seem overly mad at me, but maybe I have the Percocet to thank for that.

Tee's friends and the Chowders are taking turns bringing meals and watching the Minions after preschool. Apparently I can no longer be trusted with the Minions, so any time I spend with them is highly supervised by Luke or Saff, as if I'm a kid myself. But aside from that, Luke's giving me the cold shoulder. In a strange way, I kind of miss his lectures. It's almost like he's detached himself, cutting his losses, deciding I'm no longer worth the time to lecture. I wonder if I remind him of his brother. Of my dad.

And Saff is even worse. She morphs into this overly cheerful phony, chirping merry morning greetings, bouncing around the kitchen, preparing breakfast, heading off to school—with no offer to drive me in Tee's car and no evident concern about me opting not to go. I know there are layers of resentment beneath this irritatingly pleasant façade.

I send an SOS text to Axel on Thursday. We've been messaging back and forth since the accident on Monday, but I haven't been able to get out of the house to see him, and with Luke and Saff standing watch, it's not like he can barrel his way in.

He responds within minutes, and I hobble out to the curb for a pickup. "I am so glad to get out of that house," I confess, trying to climb into Churro with my crutches, while my ribs scold me with every movement. This proves harder than one might think. I notice he doesn't get out of the car to help me.

"When are you coming back to school?" he asks, watching me stretch awkwardly to shut the door behind me.

"Next week, for sure." Though right now the idea of maneuvering around the halls on crutches sounds daunting.

"How you feeling?" He lets the car idle, studying me.

I shrug. "Like I got thrown around a car at forty miles an hour. Thank god we weren't on the freeway."

"Maybe now you'll wear your seat belt," he says. Seriously? Of all people, I'd figured Axel would be on my side. "Your family's all pissed at me, but we wouldn't even be in this situation if you'd just wear your damn belt."

My ribs ache as I stretch the seat belt over my arm, all sassy, and click it in extra loud, for emphasis. "Um, no. We wouldn't be in this situation if you weren't trying to street race with my cousins in the car."

"Why'd we even take them out so late? They should've been in bed," Axel snaps. "And by the way, they were okay, because they had their belts on!"

"I told you to stop. You didn't listen."

He's quiet for a moment. "Can we change the subject? I'm tired of being punished for this. Accidents happen. That's why they're called accidents."

This accident didn't have to happen. But I hold my response in, ready to be done with this conversation too.

We drive around aimlessly for a while. Our moods have soured, and nothing either of us says feels right. Axel doesn't take me back to his apartment—perhaps he has no interest in my bruised and broken body. Not that I feel like making out either, but somehow this hurts me deep in my core. Is there nothing to do together if we're not jumping off cliffs or tangling tongues?

Finally he drops me off at the library, where I hobble around and flip through books for hours. At least books can't lecture me. I feel like crying, but I pinch myself a few times, and that feeling dissipates. I distract myself by changing my phone's screensaver image to one of the Minions swinging from the play structure at the spider web park. I love those girls so much. If they'd been seriously hurt in the accident I'd never forgive myself. I feel ill just thinking about it.

I think about Ryan/Dad, and how the guilt of his choices nearly destroyed him. The parallel of our lives frightens me—both of us in a major accident senior year of high school. I don't want to get stuck in the same patterns he did.

I promise myself I'll cut back on the pain medication

starting tomorrow. They sent me home with more than I need, and I don't want to take the chance of getting hooked.

I text Micah for a ride home at seven, and he shows up, no questions asked.

* * *

My aching ribs and my cast-bound ankle make it nearly impossible to sleep. I want to prop my foot up on pillows, but Tee's confiscated all the extra pillows in the house to arrange around herself. I feel for her—she can't lie flat on her back and can hardly move her arms (I guess because the surgeons sliced through muscle), so nighttime is agony for her.

Tee's parked herself out on the couch, so it's not like I can sleep there either. And I can't complain to her, because my injuries are mere splinters compared to the hackage of her breasts. I can't even justify feeling sorry for myself when I'm around her. I've basically resigned myself to never sleep again. I may start hallucinating from sleep deprivation, but what can I do?

I'm struck by a craving. A deep want for something I know doesn't exist—for someone to take care of me. To bring me an aspirin (I've switched to non-addictive pain management) with a glass of bubbling ginger ale and a straw. To tuck the blankets around me, to help me ice my ribs, and prop up my ankle. I want my mom.

I think of the journal. I haven't read it in a long time. I hobble over to Saff's room. This time the smell of lilacs makes me want to cry again, and my throat twists up like the tears can somehow be wrung out. I swallow hard until the feeling fades.

Stealthy stealing is nearly impossible with my ankle like this, but I'm at the point of not caring whether I'm discovered.

What, would Saff be pissed at me? No problem. She's already pissed at me. So I might as well do whatever the hell I want.

Once I have the journal I hobble back to my room, edge myself down onto my bed, and start to read. I find a page that feels like it was written specifically for me in this moment in time.

WHAT'S IN A LIFE?

It can happen to you. You think it can't because you're young and confident. But everything that happens to other people CAN happen to you. Like getting pregnant before you're ready. Like losing your way. Like getting cancer. Like dying.

Don't be paralyzed by this idea. This shouldn't stop you from living your life. Keep driving your car, keep dating, keep taking risks—but take precautions too. Don't get so sucked into living in the moment that you forget you are vulnerable. You are human.

And love . . .

Love is a construct. It's a feeling, of course, but it's also a construct fed by media and books and our romantic minds. We think love will bowl us over. Sometimes it does. But mostly love is a sense of companionship, a warmth in your heart, a sense of security. Make sure you're looking for the right kind of love.

WHAT'S IN A LIFE? —SAFFRON
I know it can happen to me.
I know it can happen to someone I love.

I'm not paralyzed by this idea,
But I am haunted by it.
It weighs on my shoulders
It taunts me in my dreams.
And mostly I feel like Cayenne
Wants to rub my face in it.
She's totally oblivious to how much this hurts me.
Thank God for Fletch.
He's my companion, one hundred percent.
And thank God for Vanessa.
She's my bestie.
She's been through her own hardships—
Like when she first transitioned
And her brother stopped talking to her for a year—
And when her grandma passed
And when her appendix burst.
I've been there for her and she's been there for me
Every step of the way.

I close the journal. I craved comfort and instead I got guilt. But I wonder—did Saff write this entry before the accident, or after?

Chapter 25

Another day passes, filled with enough uncomfortable moments to make food poisoning sound fun by comparison. Trying to maneuver in the shower with my throbbing ankle wrapped in a plastic bag, my toes so swollen that they look like fat little sausages, my ribs making me feel like a cracked porcelain doll, and all this compounding the impossibility of finding a sleeping position that doesn't ache.

Even though it would be easier to keep taking the pain medication, I've committed to doing my best with just aspirin. Yes, it hurts. God. It hurts. But I'd rather not take the chance that the medication will fasten a hold on me. And there's something satisfying about giving the middle finger to the pain. "Come at me!" I want to yell. "Is that all you got?"

Besides, I'd take twice as much physical pain over the emotional ick with my sister. It sounds cliché, but I can literally feel the tension in the air. Like it's thicker, tainted with some kind of toxin, and once it enters my lungs, it contaminates me too. It feels as if I'm trying to fit into someone else's skin—two sizes too small and unbendable. There's nothing I want more than to shed myself and slither away.

I find myself texting Micah. *The world has frozen over. Saff is the ice queen.*

It takes him about ten minutes to respond, during which I gaze longingly at the chipped lavender polish on my sausage toes. My tender ribs won't let me bend down to them to apply even a single coat.

My phone message dings in. *As long as we're talking ice cream, I'll take cappuccino chip.*

You are irritating. I can't help but smile.

True. But ice cream is the best remedy for misery.

Can't you just let me be miserable?

Negative.

I resist messaging back, just to punish him, but a few minutes later he sends me a new one. *You back to school yet?*

Still home. May stay home forever. Tee wanted me back today. It's been almost a week. She says it's time.

I can pick you up this afternoon after fifth period. I have a free sixth.

If you insist . . . I make a feeble attempt at grooming: brushing my hair and my teeth, changing my clothes and applying a thin layer of rose lip gloss.

Micah texts me when he arrives. He circles behind the car, opens my door, holds my crutches, and supports my arm as I climb in. He jiggles the keys until I click my seat belt.

"You're being kidnapped," Micah says, turning the key in the ignition.

"Hmm. You might need a dictionary. Because number one, I am going with you willingly and number two, I'm a freaking adult! Why does no one remember that?"

Micah laughs. "I keep telling my mom that too. She says that she'll treat me like an adult next year when I start college

171

and I'm living on my own." He pulls away from the curb slowly. "Have you heard back from your top schools yet?"

That too-small skin feeling creeps back over me. "I missed the deadlines to apply."

He brakes abruptly. "You what?"

"Hey, hey! Safe driving, buddy! You're the responsible one, remember?"

"Sorry. I just—are you serious?"

"Yeah. I uh . . . I don't know." I don't have any explanation worth saying. "I screwed up, I guess."

He drives in silence for a little while. "You can always go to a community college for a couple years and then transfer to another school. You didn't miss the boat for that. And it's way less expensive anyway."

"Yeah, or I could get a job at Yogurt Dream. Work my way up to manager. Live off the free fro-yo." I lean my head against the window. It feels cool to the touch.

"Cayenne." Micah readjusts the rearview mirror. "This is gonna sound cheesy and maybe presumptuous, because I know you're six months older and all, but I have to say it."

"Shoot." I tilt my head toward him so that I can kind of see him, even with my forehead resting on the window.

"I don't think it matters what your plan is. Plans change all the time. Did I tell you I only got a partial scholarship to Cal, instead of a full one like I hoped? I'm gonna apply for another one, but I might still be in debt up to my eyeballs by the time I finish. So obviously, planning doesn't guarantee anything, and we always have to deal with curveballs. But you gotta *have* a plan. You gotta start somewhere."

I slump, as much as I can with stretched-taut skin. "Where exactly is that ice cream? I'd like a quart. All for me."

We both order double scoops. Me—mocha almond fudge and pecan with pralines. Him—cookie dough and birthday cake. I tease him about ordering kiddie flavors, but he tells me I'm just jealous, and maybe I am. I do like cookie dough.

He drives me to his house afterward. When we pull up, Fletcher's car is parked in the driveway. I turn to Micah, confused. He holds up his hand and says, "I wasn't joking about the kidnapping thing. You and your sister have to patch things up. I'm in cahoots with her boyfriend to orchestrate a sappy reconciliation. He brought her here after her last period."

"I cannot believe you said *cahoots*."

"So you're okay with *sappy reconciliation*?"

"Oh is that what you said? I got stuck on *cahoots*."

"You must be delirious. The ice cream went straight to your head."

I groan. But secretly, I'm relieved. I can't stand much more of this fake sugar-cookie Saffron. Makes me feel like Mary Poppins has taken her body hostage.

Micah boosts me out of the car and helps me hobble into the house. Saff is perched on a kitchen stool, and Fletcher stands behind her rubbing her shoulders. As we step through the door, I watch the sweetness melt right out of her and drip all over the floor. She twists back to glare at Fletcher. "What is this?"

Fletcher slides his hand from her upper shoulders down to her arms. "Well, basically, you're miserable. And clearly Cayenne is miserable. And that makes me miserable. So it's time to fix this."

"Plus I figured you might want to finish watching your mom's videos," Micah points out, dragging another stool near Saff's.

I totter over and ease myself carefully onto the stool, trying not to jostle my sensitive ribs. The way I'm moving, I probably look a hundred years old. Micah bites his lip, like he might crack up.

"This isn't funny," I say.

"It's a little funny." He gets a regular chair, so that my butt sits on the stool and my broken ankle rests at an angle on the chair below. Saff's expression remains flat, but her eyes have softened a tiny bit.

"So we're going to be held hostage until we make up?" I ask, trying not to sound too hopeful.

Micah nods. "In your condition, you won't get too far if you try to leave on your own."

"This is true."

"So we just have to secure Saffron. I have some rope in the garage." He says this with a totally straight face, but his voice betrays him, the humor cracking through.

"Oh, shut up." Saff rolls her eyes. "I'll play nice. Promise."

"Do we have to stay in here to supervise?" Micah asks.

"No," we both say at the same time. "Jinx," I add softly.

Micah and Fletcher leave the room, grabbing sodas and a bag of chips for sustenance on their way out. "We only have enough food and sugary beverages for an hour," Micah warns. "So talk fast."

I don't bother messing around, just get straight to the point. "Hey, Saffron, I'm sorry. I know I screwed up. I understand why you're mad, but . . ." I trail off.

She stares me down, and just when I'm feeling myself melt under the heat of her gaze, she speaks. "I'm more hurt than mad. Listen—if you're gonna treat your life as so disposable, I've got to distance myself. I'm not doing it to be mean.

I'm doing it because I can't lose another person I love." Saff looks away, picking up one of the apples in Alicia's fruit bowl and examining it carefully.

I remember what I said to Axel before our last jump. That my biggest fear is losing someone I love. "I feel that way too. I guess up until this accident, I felt like I'd rather be the one to go."

"But why does anyone have to go, Cay? We're young. We have our whole lives ahead of us." She shifts the apple back and forth in her hands like it's a baseball.

I scramble to explain myself. "I'm not saying I want to die soon. But when I do die, I want to feel like I really lived."

"So that equals ignoring safety signs on cliffs and breaking traffic laws?"

"Maybe," I say. Saff groans and turns her head away. Her frustration triggers a word tornado in me. "Well, it's not up to you. Who I am and what I do—you don't get to decide for me. I'm my own person and you can't control me."

The word tornado must be contagious, because Saff snaps back. She's not yelling, but there's fury under her words. "This is not news to me, Cayenne. I have never in my life been able to control you, or even influence you. You don't care what I think. You don't care if what you do hurts me. Cayenne Silk cares about one person and one person only. Herself."

"There you go again. Thinking you know better." The words spew from some deep dark place in my core, and I can't stop them. "I think you actually like it when I screw up because then you can be the good one, the trustworthy one."

"This is pointless." Saffron stands up to leave. "I'm not going to sit here and listen to this. I give up. I'm not going to try anymore. It's too hard." She moves toward the door, each step writing me off as a lost cause.

"Wait." Something desperate pulls at me. She turns, wary. "I'm sorry, Saff. I didn't mean to flip into attack mode."

When she speaks again, she's totally matter-of-fact, maybe even robotic—and it kills me. "Cayenne. I'll always love you because you're my sister." It's weird to see someone say the word "love" with zero emotion linked to it. "But I can't count on you and I can't invest my time and my heart in you . . . unless you can promise you'll take care of yourself. I know you think I've got it all together. But I'm on the edge too. It just looks different in me. I'm not going to sign up to be hurt and abandoned over and over again."

The stool underneath me is turning into quicksand. "I'm gonna wear my seat belt from now on. I promise." I sound pathetic, backpedaling like this, but bravado clearly hasn't gotten me anywhere. "And I'm going to be more careful in general."

"You're throwing promises around all over the place. Words are meaningless unless there are actions attached to them." She pulls back and I wonder if she plans to pelt the apple at me. Instead she sets it back in the bowl. "Fletch said you promised the girls you'd never die."

"I didn't mean for it to come out quite like that. But what I meant is that I'll do better. I never promise *anything*, Saff, you know that. So that means I'm serious about this." My words are frantic, like I can somehow stop sinking into the quicksand if I get her back on my side. "I can't stop being me. But I can try to be my best me."

"Show me." Saff says, her voice strong. She fiddles with the hem of her oversized T-shirt. "I know you mean well, Cay, you always have. But nothing you say right now will be enough on its own. I can't start counting on you again until I see the difference. So let's give it some time."

"That's fair. I guess." My foot is going numb, all tingly and prickly, but the sinking has slowed. "Are we good now?"

"We're as good as we can be. I'm willing to try."

"Micah!" I holler. "We're besties, we love each other forever, and we'll live together with our cats until we're ninety-nine. Now help me up!"

Chapter 26

"My hair is so greasy I could fry eggs on it," Tee groans. It's a Thursday night and she's standing, or rather hunching, in front of the dining room mirror. The Minions are hiding in their room. We bribed them by handing off our phones, so that Tee could have some peace and quiet while they addict themselves to mindless games.

Saff and I share a glance. Tee's much more alert and mobile than when she first got home, and yesterday Luke took her to a follow-up appointment so her drains could be removed. But to be honest, she *is* a bit the worse for wear. Swollen, greasy, bruised and cranky. Luke's been helping her take sponge baths, but they're clearly not doing the trick.

"Wanna take a shower?" Saff suggests, sweeping crumbs into a pile and stooping down to use the dustpan. "You're okay to do that now that the drains are out, right?"

"Yeah, but I can hardly lift my arms up to my hair," Tee complains. She leans in closer to her reflection, staring at her pores. "How am I going to shampoo, let alone undress myself?"

"We can help you undress, turn on the water, hand you the soap, all that," I say, wiping the table. Moving her arms seems to be hardest for her. The hospital sent home a sponge on a stick, which I'm guessing is for sudsing up her hard-to-reach places. "We can wash your hair too."

Tee turns to us, and I can tell she's considering this . . . while not wanting to consider this. She's pretty modest. "What if I get in the shower and get my hair wet—and then put a towel on and get out, and you can shampoo up my hair? And then I can get back in and rinse off."

"Sure," Saff agrees. "Let's do that."

I consider teasing her, saying we've seen naked women before and it's no big deal, until I imagine how her recently hacked skin will look. All bruised and swollen and probably misshapen. I know it'll look good after it heals because Tee showed us a bunch of before and after shots her surgeon provided, but I can do without witnessing the post-op visual up close.

"Okay," Tee says, visibly relaxing. "Thanks, girls. I know I didn't do this for cosmetic reasons and I know that it'll heal nicely. But right now, I feel like Frankenstein." Moving slowly, she gestures for us to follow her. "My greasy hair doesn't help."

In the bathroom, we get the hot water running, help her unbutton her top and remove her hospital post-surgery bra. After handing her the soap and the sponge stick, we give her privacy. A few minutes later, she hollers for her towel, which we hand over. She steps out so that we can soap up her hair with a rose-scented shampoo/conditioner combo, and then gets back in to rinse it out. Some of it drips into her eyes, which makes her curse.

But aside from her red-rimmed shampooed eyes, she exits the shower looking like a new woman. We comb through her hair and help her dress.

"Oh my god. I feel SO much better," she tells us. "I feel like a real person."

I think of all those early years when she took care of us in this way. It feels good to give back.

* * *

"Hold still," I command. I'm trying to paint a flower on Maggie's big toenail, which is barely the size of the nail polish brush. I sit on a chair with Maggie perched on the armrest of the couch so I can reach her feet without inconveniencing my ribs.

Saff seems to be having just as much trouble with Missy's little piggies. It might be the medication, but Tee finds the whole business quite humorous. She sits on the couch, sipping diet soda from a straw. Luke is wholeheartedly opposed to diet soda, but in her recovery period he seems to have difficulty denying her anything.

"Girls, you're the customers here. Make sure your toes are just the way you like them." Tee giggles. "Missy, didn't you want a rainbow on each toe? I bet Saffron can paint five different colors on each toenail."

Saff fake-glares at Tee. It's hard to be mad at her when she can barely get off the couch. "Uh-oh." Tee grimaces suddenly. "Damn my bladder. Gotta go." The problem with consuming massive amounts of diet soda is that Tee has to pee about every half hour. But she's still moving slowly, so the trek to and from the bathroom gives Saff and me plenty of time to plan our revenge.

"Maggie? I bet you could paint your mommy's toes if you ask."

Missy's head pops up. "What about me?"

"Each of you could take a foot. And I bet Mommy would like some really creative colors."

The Minions love-love-love this idea. So after their toes dry, we set them up with an array of polishes, and newspaper covering the couch. Tee tries to grumble, but she can't stay upset for long. Plus she can't hold a grudge, since we're cleaning the house, doing laundry, and making dinner. I'm doing my best to help, and while my injuries are inconvenient, I can still fold laundry sitting down. I'm also breaking my own no-homework rule and trying to complete some of the assignments I've missed.

I wonder if Saffron is seeing the difference.

* * *

I avoid school as long as humanly possible, but eventually my doctor's notes run dry, and I brave the halls. They're filled with sympathy glances and poorly timed questions. I've graduated from a cast to a non-weight-bearing splint, but I still need crutches. The complaining of my ribs has settled to a low grumble. Luckily between Axel, Saff, and Saff's friends, someone's always helping me carry my books between classes.

I'm hobbling down the halls with Saff by my side, when she asks, "What are you giving me for my birthday?"

"My never-ending love."

"It's barely a week away and that's the best you've got?"

"Do you have a better gift idea?"

"Yeah. Take a blood test with me."

I nearly trip. "Excuse me? I think we already know we're blood sisters."

"I want us both to get tested for the BRCA gene together. I've been talking to Aunt Tee about it and been researching it, and I don't think I can get tested until I'm eighteen. But that's in a few days. So I think we should know what our future holds, and we can find out together."

"Everyone acts like this stupid gene is a crystal ball. We have no idea what our future holds whether or not we take a blood test."

"Well, that's what I want for my birthday," Saff says flatly. Like she doesn't see any point in debating with me.

"Ugh." I stick my tongue out at her. "Fine. I guess I can't afford to alienate my main book carrier."

"Cool. I'll have Aunt Tee book us a consultation with a genetic counselor a couple days after my birthday."

"You're welcome."

"*You're* welcome."

* * *

I glance at the clipboard. What a nightmare. Four pages of checkboxes with every symptom known to woman. I skim the form, checking off boxes with flair until I get to "Family history of cancer." I cross off "history" and write "curse." I elbow Saff and point it out to her.

"How are you eighteen?" Saff asks.

"Oh, you know you love my juvenile antics." Some of my nervousness fades away. Humor is the cure for all ills. "Plus, in our family cancer *is* a curse."

I decide to really have fun with the form. For "Have you had excessive bleeding?" I write "every freaking month." For "are you pregnant or trying to get pregnant?" I write "Trying

NOT to get pregnant every chance I get," which is certainly one way to interpret the fact that I'm not having sex. For "Palpitations or irregular heartbeat" I write "induced by hot boyfriend."

For "eating disorder" I write "compulsion to consume frozen yogurt." For "thoughts of hurting self or others" I write "Only when filling out this stupid form."

Saff keeps peeking over at me, and a red flush is creeping across her cheeks. I'm embarrassing her. She can hardly stand to watch me writing down all this ridiculousness, like it somehow reflects on her.

"Relax, Saff. We're not in school. We're not going to get in trouble."

"Well, *I'm* not, for sure. I take no responsibility for what you're writing. My form is filled out appropriately."

"You can sit over there," I offer, pointing to a chair on the other side of the room. "That way there's no chance of guilt by association."

"I could," she concedes, a tiny gleam of amusement sparking in her eyes. "But then I'd miss out on the fun."

* * *

The Genetics Department turns out to be a tiny room, empty except for three uncomfortable chairs and a mini desk. The genetic counselor, Natalie, wheels in her supplies in a luggage-type container. I can tell the job wears her down. I can't imagine going in to work every day to hand people tainted fortune cookies.

"How'd you score the closet and the portable cabinet?" I joke, trying to ease the tension.

Natalie smiles. "Our department is rather small, and mobile. I go from site to site."

"Oh. You need some better chairs." My butt bones ache already, the chairs are that hard.

She reviews our responses to the questionnaire silently, with zero expression. Next she draws out a family tree and asks a nauseating number of questions, most of which we answer with guesses. When this is done, she launches into information overload.

"My job is not to recommend your course of action, but to educate you about your options. We recommend women consider genetic testing ten years earlier than the youngest age of cancer diagnosis within the family. Since your mother was diagnosed at thirty, the guidelines would indicate considering testing at age twenty."

"See? We don't have to worry about this yet!" I announce, way too upbeat.

Saff glares at me. "Birthday present," she reminds me. Drat.

"Here's what I want you to consider. A blood test will take ten seconds. It will inform your decisions. I can have the nurse administer it today. The results take several weeks to come through, but then at least you'll have information. In the absence of information, you both have to assume that you're at high risk, and you can begin getting MRIs at age twenty for cancer prevention. But if we get some information back that takes you out of this high-risk category, then you can relax a little. Of course, I have to add that the BRCA gene mutation is only one contributor to cancer; certainly people who don't have it can still get cancer."

"See?" I say again. "Pointless. Even if we don't have the gene mutation, it's not like we're in the clear. We can still get it. We're basically all dying no matter what."

"Lovely," says Saff dryly.

It's distinctly possible that I'm giving Natalie a headache. She pinches the bridge of her nose. "I know breast cancer is your focus, due to your mother's experience, but I also want to stress this gene's connection to the increased risk for ovarian cancer. This type of cancer is much harder to detect, and the timing for a salpingo-oophorectomy can put a deadline on your reproductive decisions."

What a clinical way to say, *If you want to have kids AND avoid being cannibalized by your own cells, start planning now!*

"These are complicated decisions," Natalie says, slowing down for emphasis, "and while you're both adults, you're both very young. I want to make sure you fully understand the risks and benefits of whatever you choose to do. Of course it's up to you whether you involve your father or aunt in this discussion, but because your decision can have such an impact on your life, I encourage you to take your time with this."

Saff has been very quiet this whole time. But as soon as Natalie pauses, she says, "We want to do it. We've been talking to our aunt about it for months—let's just get it over with."

"Speak for yourself," I say. "I'm not sure I want to know right now." I'm not sure I even want to think about it. I'd rather think about Natalie's pinched nose. I wonder if that impacts her sense of smell. "Maybe I don't ever want to know."

"Cayenne," Saff says softly. She places her hand on my arm and I forget about Natalie's nose. "You made a promise to me. And to the girls. You owe it to all of us."

Natalie clears her throat. "It's entirely your right to decide you don't want to be tested," she says to me, with a pointed look at Saff. "I can tell you both have dramatically different person-alities and perspectives on life. You each should approach this in the way that feels right for you. And you can certainly take some time to think about it."

* * *

I take Natalie up on that offer and go for a walk (aka crutch-hobble) around the medical building. I'm not one to flake on promised birthday presents, even one that involves blood loss. But to be fair, this is a *big* decision. Saffron's always pushing personal choice—especially when it relates to anything about women and their bodies. Breastfeeding in public? Personal choice. Makeup? Personal choice. Hijab or no hijab? Personal choice. Appropriate pronoun? Personal choice. Casual sex, monogamous sex, or wait-for-marriage sex? Personal choice. While I give her a hard time whenever humanly possible, I totally agree with her on this front. So I'm not sure why she isn't apply that philosophy to *me*. Genetic testing or no genetic testing? She doesn't want me to have a choice. And if I'm positive for the mutation, I'm going to have to make many more personal choices that are even tougher. This is my body, right? I should be able to do whatever I want.

Saff must be getting nervous because she calls me twenty-three times during my hour-long walk/hobble. I ignore the buzzing in my pocket. I'm just circling the building, taking frequent rests because the crutches hurt my armpits and the pressure impacts my vulnerable ribs. If she peeks outside, she'll see me.

It's like planning a jump, I tell myself. Like scouting out the terrain ahead of time, picking the spot that works best, checking what time the sun will set. That's all this is. Gathering information. It's not actually jumping off the cliff.

I make my decision within thirty minutes, but I do a few more laps, partly so I can decide exactly what to say, and partly because it's just a tiny bit satisfying to know that I'm making my sister sweat.

In the waiting room, I walk straight up to Saff and square off. "Listen," I tell her. "I'm taking this test, and I'm doing it as a gift for you, but I'm not doing it because you told me to, I'm doing it because I want to. Got it?" Which is not entirely true. I'm doing it because I think it's the right thing to do, not because I actually *want* to. Close enough.

"Thank you," Saff says quietly. "Happy birthday to me. Now hopefully I don't faint."

Saff has had a fear of needles since age three. Probably since our mom died. When Mom got sick, she was pricked for IVs way too often.

The lab tech ties a stretchy band around her upper arm, hands her a squeezy ball, and tells her to pump it with her palm. I watch the color leave her cheeks. Saff can't look. It's not the pain of the prick, it's the idea of her blood being drained from her body.

"Here. Look at my gorgeous face." I arrange myself in front of her.

Saff can't even laugh at that. She does manage to give me feedback on my mascara. "Your eyelashes look like spiders."

"You're just jealous of my technique."

"Not jealous. Terrified. I keep thinking your lashes are going to crawl off your face and onto my arm." Saff's upper lip quivers, but she keeps her head toward me and away from the blood draw.

"We need a second opinion," I say. "Let's get our phlebotomist to weigh in."

Saff's voice hikes up three octaves. "No! She needs to focus on that needle."

The lab tech pulls away from Saff's arm, wrapping a stretchy bandage around a cotton ball. "Done. Now I can cast my vote."

"You're done?" Saff's voice is still shrill.

The lab tech holds a cotton ball on Saff's arm and wraps a stretchy bandage over it. "You two are a riot. You must have a ton of fun together."

I glance at Saff. "Sometimes." I hold my arm out for my turn.

"You won't get the results back for a couple weeks," the nurse tells us as she finds my vein. "Our genetic counselor will be calling you to discuss."

"Joy."

Saff rubs her arm and opens and clenches her fist. "There should be some mathematical way to figure out what the odds are of us *both* being negative. Or both being positive. Or one of each. I mean, we know that we each individually have a fifty-something percent risk, but what are our risks combined?"

"That would require that I pay attention in math." I have a vague memory of flipping coins and charting it. Statistically each coin flip has a fifty percent chance of being heads. But if you flip two coins at once, what is the chance of them both being heads?

I feel the needle pierce my skin. I don't like to look at the needle either.

Chapter 27

The blood test must've wiped Saff out, because she falls asleep early tonight. The test did the opposite for me—my mind is catapulting in a million directions and I can't settle down. I've actually been intending to pop by and talk to her, pay my dues toward some sisterly bonding, but when I nudge her door open, she's fallen asleep on the journal. I hobble forward and slide it out from under her arms. One of her sticky notes flaps down a bit, and I see that there's writing underneath it. On the back.

Huh.

Back in my room, I carefully comb through the journal. Saff has continued her entries on the back of nearly every sticky note. How did I miss that? I ease myself onto my bed and settle in to read.

LITTLE KNOWN FACTS ABOUT ME
Continued....
Sometimes I think I love Cayenne more
Than she loves me.
I'm pretty sure Cayenne's gonna die young.

I don't think she cares.
But I do.
She's like a runaway train.
There is nothing I can do to stop her,
And I will be lost without her.

My heart folds in half. Clearly Saff wouldn't want me to see this. It's one thing to read about her liking raw carrots, but a whole different thing for her to say she loves me more than I love her. Is that true? And if it is, is that somehow a statement about my ability to love? Is she more capable of love? Because I love her more than I love anyone else in the world.

I force myself to reread her entry. I visualize myself on the train tracks, tempting destiny. Lusting after my next high, pushing any thought of Saffron out of my head. The selfishness of it strikes me fully for the first time.

I let Lorelei ensnare me in her ridiculous game of cat and mouse, thinking that the adrenaline highs were what it felt like to be truly alive. But really, they're a distraction from real life. Real life is the now. It's the mundane moments, it's the human connections, it's the things you build over time. It's not contrived risks, rushes that last thirty seconds at most and then fizzle.

I want to stomp Lorelei to tiny bits, crush her like grapes, and flush her down the toilet. How did I fall for that trick? *Never again*, I promise myself. I'm done with her.

I flip through the other journal entries—Mom's thoughts and Saff's responses. I gingerly lift up each of the half-page sticky notes to view their underbellies. And yes, there is more that I didn't know about my sister.

<u>THINGS NOBODY TELLS YOU WHEN YOU LOSE
A MOM</u>
Continued . . .
I'm not tough like Cayenne.
She acts as if she's covered herself in bubble wrap:
Her ears, her heart, her soul.
She thinks she can do anything,
Say anything.
Try anything.
Tempt fate—
No matter the consequences.

For me it's the opposite.
I see every jagged edge,
Bacteria lurking on the countertops,
Moles ready to turn into cancerous carnivores.
Never knowing what tornado's going to slam into my path
Makes it hard to let go enough
To live.

Something lodges in my throat. She's . . . not wrong.

That blood test today kind of freaked me out. I think for most of my life, I've chosen not to see danger unless I can control it, unless I know I can conquer it—unless I can get in its face, give it the middle finger, and then walk away from it. I've chosen to ignore the risks that I can't engineer myself. As long as I can orchestrate it, I feel safe, but today's blood test has shattered that illusion. It makes it hard to ignore those risks. Saff and I are both pennies, flipped high in the air, free-falling. This feeling of absolute vulnerability is awful. Maybe this is how Saff feels all the time.

FLETCH
Continued . . .
I like to kiss him. I like the way he smells.
And how we can fall asleep in bed
Without me feeling scrunched.
I kind of thought love would be
More of a rollercoaster ride. A thrill. A rush.
It sure seems to be for Cayenne.
I worry that I love Fletch because I love him,
And not because I'm in love with him.
But what's the definition of love?
Is my kind of love less real because it's less exciting?
Will I wake up twenty years from now,
Bored out of my mind?
Or will Fletch be my favorite pair of jeans,
Better and better with age?

For the first time, I get the itch to write my own entry. What would I say about Axel? He's a rush—a rollercoaster ride—just like Saff says. But sometimes I wonder if all that adrenaline covers up something empty underneath.

When I was a kid, I used to think there were cookies in Alicia's decorative cookie jars. She's got like twenty, all lined up in her living room. I spent months imagining which types of cookies were in each jar—maybe snickerdoodle, oatmeal raisin, white chocolate or macadamia nut—just waiting for her to offer me one. She never did. And when I finally got the nerve to ask for a cookie, my heart beating like crazy and my mouth watering up a storm, she laughed. "Oh, sweetie. Those are just for show." She pulled one off the shelf and tipped it over for me to see. Just dusty porcelain. She offered me a granola bar, but it couldn't compare.

So is Axel a fancy cookie jar? Do I love him for his beauty and for the excitement he sparks in me, without knowing what's inside?

THE BIG NEWS
Continued . . .
I wish I could tell Cayenne how I feel.

I have to read the front of this sticky note again, to see what else she wrote, what she wished she could share with me. I flip it over. Oh, yeah. She'd been writing about Ryan/Dad being our father, and how royally pissed she was. I wish she could tell me how she feels too. I wonder if there's anything I can do to help her talk to me. Maybe all my joking makes her feel like I can't hear her.

WHAT'S IN A LIFE?
Continued . . .
When I found Fletch
I had so few people of substance.
No Mom. Clearly.
No Dad.
And I've been losing Cayenne for as long as I can remember.
I did have her once.
As a soulmate. As a supporter. As a friend. As a sister.
After Mom died, we clung closer at first.
And then slowly, our connection began unraveling.
I've been holding on by a thread.
I may not be able to hold on much longer.

Shit.

I don't want to read any more. Clearly, as a sister, I've scored an F. She doesn't think I'm there for her, she can't talk to me, she thinks I don't value my own life or the impact I have on others . . .

And all a sudden I'm pissed. What—does she think she deserved an angel for a sister? Like somehow I've lost my right to have my own reactions to life? As if it's worse for me to make a joke than to shatter to pieces? It's not like she's the only one who's been impacted by Mom's death. I lost my mom too! I'm nearly a year older than her, but that's nothing in the scheme of things. Must be nice to be so freaking perfect. Must be nice to think she can pass judgment on me.

I return the journal to her room, and it takes all my self-control to not slam it on her dresser. I'd love to see her jerk awake. But I don't. I force myself to totter back to my bed.

It takes me forever to fall asleep, and when I do, I sleep fitfully, tossing and turning, plagued by terrible, taunting dreams. Lorelei is strangely MIA, but even in her absence she mocks me. In every single dream, I let Saff down.

* * *

My eyes are crusted shut when I wake. I'm pretty sure I didn't cry before I fell asleep—I hardly ever do—but my dreams were full of body-wracking sobs. I pick at the crusties until I can blink easily.

I limp into the bathroom to brush my teeth, but I crash straight into Saffron. Because of my bum ankle, and the crutches, I can't even catch myself properly. I tip right over on my ass. I feel the impact reverberate through my ribs.

Saff rushes forward. "Oh, I'm so sorry. I didn't see you." She boosts me up.

I'm still sort of shocked. And maybe traumatized by last night's dreams. "I'm sorry too, Saff. I wasn't thinking." And I don't just mean for slamming into her. I mean for everything. For taking needless risks. For not being someone she can talk to. Basically, for our whole lives.

Saff sort of laughs. She places both hands on my shoulders to straighten me out and steers me toward the bathroom counter. She stands behind me, and we both examine our reflections in the mirror. "I forgive you, Cayenne. You're only human, right?"

She can't possibly know what I'm thinking, but I feel like she's talking about more than just bumping into me. And just like that, some heavy weight in my chest lifts.

"I like to think that I'm *super*human . . ." I start to joke, watching her reflection in the mirror. Is this a time when she'll be irritated by my humor or amused by it?

She slings her arm over my shoulder and grins at our reflection. "Yeah, not with that morning breath. You're definitely human."

Chapter 28

"You feel like fro-yo?" Saff asks me that night.

"When do I ever not?" To be honest, I've been going through fro-yo withdrawal. Something about not being able to drive makes me feel like a little kid.

"Fletch and Vanessa are treating me—one last birthday hurrah. Come with us!"

I message Axel to invite him, but he says he's cleaning Churro—which feels like a sorry excuse. He's probably just afraid to face my sister.

I actually don't mind that he doesn't join us. Fletch and Vanessa have their own banter with Saff, but they're good about including me in the conversation. Remembering Saff's journal entry about them, I can't help wondering if my life would be different with a tight group of friends, instead of a loose collection of acquaintances and the single focal point of Axel. Though I guess the tail end of my senior year of high school is a little late to try forming new bonds.

Halfway through our yogurts, Saff and I decide we're ready to watch our next Mom video. So after Vanessa heads home to work on a paper, Fletch agrees to drive us out to the Johnsons' place. We message Micah to give him a heads up, and he meets us at the door. Micah and Fletch loiter, perhaps wanting to ensure that our truce is holding.

"Sure, you can watch with us, thanks for asking," I say dryly, and they both look embarrassed, but truthfully I don't mind having them here as a buffer. We all wedge together on the couch, with the boys on either side like crusts of bread.

The camera fumbles around. It focuses on a shabby pink piggy bank. "I remember that," I say, pointing at the screen. "Remember how we used to share it? Weren't we saving up for something special?"

"Yeah. I think we wanted one of those mini play kitchens for our room."

Mom's voice interrupts us. *"So money's a strange thing. Sometimes it saves people. Sometimes it ruins them. Do you know that lottery winners are no happier after they win than they were before?"*

"Oh my god. Did she win the lottery?" I grab onto Saff's arm. "Are we gonna be rich?"

"Chill, Cayenne. I think that was just an example."

"Rats." I snap my finger, disappointed.

"It's because of how complicated money can be—how it can insert itself into the cracks and crevices of a relationship and push people further apart—that I haven't given you any yet. I wanted to wait until you were both mature enough to handle it."

I shriek. "She left us money!" I attempt to stand up and do the happy dance, but my ankle does not cooperate. "Oh this is perfect timing. I need a new car—"

Saff pauses the video and stands up too. "If we have money, we can't spend it. We need to save it for college or grad school or maybe even a first home."

"How old are you, forty?" We're nearly nose to nose.

"Wait," says Fletch. "Don't start arguing yet. You don't even know if it's enough money to spend time worrying about."

"What I do know is that I'm not letting Cayenne waste our safety net." Saff's close enough that I can smell her bubble gum.

"It wouldn't be a waste!" I say, resisting an urge to shove her backwards. "How exactly am I supposed to get around without a car? What, you're gonna drive me everywhere for the next three years until I can save up for one?"

Fletch eases the computer screen closed, and Micah edges in between us. He smells clean, like soap and antiperspirant. "Let's wait on this one," Micah says. "Seems like your mom's right. You need to be in a better place before you're ready to co-manage money."

Fletch steps behind Saff and wraps his arms around her in a bear hug. "You can try again in a few days. Just sleep on it."

* * *

I message Axel on the drive home. *Mom left us money.*

Seriously? How much? He adds googly-eyed emojis.

Don't know. Micah made us stop watching the video. We were arguing. Growling emoji.

Does she have it stashed somewhere? Or in an account?

Knowing her, there will be a treasure hunt with clues. It's probably buried in Alicia's backyard in a tin box. I'll find out when we finish the video. I glance at Saff and Fletch in the front seat. Saff's resting her head on his shoulder while he drives.

This is great news, Cay. Just think of all we can do with a chunk of cash. He adds images of gold and stacks of dollar bills.

We?

Of course. We could get our own place, or start a business. Something cool like that. Smiley emoji.

Maybe. My own frozen yogurt shop. Or something.

Wait. Rewind. Why were you surprised when I said "we"? I'm offended. He adds a crying heart. *We're a unit. We've been a couple since forever.*

I seem to remember him telling me that he wanted to be independent, but whatever. *Sorry. I'm pissing people off right and left. It's becoming my specialty.*

I forgive you.

I'm just overwhelmed. Probably gonna save the money anyway. That's what Saff wants. She's the RESPONSIBLE one.

Phsh. Being responsible is overrated. Speaking of which, I have some new ideas for our Pinnacle Peak jump, for when you're able to use your foot again.

The last thing I want to do is jump off another cliff, but I'm not sure how to tell Axel that. *Well, I have some new ideas for activities that don't involve putting weight on my foot . . .* That should redirect his train of thought.

Staring at a screen while I'm in the backseat is giving me a nauseating headache, so I put the phone away.

Chapter 29

Saff ignores me all through dinner. Maybe I should listen to Micah and Fletch. I don't care about the money if it's going to drive a bigger wedge between us. I should forfeit. Just let her do whatever she wants. Needless to say, I find this infuriating.

Every single person we know would say Saff's more responsible than me. But aren't there different ways to be responsible? Aren't there different ways to get the most out of life? Just because I do things my own way doesn't mean my priorities are all wrong.

I remember what Micah told me: *I don't think it matters what your plan is . . . But you gotta have a plan.*

I'm sitting at my laptop stewing about this when inspiration hits. Moments later I'm looking at the home page for Coast Community College.

Just because I didn't apply to any universities doesn't mean I don't want to go to college. I could knock out some classes at a junior college and then transfer somewhere else. When I close my eyes and think about my future, I always envision myself doing something supremely cool like physical therapy or psychology. Obviously those jobs require graduate school on top of a basic college education. Sure, swirling yogurt in a shop would be fun, but in the long run I know I need more than that.

I scan the courses. Names like Physics 101, Intro to Greek History, and Principles of Retailing make me want to pull off my toenails one by one. I consider Hip Hop A: The Fundamentals. Can you really get college credit for that?

I scan the culinary courses. Basics of Tuscan Cooking, The Essentials of Pan Sauces, Chowdah!, Pretty Pastries, Cooking with Herbs and Spices . . . Huh. That might be fun, actually. Maybe I can start out with a non-academic class, just to get my feet wet.

Cooking with Herbs and Spices meets Wednesday evenings during the summer semester. That sounds like something Mom would've liked, what with her whole spice obsession. Maybe.

I think I'm starting to see what Micah meant about making plans. They don't have to confine me or define me. I'm not limiting myself to a certain path, I'm just opening up possibilities.

And I know I don't need a surprise inheritance to do that. Plus the money from Mom doesn't feel real. It's like Monopoly money. My visions of a car were just make believe, like fantasizing about moving into a mansion or marrying a millionaire. I can manage fine without all that.

Saff's right. Though I won't admit it unless pressed.

* * *

I can't sleep. I've counted sheep, sucked in meditative breaths, and visualized myself on a beach. Normally I'd read a journal entry, but I've gone through them all. So I grab a stack of half-page sticky notes and try to compose my own entry. I'm not sure I'll ever let anyone read it. But I figure I'll keep it in my room, in case I eventually want to stick it into the journal.

LITTLE-KNOWN FACTS ABOUT ME —CAYENNE
I believe chocolate should be a vegetable, and Hot Cheetos a fruit.
I am a secret toenail biter. (Yes, I can reach.)
Sometimes it's hard for me to show people how I really feel. I communicate my feelings in my own secret language. My jokes are my hugs, my jabs are my kisses.

I pretend I'm responding to Mom's entry. The idea of responding directly to Saffron feels too exposing or something. A visual pops into my head: me standing post-shower, totally naked and trying to cover myself with the journal and my hands. But why? Why can't I let Saff see who I am? Why is it safe to write to my dead mother but not to my sister? It's not like she hasn't earned my trust. All our lives, Saff's been my rock.

I pick up my pen and add one last bullet point.

There is no one in this world I love more than Saffron Silk.

Chapter 30

"I've been thinking . . ." Saff dumps three cups of frozen berries into the blender.

"Ooh. Don't do that. It causes all kinds of problems." I hand her a carton of low-fat milk. Our recipe calls for juice, but we always like creamy smoothies as our after-school snack.

Saffron turns to me as she pours the milk in. "Listen, I'm not sure I want the money Mom left us."

I'm stunned. I've been meaning to apologize to her, but maybe she's beating me to it. New car, here I come! I'm considering breaking out the happy dance when Saff goes on, "Instead of this money making me excited, it just makes me sad."

I think for a moment. The idea of the money does give me a hard-to-define feeling deep in my gut, one that's not particularly pleasant. But how can money be a bad thing?

"I'd rather have her, you know? The money, however much it is, doesn't make up for losing her." Saff peels a banana and dumps it in, then starts the blender, and the whirring blurs out anything else she might be saying. After the frozen berries are sufficiently smashed, she turns it off.

"So I kind of don't want it." She pours the deep purple liquid into glasses.

"You could donate your share to me," I suggest.

"Shut up." Saff rolls her eyes and pointedly sets one of the smoothie glasses out of my reach while sipping her own. "I think we just need to press pause on this whole thing. Maybe we're not ready. If we just keep the money where Mom left it—in investments or savings accounts or whatever—it'll keep growing, and that will give us time to think. Let's hold off on deciding anything for, say, five years."

I grab the smoothie. "Personally, I think we're as ready as we'll ever be, but I guess there's no hurry. We've been living without this money for fourteen years. I'm okay with waiting until we're in a better place to hash this out." I really am. Something shifted in me overnight. "And if we can't agree on a joint purchase in five years, we can just split it down the middle."

My phone buzzes on the table, and I peek at the number, but I don't recognize it. "Telemarketer," I pronounce, choosing not to pick up. A minute later, "voicemail" previews on my screen.

Just as I go to listen to the message, Saff's phone rings. She checks the screen. "It must be telemarketer afternoon."

"Let me see."

Saff holds up her phone and the same number previews on the screen.

"Uh-oh. Maybe there's an emergency. Pick it up."

Saff puts her phone to her ear. "Too late. It just went to voicemail."

I listen to my message. "Hi Cayenne, this is Natalie, the genetic counselor with Nola Health Group. I'm calling you to set up an appointment for you to come in so that I can review your BRCA test results."

The message for Saff is identical, down to the inflection in the way Natalie says her name. I pull Saff over to the kitchen table. "Let's call her back. Put her on speaker."

Saff dials, and we sit, knee to knee, listening to the shrill ring. "Genetics at Nola Health Group, this is Natalie."

"Uh, hi, Natalie. This is Saffron Silk and my sister Cayenne. We have you on speaker phone, and we're just calling you back."

"Oh hi ladies." Her voice is lightly gravelly, as though years of sharing bad genetic news has scraped up her vocal cords. "Let's set up a time for you to come in for an appointment."

"Any chance you can just tell us over the phone?" I press. "Save us the gas money?"

Momentary pause. "I'm afraid our protocol is to go over the results in person."

We set up appointments for Thursday afternoon, and hang up the phone. "This can't be good news," I tell Saff, and my own throat is gravelly. "She'd have told us if we were negative. Shit."

"We don't know for sure, Cay," Saff says. I decide the graveled throat phenomenon is contagious. Because she's got it too. "We have to wait and see."

* * *

Waiting for our genetic appointments makes my body heavy and sluggish. The night before our appointments, I craft my next journal entry response.

HERE'S THE THING—YOU DON'T KNOW ME.
Maybe no one knows me.

If nobody gets close, then I can't be hurt. Then I can't lose anyone.

I've taken great pains to lower expectations. If I don't try then I don't have to hope. There's no pressure, no one being let down if I stumble. If nobody expects anything from me, and if I don't expect anything of myself, then there is no disappointment.

Maybe, Mom, I was this brilliant, fragile little china teacup. And maybe when you died, I cracked. Tiny spidery cracks etched along my teacup sides. And maybe the only way to survive— to hold onto any usefulness—was to mend myself with thick clumpy clay, sealing the cracks shut. Not so brilliant and shiny anymore, but a helluva lot more resilient.

I don't care to be that brilliant fragile little china teacup anymore, Mom. I'm sorry to disappoint you. I am no longer the little girl you knew. Frankly, I'm not sure I want to be.

Tomorrow I find out whether we have this broken gene, whether I'm likely to die young like my mother, or whether I could live to be old enough to wrinkle. I try to picture myself shriveled up like a prune, with lines that fan out from my eyes and crease the corners of my mouth.

I fail. I cannot imagine myself old.

I know in my heart that an early death is lurking in my cells. I just hope the Silk Curse spares Saffron. Please.

* * *

My appointment is first. Saff sits in the waiting room with Ryan/Dad, who decided to come along for moral support. Natalie's office feels even smaller and more confining than last time.

"Let's cut to the chase here," I say to Natalie as soon as I sit down. "I appreciate the small talk and I'm sure you're a nice enough person, but I already know what you're going to say."

Natalie rests a stack of papers on her lap. "I'm afraid you're positive for the BRCA 1 gene mutation."

Shit. I knew it.

She rushes to add, "But I'm here to reassure you that there are many options."

Natalie probably talks to me for another half hour, but I can't retain anything she's saying. "With this gene mutation, about fifty-seven to eighty-four percent of women develop breast cancer by age seventy. Risk of ovarian cancer is up to fifty-four percent. And remember, ovarian cancer is often difficult to detect. Also, the family history of cancer can either increase or decrease this risk." I'm nodding and listening, but I feel underwater. All her words slur together in my waterlogged brain, and I can't wait to leave. Weirdly enough, my brain exits the room long before my body does. I send all my mental energy to Saffron, and hope her results are negative.

Back in the waiting room, Saff looks at me expectantly. I go to high-five her and joke, "I'm in the club."

Saff's face crumbles. She stands up slowly and follows Natalie to the exam room. She looks like she's walking down death row. Ryan/Dad picks at his fingernails. The corner of his thumb is starting to bleed but he keeps picking.

Saffron stays in the room forever, probably asking a million questions about her results. With every minute, my heart sinks further. When she steps out, her cheeks are streaked with tears, and she's turning interesting shades of pink and purple.

I'm beyond pissed. Of course we *both* have it. We're the random coins, flipped simultaneously, and both landing on our heads.

I *hate* this curse! Poor Saff. She's silent-crying all over herself. "It's okay, Saff," I tell her. "We have lots of options. We're young. We don't even have to think about this for a couple years, remember? Not until we're twenty."

Maybe the stale Genetics closet has waterlogged her brain too, because except for her gaspy-crying breaths, she stays quiet all the way home.

When Ryan/Dad pulls up to the curb, he leaves the car running. We all sit there, wasting gas and polluting the environment, until he finally turns the key to settle the engine.

"The Serenity Prayer. You ever hear of it?" he asks. His cologne is too strong. I shouldn't have chosen the front passenger seat. Saff is sitting in the back, her head pressed against the window, and her body curled up like she's trying to fold herself in half.

"What is with your strange habit of throwing out non sequiturs?" I'm not in the mood for Ryan/Dad to get philosophical with us.

Ryan/Dad seems unfazed, which irritates me even more. "They say the Serenity Prayer at the end of twelve-step meetings. It's about having the grace to accept the things we can't change, and the courage to change the things we can, and the wisdom to know the difference."

"Wow, thanks for the fortune cookie."

He taps his fingers on the steering wheel. "It's just—those words helped me through the hardest times in my life. I watched your mother die—I watched the cancer suck the life out of her, no matter how hard she fought. I don't ever want to"—his voice breaks and he shifts in the front seat, turning slightly away—"to watch either of you go through that."

"I don't think it's up to you," I snap at him, too angry to care that he's clearly in pain. "You can't control the Silk Curse. No one can."

Hearing my words out loud makes them feel real. For most of my life I've assumed that I'll die young, that it's inevitable. I think taking risks made me feel like I could decide how I live and when I die, like I could pull the puppet strings. As if I could dictate the course of my own life. As if that could somehow protect me from losing someone else. Which makes no sense. It's like quarterbacks wearing their lucky undies before a big game.

"Well, that's the thing." Ryan/Dad runs his hands through his hair. "You can control one thing."

"What!?" Saff and I both retort, in sync for once, equally pissed. Who is *he* to offer us advice?

"Yourself." He says. "You can decide how you manage this risk."

"Lovely. Tell me how to control *her*." Saff kicks the back of my seat.

"Weren't you paying attention, Saffron?" I snark back. "You can't. You can't control me and I can't control you. And we can't control cancer." I push open the door and get out. Before I slam it shut, I lean back in and yell, "Great pep talk, *Dad*." I push the last word out of my mouth like it's the biggest insult in the world.

Chapter 31

Saff talks to Aunt Tee in the kitchen while I'm hogging the bathroom, taking the longest shower in recent California history. By the time I emerge, Saff has retreated to her room and Aunt Tee insists on taking me out to dinner. I can't remember the last time the two of us went out on our own, and it's obvious that the test results are the trigger. I assume she'll be doing the same thing with Saffron sometime in the next few days. As far as consolation prizes for death sentences go, I'm sure I could do worse.

Luke drops us off at a restaurant Tee likes, and Tee rambles innocuously while we wait for our food.

"It's *so* nice to get out of the house. Other than the support group, it feels like ages since I've been around any humans I'm not related to. Not that I'm complaining."

She unwraps a straw and hands it to me, like she used to do when I was little. I accept it and insert it into my ice water.

"So listen, Cay. I'd love for you to come to a support group meeting with me sometime. There are some women I'd like you to meet. Ladies who've done all kinds of different things to manage their risks—some surgery, some other techniques.

There are a couple of younger women—one who opted for an early oophorectomy but has saved her eggs, and another who's scheduling frequent screenings."

"You're ruining my appetite," I point out.

"Cayenne . . . I'm so incredibly sorry you have the mutation. But from now on, these considerations have to be a part of your life. You need to fully explore your options."

"No thank you," I say sweetly. We're out to eat after all. No need to make a scene.

"How can I help you when you're so guarded all the time?" Tee folds her napkin and sets it on the table, like she's giving up on dinner already.

"Tee, I appreciate everything you do for me, but the best way for you to help me right now is to not make a bigger deal of this than it needs to be."

Another sigh from Tee. "Cayenne. I know you like to think of yourself as confident and sure of yourself, but it's okay to admit you're scared. Or even confused."

"Great, well, it's okay for *you* to not treat me like a little kid." That doesn't come out sounding as mature as I would like, but I can't help it.

"I know you're not a little kid, Cay. But you also don't have to pretend you have everything figured out." She gives me the smallest possible smile, one that's more wistful than amused. "That's one way you remind me of your mom, actually. You're someone who's constantly seeking. Seeking a sense of a control, seeking an identity, seeking reassurance of your value, seeking safety."

"Safety?" Does she even know me? I dodge safety. I give a mental middle finger wave to Lorelei.

"Yes, in a counterintuitive way. You try to predetermine

your risks. And on some level that makes you feel safe. It's the unknown that's hard for you."

Our salads are delivered to the table, but my appetite is waning.

"I think that's why you never study for tests," Tee goes on. "If you were to study and fail, you'd feel inadequate. So instead, you don't try . . . then if you fail your excuse to yourself is that you didn't try and you don't care." This stings a bit. "To truly care and truly try, to truly work toward building a future—that makes you feel vulnerable. Because it means you have to step up to the plate and be responsible for your life."

This whole conversation feels insulting. I'm immediately on the defensive. "To be fair, life is shitty." My voice catches, and I hate it.

"Yes, life is shitty." Tee grabs my hands in her own from across the table. She nearly knocks over an ice water. "It's shitty and wonderful and unpredictable and you can't extricate one component from the other."

"Yes I can." I just feel like arguing. Aren't we supposed to be bonding here?

"Well, I think you're missing out. You're building walls around yourself that keep you from seeing possibilities—the good ones along with the bad."

"And where did you get your psychology degree?"

"The choice is yours, Cayenne. You're an adult now. You get to choose how to live your life. All I'm asking is that you consider options, even uncomfortable ones. Accept knowledge and input. Accept support."

My meal is ruined. I can hardly swallow the chopped salad because of the tightness in my throat. Plus the lettuce is wilted and I hate that.

My cluster of sticky-note journal entries is growing. I haven't placed any in the journal yet. If I ever do, I may have to glue them on, because the sticky strips are weakening.

THINGS NOBODY TELLS YOU WHEN YOU LOSE A MOM —CAYENNE

How bad it'll hurt at first. Heavy compressed pain, as if your entire self has been bound up and packed into a tiny metal box an eighth of your size, and you don't fit. You're bound so tight you can think of nothing else but survival.

How you get used to it after a while. You stop feeling that confinement, and then the hurt scabs up and over, covers you with a crusty outer coating that protects you. How you never ever want to peel that off. Because underneath, you're raw, you're bloody, you're exposed.

How once you're scabbed over and crusty, you're also kind of numb. How sometimes doing reckless things makes you feel alive again—if only for a moment.

How this is kind of addictive. How it's hard to stop. Even if you know you might lose the person who matters most to you.

I chew on the back of my pen, leaving teeth marks in the plastic. I compare my entry to Saff's entry. Mom's death affected her in a totally different way. I guess that every person has a unique reaction to loss. I haven't spent much time trying to understand that.

* * *

Saffron knocks on my door, two quick taps. I slide my Sticky note entries under a book just as she barges in. Her face is swollen. She's engulfed by a large sweatshirt, with the sleeves pulled over her hands as if it's eating her alive. Man, she's taking this hard.

Saff has done everything right, always chosen the careful path. It's not fair for the curse to snag her too.

"Saffron." I reach for her. We haven't hugged much since we were little, but I stand up and pull her in. "It's going to be okay, you know. I know you're not a fan of medical procedures, but we'll schedule our surgeries together so we can sit on the couch for weeks and critique bad daytime television." Truthfully I'm not sure I'll be signing up for the whole surgical disfigurement deal, but it seems the right thing to say. "Anyway, even if we start MRIs at twenty, we don't need to seriously consider surgery for years. We don't have to stress yet." Saff starts sobbing. I consider trying to lighten her mood by suggesting she bump up a couple of bra sizes, but I restrain myself.

"Now." She presses against my shoulder, trying to get something out in that hiccupy-gaspy middle-of-crying way. "We—have—to do it now."

I pull back to examine her, and for a split second the ground drops away from me. "Now?" My voice jumps up an octave. "Um. You just turned eighteen. And I'm not even nineteen."

"I know you—Cayenne. You're going—to pretend this

214

doesn't—exist. You're not gonna d—eal with it. No matter what you say, no matter what you promise me, I kn—ow you. N—othing you say will r—eassure me. Unless I see—you do this—I won't be able to relax."

I still feel incredulous. I'm so surprised that she's not obsessing about the medical part of all this. The girl's scared of a freaking needle . . . I can't imagine her facing a scalpel. "Wait. You're going to have an elective mastectomy a *decade* before you need to, just because you're afraid I'm not going to follow through on mine? I think your logic is a little off."

"There is no logic with you, Cayenne!" She's scream-crying now. "I don't want to lose you! I'll do anything I have to. Anything!" There is snot dripping down her face. I've never seen her cry like this before.

I can't stand to see her in so much pain, as if she's being ripped apart. I want to fix this for her. "Hey. After the accident, I made a promise to myself and to the Minions. That I'll be there for you guys. I won't let you down again."

She stares at me, like she's not sure she believes me. "If that's true, we at least have to make a plan now. There's op—tions. I asked Nat—alie a ton of q-uest—ions to—day." So this explains her being in Natalie's office for so long. Her face breaks into pieces. "Promise?"

"I need to think, Saffron."

"You don't have to promise details, Cayenne. Just pr-omise we'll d—eal with th—is together?" She asks between sobby, hiccuppy breaths.

"Promise," I say, regretting the word before it's even out of my mouth.

* * *

215

It's been less than twenty-four hours since the solidification of the Silk curse, but Saff has already engulfed herself in planning. She's more than on a roll, she's on an avalanche, and it's picking up speed. Truthfully, her enthusiasm is a little frightening.

Apparently the first available consult with a specialist is six weeks out, since our situation is not "imminent." So in addition to arguing with some intake coordinator about the meaning of *imminent*, she's printing a whirlwind of online articles, which she's analyzing and taping up around her room. And *I'm* supposed to be the unstable one? The girl is losing it.

I need a break. I text Vanessa and ask her if she can come over to distract Saffron, because she shouldn't be alone when she's like this . . . and when Vanessa says she's game, I escape.

Do I hate asking Ryan/Dad for a lift after our last conversation? Yes. Am I relieved that he's willing to drop me off at the secret garden and available to retrieve me whenever I want, no questions asked? Absolutely.

I spend four hours at the garden. Thinking.

The idea of doing this right *now* totally terrifies me. And will a mastectomy satisfy my sister, or will she push for us to get our ovaries removed as soon as possible too? I need to buy us a little time.

I've never wanted to get married and have kids. But now there's a tiny seed of doubt sprouting inside me. What if in five or ten or fifteen years, I realize I do want kids, and by then it's too late?

I don't think I've met any straight guys who aren't at least mildly obsessed with boobs. It's hard to imagine someone being attracted to me without them. And my ovaries? Without those I won't have the ability to create and sustain life. And isn't that, at its core, what makes women different from men? I remind myself that that's not always true, that I really should stop defining womanhood so narrowly, but when it comes to *my* body, I don't like the idea of giving up that aspect of myself. Of limiting what my body is capable of.

I run my fingers down my mid-region, circling my belly button. A baby could blossom in there. A child. A beautiful, perfect child. Someone I create.

Shit. This is so stressful. I try to quiet my brain. I lie on my back and stare up at the leaves. At the way the sun shines through the cracks. At the tiny slivers of blue sky. I breathe in the earthy smell of the grass, and I focus on my breathing. In through the nose, out through the mouth.

I must be near sleep, because Lorelei hovers.

It occurs to me that sparring with her won't make me feel any less overwhelmed. I devised this cat-and-mouse game to protect Saff and Tee and the Minions from her wrath. But the ridiculousness of this hits me. Nothing I've done has helped Saff at all—we both have this gene mutation. Death isn't some sort of strategic game. Me dying doesn't mean Saff is any more likely to live. Me living doesn't mean Saff is any more likely to die.

I hope you know I'm not afraid of you. When we do this surgery, that decision will come from a logical place, not from an emotional place.

Fear gets a bad rap, in my opinion. She's got a creepy Cheshire cat grin.

Well, your opinion doesn't interest me. I'm starting not to care about you at all.

Lorelei snickers. *Clearly I'm making progress. You're just too self-obsessed to see it for what it is.*

I corral every ounce of strength in my mind to push her away. She swirls up, as if caught in a tornado. I know she's a figment of my imagination, but I've never before been able to exert so much control over her.

Goodbye, Lorelei.

For now.

Once her laughter fades, I center my mind again, focusing on my breaths. Gradually my thoughts return, but not in a rapid misfire kind of way. Now they float past like they're drifting down a lazy river. I consider each one in a removed manner, almost as an observer. As my mind settles, my options become clear.

Chapter 32

Axel's man cave is the perfect setting for an after-school TV marathon. His bed sits against the wall, covered with neatly placed pillows, all smelling like his coconut hair gel. He keeps the lights permanently dim—"mood lighting," he calls it. His room is clean and organized, totally not what you'd expect from a teenager living on his own.

We lie on his bed, under the covers, watching (and not watching) HBO. His arm drapes over my shoulders, resting on my belly. He drums his fingers there lightly. I twist toward him, ignoring the faint ache of my ribs. I get my walking cast tomorrow, and I'll be so glad to kiss my crutches goodbye. I wrap my arms around his waist, gently pulling him on top of me. We haven't had much of a chance to make out since the accident, and I miss it.

The weight of his body lulls me, and I sense the impermanence of my own skin. My breasts are only visiting. My ovaries only temporarily harvesting estrogen, let alone eggs. They're on borrowed time. I have this urge to use them. To maximize their potential. I slip my shirt off and unhook my bra.

Axel's lips part appreciatively, and he dips his head toward me, kissing me hard and deep. He runs his fingertips across my side. I grab them and lead them to my breasts. The nerve endings there blossom, and I let myself succumb to the pleasant throbbing that resonates in every cell.

He kisses the crook of my neck and I tilt my head away to give him fuller access. "You ever think of getting married young?" I ask, goose bumps prickling up all over my skin.

Axel stops working on my neck. "I thought you were anti-marriage."

"I was. I am. I just . . ." I can't concentrate with all the goose bumps. I want him to shut up and go back to my neck. But I also want to get this out in the open. "I have that gene mutation, Axel."

"That what—oh. Really?" He sits up, digesting. "Shit, Cay. That's terrible." He lets his eyes fall to my breasts, and they linger there as if he's painting a Renaissance picture in his mind. "What do you think you'll do?"

"I'm leaning toward herbs, alkaline water, and acupuncture."

"Be serious."

"Well, I forgot to apply to college, so I was thinking I'll pop out a couple babies and then pull an Aunt Tee—kiss it all goodbye. I promised Saff I'd make a plan—that's the best I got." I'm grateful that my constant joking makes these words so easy, even though I'm being one hundred percent serious. "Wanna make a baby? I hear it's fun. . . at least the first couple minutes anyway. The next nine months are kind of a drag, but that wouldn't affect you." I decide not to mention the subsequent eighteen years.

His face stays somber, but with a flicker of irritation. "Come on, Cay. You don't want kids."

"I don't," I agree. "But I do like the Minions . . . so I got to thinking . . . what if I change my mind and it's too late? I figure

I should produce a few early, before I remove my equipment."

The irritation has now consumed any other emotion Axel might be having. He scoots away, and I'm thinking he has no plans to go back to kissing my neck. "Cayenne. You make a joke out of everything."

"So I've been told." I'm a tiny bit hurt that he's not at least playing along, but I barrel ahead. "So whaddaya think, wanna make a miniscule alien creature who will take over my womb like a parasite?"

"Whoa." Axel holds up his hand. "I can't believe you're throwing yourself at me and I'm turning you down. I've wanted to be with you for so long. But this isn't right. I don't want to take advantage of you when you're like this." Axel climbs out of bed and pulls on his jeans. "Listen, Cayenne. Maybe we should take a break."

"*What*?" That tiny bit of hurt swells into something bigger.

"You're kind of freaking me out."

"I just told you I'm on the genetic high-speed railway to cancer and now you're saying we should take a break?"

"Uh, well, you suggested that I get you pregnant, which feels like a pretty big red flag to me. You know I don't want kids, and by the way, we're still in high school! Why the hell would I be cool with that?"

White-hot embarrassment flashes through my whole body. "Okay, so maybe I'm going a little overboard. Sorry. I'm not trying to like, entrap you or something."

"No, you were just thinking about what *you* wanted, like usual."

"That's not—that's not fair." Especially coming from Axel, the guy who supposedly loves my free-spirited independence. "I'm sorry, okay? I'm just a little freaked out, I guess."

Something bursts inside me, and despite my best efforts my eyes start to water.

"Look, Cayenne. We make a great team. We have a ton of fun and all that. But I'm not into long-term commitments. This is getting way too real for me."

"Oh, that's right." I wipe my chin, because now the tears are literally rolling down my cheeks and dripping off my chin. "You're the fun boyfriend. You're the guy who's all about having a blast, and not about anything real. I cannot believe I just offered to have sex with you."

I stand up, blindly searching for my bra, which has somehow gotten tangled with my shirt on the floor. I don't want to stand here and wrangle with my clothing in front of him, so I stumble to the bathroom. There's a freaking flood pouring out of my eyes. I try not to look at myself in the mirror, but I catch a glimpse by accident. My nose and eyes have puffed up. Wet cheeks. Blotchy skin. My flesh is raw, fresh, young . . . my breasts full . . .

I hook my bra, yank my shirt over my head, and grab my crutches. I storm out of Axel's apartment, still grasping my shoe in one hand, which is hard to do while also holding the crutch steady. I'm not supposed to put weight on the splint, but it's so tempting. I hobble down the apartment steps and propel myself down the sidewalk as fast as I can.

I get about two blocks before the blisters begin on my left foot and under my armpits. My ribs protest against the extra pressure from the crutches. Since I still have my shoe in my hand, I ease myself down on someone's lawn to put it on. My angry ribs make this descent awkward, painful, and probably hilarious to watch.

I text Saff. *Ride, please? Fight with Axel.*

It's suddenly raining. I duck my phone under my shirt, but the fabric soaks within seconds. Wait, not raining . . . sprinklers! The water transforms the lawn into a grassy puddle. I ease myself up and onto the sidewalk as fast as I can to protect my phone.

I text Micah. *You busy?*

Never too busy for you.

Can you pick me up? I'll pay you gas money.

No way.

When those words appear on my screen, it feels like the water from my shirt is permeating my skin, drowning my insides.

I mean "No way" about paying me gas money. "Yes way" about picking you up.

Glad you clarified. It may take a while for my waterlogged heart to wring itself out.

Where are you?

I survey my surroundings. *263 Blossom Street.*

On my way. You're lucky I'm just sitting around, messaging my roommate-to-be.

I feel ten miles from lucky. If anything, "unlucky" has sucked onto my forehead like a parasitic leech.

Saff messages me back five minutes later. *You okay? Fletch and I are watching the kids, and I don't have any car seats. You want me to send Fletcher?*

No, it's okay. Micah is coming.

Sorry you had a fight with Axel.

He's an ass.

Agreed. She responds so quickly that I feel like she's just been waiting for an opportunity to trash Axel.

Why do I like such an ass?

You are one of the world's greatest mysteries, Cayenne.

Chapter 33

Micah spends a good ten seconds laughing at me when he pulls up to the curb. I'm sitting on the sidewalk, comically miserable. My wet shirt still clings to my skin, and my hair's matted around my face.

"This is way more entertaining than messaging a stranger or working on my econ paper." He hops out of the car and comes around toward me, offering me a hand up.

"Gee, how flattering."

As soon as I'm standing face to face with him, his amusement fades. "What's wrong, Cay? You've been crying."

Something about the way his tone softens and his brow furrows causes tears to spring back into my eyes.

He pulls me into a bear hug. I haven't hugged him in so long that I stiffen at first. But the thing with bear huggers is that they go in for the squeeze full force, and they hang on. He keeps me wrapped between his arms, pressed against his chest, despite the dampness of my shirt. I thaw there, and finally hug him back.

"You don't have to tell me what's going on." He speaks into my hair, his arms still around me.

"Thanks." I feel a little weird about still hugging him but also don't want to pull away.

We stand there for a little while, until he asks, "Want to go?"

"Yeah. I think I've been loitering in front of this family's house for long enough."

He releases me and leads me to the passenger side door. "Where to? Home to change?"

"Not home. Let's go somewhere else."

"I know just the place." Micah grabs an old beach towel out of the trunk and spreads it over my seat. "No offense. Just—you're pretty wet."

Micah waits to start the engine until I've strapped on my belt. I relax into the beach towel, turning my head toward the window. The scenery blurs past. Micah plays some tunes, quiet though, and I close my eyes. I may have fallen asleep, because when I open them, he's parked in the shade, the windows rolled down. A light breeze brushes my cheeks.

"You up?" He asks. "You kind of crashed."

"Yeah."

"I grabbed you a caramel latte."

"Thanks." I make a feeble attempt to smooth my knotted hair and my still-damp shirt. I take a sip of the latte, and it slides down my throat, coating it with warm sweetness. "Where are we?"

"My favorite beach. The waves suck here, so no one ever comes. But it's quiet and the breeze is just right. You wanna go out and sit, or stay in here?"

"We can go out."

Managing my splint and crutches in sand turns out to be challenging, so halfway there he deems this a ridiculous

225

attempt and guides me to a smooth rock that I can perch on and angle my ankle against. He returns carrying my latte and his own warm drink.

"What're you having?"

"Uh, none of your business," he says nicely enough, but he doesn't sit.

"Maybe not. I'm just making conversation."

"Okay, if I tell you, you must guard this secret with your life." He theatrically examines his surroundings as if there are spies hiding behind the rocks.

"Got it." I pat the rock next to me, in case he wants to join me.

"It's vanilla milk." He leans forward to whisper this.

I have to laugh. "Weirdo. You don't like any of those sweet coffee drinks?"

"Nope." He straightens up and sits next to me. "I'm a vanilla milk kind of guy."

"Is it hot?"

"Yep—steamed milk and vanilla syrup. You want a sip?"

"Sure." I reach for his paper cup and take a tiny sip. "Oh, that's good. It makes me think of cut-out sugar cookies."

"Yes. I'm a child. I sleep with the bathroom light on too."

This makes me want to hug him again. "You might be in trouble when you go to college. Your roommate could prefer pitch-black."

"True. I've been thinking of sending myself to darkness-sleep-training but they won't let me bring my teddy."

I sock him in the arm. "Maybe you should just stay home. You might be able to convince me to go to community college with you." I don't tell him that I've already been considering community college options.

We sit in silence for a really long time, just listening to the comforting sound of waves crashing on the shore, the birds squawking above, and the gentle shushing of the breeze. I try to find a pattern in the way that the waves crash, but they're each unique, like cobwebs and snowflakes. I've drunk most of my latte when I finally speak again. "How'd you know caramel lattes were my thing?"

"Asked your sister."

"Oh." I wonder how much else he knows. "Did she tell you what's going on?"

"Some of it." Micah picks up a rock and turns it over in his hand. "That you and Axel had a fight. And . . . about the cancer gene."

"Yeah, that pretty much sums it up for today." I put my latte to my lips but don't take the last sip. "At least I don't have the bubonic plague."

"True. Way to look on the bright side. And at least you don't have a broken ankle." He nudges me and smiles. "Oh, wait, you do."

I smile back. "Hey, that's my move."

"I know. I pulled a Cayenne—I turned something that sucks into a joke that sucks." He wraps his fingers around the rock. "But seriously. I'm sorry, Cay."

"Me too." I reach over and peel his fingers away from the rock. It's smooth. "Honestly, the gene mutation just tells me what I already knew. Big surprise—Saff and I'll probably get cancer. I could've told you that without a stupid blood test."

Micah offers the rock to me. "Yeah, but this gives you a statistical probability. I've been researching it online. It's kind of a big deal."

"I know." I accept the rock. "And I've always kind of

thought I'd die young, so I might as well cram as much fun in my life as possible. I just—I didn't want Saff to have to deal with all this." My voice catches. "She thinks we should do the surgery now. Mostly because she's afraid I won't follow through if we put it off till later." I extend my fingers, with the rock flat on my palm.

"It doesn't have to be like that." Micah squares off so that we're nearly eye to eye. "There's a middle ground. You're eighteen years old, come on. You could probably make a plan to monitor closely for the next few years. If you had the surgery before thirty, that'd be plenty proactive. I bet most people don't do it until much later."

"It just . . ." Perhaps it's the topic or the fact that his nose is nearly touching mine, but I'm having trouble finding my words. "It will color every decision I make. I wasn't really planning on having kids . . . but now I'm not sure I'm ready to rule it out completely. I don't know that I can decide now for forever."

"Saffron's going to hate me for saying this, but don't decide now." Up close, his eyes are gray with flecks of amber. "Start planning now, sure. But give yourself a chunk of time to grow up and then you can decide."

"Look who's talking about growing up, vanilla milk boy!" I twist away as if we're done with this conversation. "And you're a stealth milk consumer too, hiding it in a coffee cup. For shame."

"Yeah, yeah. I know." He slings his arm around me and squeezes my shoulders.

Now that we're not facing each other anymore, I feel brave. "I have a strange question for you."

"Go for it."

"So you're a guy," I start, twisting even farther from him.

"I've been under that assumption for the last eighteen years."

"A guy who's into girls."

"Definitely."

I let my eyes travel along the coastline, while I ask what might possibly be the most awkward question in the history of womanhood. "So . . . would you date a girl who didn't have breasts?"

"Hmm." I can tell my question surprises him but doesn't scare him. "I do like breasts." He drums his fingers on the rocks. "Would this hypothetical girl be completely breast free? Like no reconstruction or anything?"

"Possibly." I watch a lone bird soar, then dip down toward the water.

"Would this girl have a fun personality—some sarcastic wit, a bit of a prickly exterior but a secret sweet side?"

"Okay, let's give her that." I allow myself to edge back into his line of vision, because I want to see his expression. His lips are flat, but there's a subtle humor in them. "Good personality, intelligent . . . let's say you're attracted to her . . . just no breasts."

"You want honesty here?" he asks, and he waits.

I peek back at his gentle eyes, and they are full of warmth. "Yes. Total honesty."

"If I loved her, it wouldn't stop me for a second. If I thought her breasts could kill her, I'd want them gone. I wouldn't want her to be impulsive about it, I'd want her to think it through and find the right time for herself, but I would support her no matter what."

Now that I can see his face again, it's harder to ask these questions. I force myself to go on. "What about a girl with no ovaries? Would you marry someone who couldn't make babies with you?"

He examines his fingernails, but just for a moment, and then he's back. "You're asking hard questions."

"I need to know. You're a guy. You know how guys think."

"I know how *I* think. I can't speak for other guys." He hesitates. "Okay, so for me—I want to have kids someday. That's important to me. So ideally, I'd want to marry someone who could have kids. But I'd be totally okay with her like freezing her eggs or something. Or with getting rid of her ovaries *after* we had a couple kids." He stops, but I can tell that he's not done, that he's just pulling his thoughts together. "But . . . if I fell in love with someone who already didn't have ovaries, it wouldn't be a deal breaker. There are other ways to have kids. And a lot of couples can't get pregnant for all kinds of reasons. So if my wife and I couldn't, we'd adopt or something. I mean, there are so many ways to be a parent. Like just because Aunt Tee didn't give birth to you doesn't mean she's not a mother to you."

I nod, absorbing what he's said. "Yeah." And suddenly I'm so grateful for his openness—his thoughtfulness. "So . . . is it weird to be having this conversation?"

"A little," he admits, smiling. I focus on his dimples, fighting the urge to stick my finger in one. "But hey, we've known each other our whole lives. My mom's got some photos of us in the bathtub when we were toddlers."

I groan, picturing that. "Yeah, well, it's awkward for me too. But thank you for being honest. It's helpful to get your perspective." I place the rock back in his own hands, but my fingers linger. "Just so you know, I wasn't asking if you'd want to date me, or anything. It was just a hypothetical."

He doesn't pull his hand away. "Well, just so you know, I would."

"Would what?" I'm confused, and I pull back.

"I would date you. With or without breasts. With or without ovaries." He says this with a straight face, and a tenderness I haven't seen before.

"You would?" If I'd known the conversation was going to veer off in this direction, I'd have made a point to be examining my fingernails or something. But I didn't.

"I would." He shuffles the rock from one hand to the other, absentmindedly. "But I don't think I'm your type. And that's okay. I don't take offense at that." He chuckles. "Based on your boyfriend, I'm not sure I want to be your type."

"Not a fan, huh?" I ask. My voice sounds convincingly light, but my heart rate has gone haywire. Did Micah really just say he'd date me? And why does that sound so appealing?

"Nope, not particularly a fan of Axel. He doesn't seem like a bad dude, just kind of self-absorbed. You deserve better." Micah checks his phone. "Your sister just messaged me. I better get you home. Is she always this much of a stress case?"

I don't want to leave this moment. The serenity of the beach has balanced out the awkwardness of our conversation, and I just want to stay in this safe spot with Micah forever. But real life beckons, so we make our way home.

* * *

That night I lie in the dark, thinking. Saffron has been super emotional all evening. I guess this whole gene thing is really messing with her, even more than I'd have thought it would. I texted Fletcher after dinner and asked him if he could come keep her company, even though he was just over this afternoon. He didn't hesitate—just called out of work to spend the evening with her.

So what is it about Saffron that leads her to pick a guy like Fletcher? And what is it about *me* that makes me love a guy like Axel? Yes, Axel's fun. Exciting. And we have chemistry. But if he doesn't care enough to want what's best for me, then is our connection anything more than an adrenaline rush?

And what is it about Micah that's so intriguing? He's safe, I guess. Reliable. Kind. Not my type, true. But isn't my "type" allowed to change over time?

I take out my phone to text Axel. *You're right. Let's take a break*, I type, and I press send before I can change my mind.

I wait an hour for him to send an apology text, saying he wants to stay together after all, but he doesn't. That opens up an empty pit in my stomach. I thought for sure he hadn't meant everything he said back at the apartment. I mean, of course it's a huge decision to make a baby, and it should be mutual, and I know I shouldn't have been so pushy and impulsive about it. But he didn't have to abandon me completely! I haven't even gotten a basic acknowledgment—no "Glad we're on the same page" or "Okay, take care." Nothing. What did the last year mean to him?

My hands start to shake as I think about the fact that I almost had sex with him and he doesn't have the freaking courtesy to respond to my text.

My thoughts spiral: What if we'd had unprotected sex, and I'd gotten pregnant, and I'd had the baby? What kind of father would Axel have been? Better or worse than Ryan Channels?

What choices would I have made for myself, for my kid, if I'd found myself in that position? Better or worse than my mother's choices?

Luckily I don't have to find out. But the near-miss of it unnerves me. I was so certain about Axel—so certain and so completely wrong.

My mom's words from the journal filter back to me. *I want to give you permission to make mistakes. Mistakes are how we learn. So give yourself a break here and there.*

I settle down with a sticky note and write my next journal entry response.

THE BIG NEWS —CAYENNE
    I forgive you, Mom, for being human.
    I forgive you, ~~Ryan~~ Dad, for being human.
    I will try to forgive myself too.
    I will, at the very least, understand that I am still evolving.
    I am a work in progress.

Chapter 34

Over the next two days, something settles within Saffron. I give half the credit to Fletcher and her supportive gaggle of friends, and half to the six weeks we'll have to wait to see a specialist. Saff's forced to shift her focus—to sleep and eat and do homework and think about ordinary things. Maybe I get a teeny tiny bit of credit too? Like one percent? Because I keep promising her I'll be proactive. I'll listen to the doctors. I won't make her get her boobies hacked all by herself. We'll do it together.

So in the spirit of moving on, we've decided to finish the next Mom video. One of Tee's friends has whisked her and the Minions off for a thrilling afternoon at the community pool, so Saff has Tee's car. I've graduated to a walking cast, and I can't believe how free I feel. Just ditching those crutches has rebirthed me. I can actually bend to search for the hidden key from the flowerpot on Micah's porch.

Turns out I don't need the key, though, because the door to Micah's house is unlocked. This is strange because Alicia and Micah have driven up to Las Vegas for a cousin's wedding. You'd think they'd lock the door when they're out of town. Maybe Micah's dad is in and out between flights.

Unlocked doors always freak me out—my mind fastens on sinister intruders. The truth is lots of people choose not to lock their doors. Axel and his roommate never lock theirs. They're more worried about being locked out themselves when they forget a key than about someone getting in. Luke, on the other hand, is a fanatic door locker.

The darkened house sits cool and still. "Hello?" I call out after Saff and I enter. I flip on lights. Everything's normal—cluttered, of course, but Alicia's typical level of disarray.

The enclosed porch, however, looks like it's been ransacked.

"Did we have an earthquake that I missed?" Saffron jokes. I think this might be her first wisecrack in days.

"Micah and Alicia were probably looking for something and didn't have time to put it back."

"You don't think someone robbed them, do you?"

"No. You think someone's after all the treasures in this house?" I lace the comment with heavy sarcasm. If Alicia sold everything under her roof in a garage sale, she'd walk away with less than a thousand dollars. It's all junk with sentimental value.

Except for the technology, of course. I open the desk drawer that holds the laptop and charger. It's empty.

"Wait. Where's the laptop?"

Saff peeks inside. "It's usually right here. Maybe someone did take it."

"It's probably worth more than everything else in the room combined. Maybe someone came searching specifically for it." I reconsider the unlocked door.

"That video—the one we were in the middle of watching— she was starting to tell us about the money." Saff sinks down onto the couch. "Possibly large amounts of money."

"Yeah but a thief wouldn't know that. No one knows that," I remind her.

"Except Micah and Fletch."

"And Axel—I told Axel," I remember.

"Oh. My. God." Saff stands up. "Do you think Axel took the laptop?"

"Why do you go straight to him?" I'm offended. "It could've been Fletch."

Saff gives me an "oh please" look. Fletcher once drove fifteen minutes back to the grocery store when he realized they'd given him too much change. "Maybe Micah has it. He was the one who told us to stop watching. Right in the middle of Mom explaining about the money." Saff's voice turns shrill. "Cay— those videos and that journal are all we have left of Mom! We have to get it back!"

"We will," I promise, sounding way more confident than I feel. "Don't panic. Let's think this through. Micah's had access to the laptop all along. Why would he take it? He could just keep watching the videos without us knowing. Maybe he's even watched all of them already."

This idea unsettles something in my stomach. Maybe Micah knows how much money we're getting. Maybe this is why he's been so nice to me. Maybe this is why he said he wouldn't care whether I had breasts or ovaries. *I'd* have watched ahead if I were him. I've been reading Saff's journal entries— same difference, right?

"You're right," Saff says, talking fast. "It's not Micah. It's Axel. You opened your big mouth about the money, and when he realized you were breaking up with him, he came here and snatched it. Simple."

"He can be an asshole," I admit. "But he wouldn't do that."

"Wouldn't he? Didn't he break into Donut Diva after he lost his job?"

"Yeah, but just to take the money they owed him."

Saff looks pointedly at me. "And you don't think he feels like you owe him something?"

I digest this thought for a long time, so long in fact that Saff probably thinks I've short-circuited. I remember texting him to say that Mom probably buried the cash in a tin can, or came up with treasure hunt clues. Finally I say, "Let's pay him a surprise visit."

* * *

I've never seen Saff drive this fast. She's whipping around turns, tires squealing, like she's training for NASCAR. We screech up to Axel's apartment.

"We just gonna walk in?" Saff asks, climbing out of the car.

"For damn sure." I slam my door. "I'm not giving him a heads up."

I turn the front doorknob slowly. Unlocked, as usual, but that doesn't mean anything. It's eleven o'clock in the morning. Will Axel be lounging in his bed, watching Netflix? Or out spending our money? The thought breaks me apart like a chisel to ice.

The place is empty. Dirty dishes in the sink. Coffee stains on the counter. Laundry piled up in baskets and hanging from doorways. Axel's roommate is not the neat freak he is. I close the door behind me.

"Should we dig through his stuff?" Saff whispers, and I nearly laugh.

"You're asking me? Your morals trump mine by far. So if you're good with it, so am I."

"Surprisingly, I feel totally okay about this. I kind of hate Axel, and I don't normally hate anyone."

I tug her toward Axel's room. "You are becoming one with your angry side. This means you are no longer a saint. Thank god. Welcome to humanhood."

Saff holds back, hesitant. "Do you think you should message him to see where he is? What if he walks in on us?"

"I say, bring it on."

And with that, we comb Axel's place. His room is military-organized and sparse. In one drawer we find a thick stack of cash bound with a girl's hair band (oh my god) and five phone chargers (who needs that many?). Under his bed I find a lacy underwire bra (that does not happen to be mine—OH MY GOD). In his roommate's mess of a room we find a long-lost remote control and two cockroaches (dead and crispy).

I sit down on the floor, seething with fury. I cannot believe he has someone else's bra! *Don't think about that right now. Focus, Cayenne.* I spread the money in a half circle around me and start counting. Three hundred and seventeen dollars. Asshole. It's one thing to be a self-centered reckless jerk, but to steal from me? And from Saff? Scum.

"Should we steal it back?" Saff whispers, her eyes flashing with the excitement of revenge.

"Absolutely." I struggle to calm myself. "Maybe then he'll think to lock his freaking door. Take basic precautions like a normal person." Of course, I don't have much room to criticize, given that I couldn't even be bothered to wear a seat belt until recently . . . I shake my head. That was the old Cayenne. I'm no longer that person.

I stack the money back up and slide it into my purse. It's too thick to fit in my wallet. We return the chargers and the remote to their places. I keep the lacy bra—I'll destroy it later. I'd love to put the crunchy cockroaches in Axel's bed, but I can't bear to pick them up.

We scramble back out of the apartment, tripping over each other, and tumble into the car. My adrenaline shoots up, and with that flash of energy, an image of Axel bursts into my mind—as well as his smell, his touch, the texture of his skin. Although I've known for a while that Axel spells bad news for me, it's not until this pivotal moment, running from his apartment, that I feel a complete severing from him. No going back. No repairing this relationship. I'm done.

Saff zips down of the street, spinning around corners with the same fervor she showed on the way over. I tilt my head back and werewolf howl, prompting her to join in, which sets off a serious case of giggles. As we regain our breath, my pulse slows, and so does her driving. "Cayenne?" Saff works the words out of her mouth carefully, and with effort. "This is a lot of money, sure, but I was kind of thinking Mom would be leaving more than this. Otherwise why all the theatrics? Sure, this is a ton of cash for binge spending, but as an inheritance, it's basically nothing. A few new outfits for each of us."

I absorb what she's saying. "Huh. Good point." I pull the bills out of my purse.

"What if this isn't our money?" Saff's voice cracks. "What if Axel just doesn't believe in bank accounts, and keeps his life savings in his underwear drawer?"

I smooth the bills and place them back in my purse. "Then that would mean two things. One—we're officially burglars. And two—someone else took our laptop."

Chapter 35

We drive all the way home and zombie-watch a half hour of bad television before we decide we've made a terrible (and criminal) mistake, and that we've probably left our fingerprints all over his filthy apartment. We can't agree whether this would be a misdemeanor or a felony, but either is bad, really bad. So we decide to go back, preferably as fast as possible without getting pulled over.

I feebly argue that regardless, Axel deserves this for having SOMEONE ELSE'S BRA on his premises, but this argument falls flat. My adrenaline surge rebounds, double strength. Not that I *wanted* Axel to steal from us, but I can't tolerate the possibility that Micah did. Saff refuses to consider Fletcher as a suspect. Plus Fletcher has a solid after-school job and well-off parents. He clearly isn't hurting for cash.

While Micah has this stellar house, I know about his dad's gambling problem, and that he'd been hoping for a full scholarship for college but only got a partial. Would he have watched the video and taken the money? I can't wrap my mind around this idea.

I text him while Saff drives. *Can't find the laptop. We're ready to hear about the $.*

No answer for a long time, and staring at my phone while Saff whips around turns is making me dizzy. Finally he responds, *I took it. Sorry. I need it right now . . . probably more than you do. My second scholarship didn't come through.*

I'm not sure I've ever felt truly incredulous in my life other than this moment. Disbelief hijacks my every cell. "Micah took it! He admits it!" I practically spit the words out like they taste bad. "What a faker. He acts like this stand-up guy and then meanwhile he's stealing from us?"

"Whaaat?" Saff swerves.

"He said his scholarship didn't come through. But come on, this is way over the line—"

"Um, Cayenne?" Saff pulls to the curb back at Axel's. "I think we have bigger problems now." She points to Axel's apartment building, where a police officer presses the buzzer. I instinctively suck in a deep breath. From our spot on the street, we watch. Axel opens the front door and speaks to the officer, waving his hands wildly.

"Oh-my-god-oh-my-god-oh-my-god." Saff slumps forward on the wheel as if praying to the dashboard. "I can't believe we did this."

"We can fix it. We'll put it back."

"How?" Saff practically howls. "Axel's at home, there's a cop here—how can we put it back without getting caught?"

"I'm still thinking." The truth is, I have no idea. It's not like I can slide it through his window or under his doormat. What if I hobble up there and claim I grabbed it by accident when packing up? Maybe I can say that I scooped it up along with my clothes when I left?

In the absence of a better plan, and feeling urgency to act quickly, I unclick my seat belt. "I'm going up there. Stay here."

Saff nods weakly, probably relieved that she doesn't have to be involved in returning the money. She's a terrible liar anyway. She'd probably break down and confess immediately.

I hobble over to the building, pulling the cash and the lacy bra out of my pocket. I wrap the bra around the money. It doesn't fit neatly, of course, but it binds the loose bills, and it makes a point. Maybe I'll hand this combo to Axel and say, "Oh, sorry, I realized I got home with the wrong bra, you asshole!" And then he'll know that I've realized what a creeper he is. Adrenaline propels through my veins. I'm pissed. More than pissed. Righteously pissed.

I open the door without knocking. My confidence rises when I realize the cop is a forty-something woman wearing a this-is-a-waste-of-my-time expression.

"Hi there, officer. I'm sorry to interrupt. I just have to clear some things up with my ex." I turn to Axel. "How long have we been broken up, Axel? Two days?"

"Uh—" He glances around, like the answer is on the walls.

"And when I came to pick up my stuff from your room, I accidentally grabbed SOMEONE ELSE'S BRA."

"What? Wait, that's not what it looks like—"

"Two days!" I add to the officer for emphasis. "After a year together."

"That's not what happened." He moves forward, lifting his sweaty arm. "I've had that bra for six months."

"You WHAT?"

"I mean years—six years." He seems flustered.

"Six years ago you were twelve." So that settles it—he's been cheating on me. "Oh, you are so disgusting. I can't believe I—" I swivel toward the cop. "Can you arrest him for being a royal asshole?"

I throw the bra at him, and as the fabric spirals, it loosens and the money inside flies out everywhere. "I am so glad I never had sex with you! Oh, and by the way, here's the money you said I could borrow."

"Wha—?" His eyes widen.

I spin on my heel—well, as much as I can with my bum ankle—and hightail it out of there. If only I had time to snap a photo of Axel's bewildered face and the way the cop is appraising him with a layer of irritation and disgust.

I am so out of here.

Chapter 36

"Las Vegas, here we come!" It's road trip time.

We pack up Tee's car with a ridiculous number of snacks, crank up the music and roll down the windows. Both seat belts securely strapped (Saff double checks mine), we car-dance along Interstate 15. We snagged Micah's cousin's wedding invitation from the Johnsons' fridge, so I enter the address into Saff's GPS. Our destination is approximately four hours away.

I send Micah twenty-three texts, none of which he answers. Maybe his phone's off, or maybe he's gambling with our money, trying to increase his haul. So now, we're tracking him down. Or rather, we're tracking his mom down. Because we're planning to tell on him.

"Men are scum," I say, checking my phone to see if Micah's magically texted me in the last five minutes. "Axel cheated on me. Micah stole from us."

"There's got to be an explanation. I totally believe Axel would steal from us. Micah—I just think there's got to be a reason for this."

"I know the reason. He's 'borrowing' the money—he's trying to win more in Vegas so he doesn't need to take out loans. He probably plans to pay it back eventually, assuming he doesn't lose it all. Simple."

"I don't think so, Cay. That's not his character."

"Character shmaracter. People take care of themselves."

"Yes and no. I mean, of course, if someone's starving or something, they do drastic things," Saff says. "But except for super dire circumstances, people make choices based on who they are."

"Okay, then how do you justify the 'breaking and entering' we just committed in the name of revenge? That's not *your* character. You're law abiding to a fault. You might be the most honest person in the history of the world."

Saffron is quiet for a few moments. Finally she sighs this long, drawn-out, leaky-tire kind of sigh. She pulls off the road and turns down the music. It kind of freaks me out. "Um, Cayenne?" Saff's voice is tiny, almost childlike. "I have to tell you something." Saff sucks in a huge breath. "I, uh . . ."

"Spit it out. Are you a vampire? Or a spy?"

Saff's face is serious. "I don't have the gene mutation."

"Whaaaat?" It takes me a few moments to register what she just said. "That's fabulous!" The pressure that's been in my chest for weeks dissipates. "Wait. Why the hell did you tell me you did?"

"I didn't actually tell you I did. I just didn't tell you I didn't." The classic lie of omission.

I study her face, trying to understand. "But we were planning joint surgeries. To do it together." Complicated emotions are flickering in my gut. Relief—she doesn't have it, she'll be okay. Anger—she convinced me she had it and pressured me to make a decision. What if I'd had sex with Axel and gotten pregnant? Hopefulness—maybe now I can buy myself more time to figure out how to handle this . . .

"I'll still do it with you. Look, our family history is horrific, whether or not I've got the gene mutation. I bet insurance will still cover the surgery as a precaution."

I might cry.

This is maybe the most generous thing anyone has ever been willing to do for me. I intend to talk her out of it, but I'm too choked up to get anything out. So Saff goes on, "I wish I was the one who had this stupid gene mutation. I'd trade with you in a heartbeat. I know I'd do the right thing. I'd be proactive. I'd do anything to be here for you. And I've been afraid you won't do the same for me. Me telling you this—it can't change anything."

"Yeah, but it does. For you—not me. It has to change *your* outlook." I put my hands on her shoulders and awkwardly twist her so that she's facing me squarely. "I promised you, Saffron. I'm going to take care of myself. And now, I'm going to make you promise me something. That you'll make the best decision for your specific medical risk. Not for mine. You're right that you still have the family history, and you could still be at risk. But you do not have to have surgery just to make sure I do. I'll do it because I want to be here for you—and for myself, because I want to be here too. Let's just keep the appointment with the specialist, and we can figure out what's best for each of us."

"Okay." We do an awkward car-hug, and it feels like we're sealing a deal.

We could sit here on the side of the freeway forever, but I really do want to find the laptop. "Any more bombs to drop before we hunt Micah down?"

"Nah." Saffron wipes her eyes and starts the car. "We better get on this. What're we going to say to Alicia?" She pulls back onto the road.

"Your kid stole our only connection to Mom. We want it back. Let's not make it about the money."

"Sounds about right."

"You know what?" I swallow a bite of licorice. "It's *not* about the money. I don't even want to know how much it is. I just want to watch the rest of the videos."

"For real, Cay?"

"Yeah. At first I was hung up on the idea of a new car. But now that you're my chauffeur, maybe I don't need one anymore. I'm a much better car dancer when I'm not trying to drive." I wave a Dorito under her nose. "Want one? It's Cool Ranch."

She snatches it from my hand with her teeth, which is a questionable move given that she's driving. And she's supposed to be the responsible one. Mid-crunch, she says, "Okay, so Cayenne, I have a suggestion. Let's just agree now, let's make it official, that no matter how much money Mom left us, we'll leave it where it is for five years."

"It pains me to agree with you. But okay. Even if I go to college, I can take out student loans. I don't have to pay them back until I'm done."

"Did you just say college?"

"I've been considering it."

"Wow." Saff tips her sunglasses down to her nose to study me. I point back at the road, which is where her eyes should be. "Hey, uh, will you be disappointed if it's not much money? It might not be."

I can't deny that having a nest egg would be nice. "A little," I admit. But everything about Mom's gift to us—seeing her face, hearing her voice, getting access to her innermost thoughts—is more than we ever expected to have. It's rarely occurred to me to think of us as lucky, but considering that I assumed I'd live the rest of my life without a real sense of connection to our mother, I can't think of any other word.

* * *

"You are not a good influence on me," Saff tells me from the next stall. It's an hour later and we're hiding out in a hotel bathroom, changing from our shorts and T-shirts into the dresses we wore to Tee's hospice fundraiser gala last year. "First breaking and entering. And now, crashing a wedding."

"In your case, I take that as a compliment." Her flip flops and wrinkled clothes are on the bathroom floor, which is kind of grossing me out. It's a clean bathroom, but still. I pull my deep purple spaghetti strap over my shoulder, gather my stuff, and step out of the stall to examine myself in the mirror.

"At least it's a big wedding. No one will realize we don't belong. They'll each think the other side of the family invited us." I pull out lipstick and eye liner, leaning in to the mirror to apply.

Saff joins me, wearing her clingy teal dress—a thrift shop discovery for which I take full credit. We jokingly call it the Barbie dress because it makes our breasts look big and our waists small. The fact that Saff once wrote a persuasive paper on the problematic nature of Barbies' unattainable chest-waist-hip ratio did not deter her from adopting this name for the dress.

I grin at her. "You look hot, girl."

Our eyes connect through our reflections and we smile. "You don't look so bad yourself," she tells me. "Too bad we're here to harass Micah, not to find you a new boyfriend."

"Hey—I know you're not a big fan of eyeliner, but can I just use a little?" I see her hesitation. "I promise I won't blind you or make you into a clown." I think that's partly why she doesn't wear it, because if it's too heavy it comes off as garish. But if it's light and smoky, I think she's gonna look amazing.

For a second I think she's composing a snappy comeback, but instead she just agrees.

I pull her toward me and go to work. "Okay. Stay focused. We have to find Alicia, pull her aside, tell her what an unbelievable asshole her son is being, and get that laptop back. In and out, you understand?"

"In and out," she agrees, staring up so I can line under her eyes.

Once I'm finished I pull her hair out of her clip so that it frames her delicate face. I tousle it a bit and I spin her toward the mirror.

"You are beautiful, Saff," I tell her. "If Mom was around, she'd be telling you that all the time. Tee's not the type to say those warm-fuzzy things, and neither am I. But you are drop-dead, model gorgeous."

Her expression tells me what she wants to say—that it doesn't matter, that beauty is only skin deep, and who you are is what's important. All those things are true, and I'd agree with her if she said them. But I think it's also important to be comfortable in your own skin. Some of the time I'm not sure Saff is. So when she takes a deep breath, that glimmer of flush crosses her face, and she says "Thanks, Cayenne," it feels so freaking good.

Saff examines herself in the mirror, seeming pleased. "You did a good job," she tells me. "Honestly, I like myself best without makeup, but every once in a while it's fun to do something different. Though I'll never understand why you do this to yourself every day. It takes so much time!"

I try not to laugh. How can sisters be so different? I love lining my eyes. It's comforting and part of my routine, like brushing my teeth. It doesn't feel like a waste of time to me. But that's the point, right? We should do whatever makes us comfortable. We each get to choose.

I snap a few selfies of us, and when I scroll through the images to view them, I'm reminded of the videos I took of the Minions. I still want to compile them all for a gift for Tee, and truthfully, for myself too. So I don't forget their four-year-old sweetness when they're snippy tweens.

By the time we step into the reception hall, we've missed the meal. Waiters mill about the room, gathering used plates with gloppy food remnants.

The two brides are swaying together in the middle of the empty dance floor, finishing up their first slow dance. They've coordinated their outfits, and their pearl color scheme matches perfectly. One wears a floor-length gown that's lacy across the shoulders, and the other a fitted strapless dress and dangly earrings.

The DJ speaks over the microphone. "Okay, now. Let's get our Dear Old Dads out here for the father-daughter dance."

Two middle-aged men step in to dance with their daughters. "This is really sweet," Saff whispers behind me. I'm not one for tearing up at weddings, but my eyes are welling. Everyone looks so comfortable with each other and with themselves. If I ever get married, I hope I feel the same way.

"Can you picture Dad dancing with you at your wedding?" I ask Saff.

She sucks a breath in, like the thought surprises her. "Yes," She says, side-hugging me. "I totally can."

"I can too. Which is strange—because for most of my life

I didn't think I'd ever get married, and of course I didn't think we'd know our father. Go figure."

Saff nods. "I've been super hard on him, but I know he loves us. Like, that's not even a question in my mind. And he wants to be there for us, in his own awkward way. Even if I think he let us down in the past, I wouldn't *not* want him to be part of our lives now, you know?"

I nod. Now that she says it, I know I feel the same way.

"Okay, let's do this. In and out!" Saff disappears back into the crowd. I can't pull myself away from watching the dance floor. I've always been a people-watcher, but in this moment, I find myself studying all the women especially carefully. We're each so unique—there are so many ways to be a woman. So many ways to be a wife. And a sister. And a friend. And even a mother. We come in a million flavors.

A hand taps my shoulder. I spin, feeling guilty for stealing part of this couple's wedding experience.

Micah. In a suit, with his hair gelled to the side, and smelling delicious. "You look amazing," he says, not seeming all that surprised or alarmed to see me.

"I came to rat you out. Where's your mom?"

"Well that's a nice introduction." The music and chatter are loud enough that I'm half lip reading and half listening.

"I texted you a thousand times."

"Your fingers must be sore," he teases. When I don't smile, he adds, "Cayenne. I turned my phone off during the service. Which was amazing, by the way. The entire wedding party danced down the aisle. Everyone was so pumped!"

I ignore his wedding commentary. "I'm sorry about your scholarship, but that's no excuse to take our money."

Micah's face bunches, as though he's fitting puzzle pieces

together in his brain. "I took the *laptop*, which is mine by the way, so that I could revise another scholarship application essay. I would never take your money!" His eyes are wounded. "How could you think that?"

Ohhhh. Well, that makes a lot more sense. Why does Saff always have to be right?

"So this had nothing do with my mom's videos?"

He flushes. "Well . . . the thought did cross my mind. I didn't think you and Saff were ready to finish the money video. I figured it wouldn't hurt you to wait another week or so."

"This is very confusing. You are confusing."

Micah places two hands on my shoulders. His skin is warm. "I love you guys, Cay. I want this to go well for you."

I freeze, fish-hooked by the "L" word. "You lov—"

"I love you," he reasserts. "You've been thrown a helluva lot of curveballs. Some of them you've thrown yourself, some were just handed to you. This money can help you out. But not if you're going to fight over it."

Part of me wants to step away from his touch. Part of me wants to curl into it like it's a blanket. "Well, you're in luck. On the drive here, I decided I don't care about the money. I can take out a loan if I go to college. Saff and I are on the same page."

His deep-dish dimples indent with confusion. Those are some multi-purpose dimples—they jump into action for an array of facial expressions. "I'm sorry. The music's kind of loud. Did you say *college*?"

"Sheesh." I place my own hands on his, and my elbows bend up, making me feel like a chicken. I pull his hands away from my shoulders, but gently, and I hold on to them. "Why is that so surprising?"

Someone bumps into me from behind. "I found Alicia!" Saff hollers over the music, holding a plate of tiny cakes in her hand. She points toward the dessert table, where Alicia—who's ditched her farmer garb for a svelte red dress—stands chatting with a group of women. "We're going to tell your mom what you did!" Saff hollers at Micah. Her threat probably would have been more impactful without the tiny carrot cake square, the lemon meringue circle, and the double chocolate fudge block that she's waving in his face.

I quickly explain. "Saff, he just wanted to use the laptop— he wasn't going to take our money." While she digests this, beet red with embarrassment, I turn to Micah. "You'll have to forgive us for jumping to conclusions. But I think we deserve props for bringing tattling back into style."

"It *is* a dying art form," Micah agrees, his cheeks dimpling. "It made a brief comeback in early elementary school, but began losing followers by third grade."

"We'll try to do it with style," I reassure him, still holding his hands. "Perhaps over the microphone at this lovely wedding?"

Saff nearly drops her plate of sinful indulgence when she sees our intertwined hands.

"Although, I suppose we could make a deal," I concede. "Spare you all that public humiliation, if you can hand over the goods."

"Strategic move," Micah says. "I hear blackmail is a hot new trend."

Saff holds the plate out to Micah. "How about bribery? Does that work?"

He drops my hands to take the plate. "Tempting."

"I'm not sure I can handle committing any more crimes," Saff says a little plaintively.

"Her stamina was impressive today," I inform Micah. "But when her conscience kicks in, we all need to take cover."

Micah surveys the room. The dessert cart has created a massive sugar high, and the dance floor is full. "Well, in the spirit of self-preservation, I say we ditch this party and go get that laptop. It's in my hotel room."

I high-five Saff. "See how easy that was?"

She grimaces. "Yeah, if you don't count our run-in with the law and our four-hour drive . . . pretty easy."

*　*　*

Twenty minutes later, we all sprawl on Micah's cushy king-sized bed, with the laptop in front of us. He backs up the video clip by a few seconds. I gaze at Mom's bony hands, holding the shabby piggy bank. "—*how complicated money can be, how it can insert itself into the cracks and crevices of a relationship and push people further apart . . . that I haven't given it to you yet. I wanted to wait until you were both mature enough to handle it.*"

I kick Saff. "Whaddaya think? We mature enough?"

"That's debatable, but let's go with this."

"*You probably know that although I had a solid job, with good benefits, I didn't make a ton of money. And since I'm leaving this world pretty young, I haven't had many years to build up a nest egg for you both. But there's one thing I did right. When I gave birth to you, Cay, and I realized that I'd likely be a single mother, I took out a life insurance policy on myself. For five hundred thousand dollars.*"

I clap a hand over my mouth.

"*I selected Alicia as the trustee, and you two as the beneficiaries. I instructed Alicia to use half of the money to pay Aunt Tina a stipend every month. Right now she's working at a frozen yogurt shop, for*

Pete's sake. There's no way she can raise two little girls on that kind of money. So each month for the last fourteen years, Alicia has been sending her a check for your living expenses."

Micah pauses the video and whips out his phone to do the math. $250,000 divided by 14 years equals $17,857 . . . divided by 12 months a year equals $1,488 per month.

"Wow. We should've gotten everything we ever wanted for that kind of cash." For a moment I think of the Barbie Dreamhouse I begged for but never got.

Maybe Micah can see my wheels turning, because he tells us, "Don't forget, she had to pay her rent, and now her mortgage. She paid for your school supplies, for doctor and dentist visits, for clothes, for birthday presents . . . and I believe you did have a car before you demolished it, right?"

"Oh yeah. That." Fair enough. Barbie Dreamhouse would only have been fun for about a week anyway.

Micah presses play.

"The remaining half has been invested by Alicia for you two. It may have grown or it may have shrunk in the last fourteen years. My hope is that you're responsible enough to handle this kind of money. I know you'll have college expenses very soon, and that is why I'm giving it to you now instead of later."

College. It keeps coming up.

The camera focuses on a piece of paper. The life insurance policy.

"Ideally, I'd love to see you both keep this money in investments for as long as possible. But if one of you needs to use your half of this money, Alicia's instructions are to split it evenly between the two of you. One of my biggest fears is that this money will divide you. Please don't let it do that. This is a gift to ease the struggles of life. Please don't allow it to be a burden or a stressor."

"I changed my mind. I want a car." Both Micah and Saff whip their heads toward me with alarm scribbled all over their faces. "Joking!" I insist.

"Alicia has the account information. Please consider just keeping all the investments in place until it's absolutely necessary to move them."

The camera shifts again to the piggy bank. *"Good luck, sweets."*

"That's a lot of money." Saff speaks breathlessly. "Even split in half."

"Then no more sharing desserts," I say. "If I've got this much money in the bank, I'm getting my own."

Saff smiles. "I can live with that."

Chapter 37

A year ago, if someone had told me I'd wake up hundreds of thousands of dollars richer, I'd have envisioned sleek cars, fancy coffees, and a multi-flavor frozen yogurt dispenser in my kitchen. The reality is that nothing concrete changes. I feel different though—in a way I can't quite describe.

I can't pin this change on the money. In fact, it's not about the money at all. It's about the cluster of events that pushed me forward. Mom's messages to us. The accident. Tee's surgery. Axel being an asshole. Me *realizing* that Axel was an asshole. Finding out I have that gene mutation. Reconnecting with my dad—slowly but genuinely. I've been helping him with the pet-and-plant-care part of his housesitting business lately, and there's something about working as a team that makes me feel closer to him, even though he still can barely hold up his end of a conversation. And Micah . . . something's shifting with Micah. I never used to notice how he smelled, but now every time he's near me I breathe him in.

It's like I'm seeing the world through a different lens. Like I've been walking around with poor eyesight for my whole life, thinking I'm seeing just fine. And then someone hands me a pair of glasses. I'm seeing everything now—both the grit and the glimmer—noticing the fine details I've missed forever. Some of those details are ones I'd rather not see, but now that I know they're there, I can't un-see them.

Luke *wanted* to be pissed when he found out we took his wife's car on an impromptu road trip to Las Vegas, but we're both eighteen, so it's not like he can really do anything about it. Seems like he's been backing off a little ever since Ryan officially took the title of "Dad."

And it helped that Tee was chill about the road trip, calling it a bonding experience, with the caveat that a-little-communication-with-the-people-who-love-and-worry-about-you-never-hurts. Her energy level is way up, which has put her in a good mood. She's going back to work soon, and in the meantime she's started teaching the girls to knit, which is hilarious to watch. I record one of their knitting sessions, thinking if I share it with them in ten years, they'll be rolling on the floor with laughter.

A couple weeks after the wedding, Micah comes over to watch a movie at my house. We sit together on the couch. Luke's been overly enthusiastic with the thermostat, so it's freezing inside. I spread a quilt over my lap. My walking cast is now off, and I'm relishing my newfound ankle freedom.

"You gonna hog that blanket?" He asks, dimpling.

"Yep. I was planning to."

And now we're in a tug-of-war, yanking the quilt back and forth. He's stronger than me, though, and I suspect he's grounding his feet as leverage, so I lurch forward and land in his lap. No cologne this time, just a combo of soap and light vanilla, like maybe he borrowed Alicia's scented hand lotion.

"I *suppose* this quilt is big enough to share," I grumble, but

I don't mind. The truth is, I'm confused about how I feel about Micah. I want to snuggle in with him under the blanket, lean my head on his shoulder, and let his warmth wrap around me. But do I want that because I'm missing Axel? Or do I want that because I want that?

I definitely don't want a rebound. And I don't need a new boyfriend. I'm fine on my own. So why do I want to curl up next to him?

I'm struggling with these questions, plus he smells so freaking good that I can't concentrate on the movie. So I press pause and turn toward him. "I've always thought we were practically cousins."

His smile is knowing, as if he's had this same thought himself and he appreciates me sharing it. "Me too. But that's silly. We're not blood relations."

"Yeah, but I've known you since we both pooped in diapers and stuck our hands in our mouths and picked our noses." It's hard for me to shake the idea of him as family, but bit by bit I'm shedding that mindset. Just like Ryan/Dad morphed from random step-uncle to father, maybe Micah's transforming from family friend to something more. It's strange how something can feel so permanent, and then shapeshift and surprise me.

"We do have history." He deepens his voice in an over-the-top soap opera kind of way. "But maybe that just means we have a foundation for building something else."

Huh.

"Feel like wearing an uncomfortable dress and uncomfortable shoes?" Micah asks out of nowhere.

"Uh, not particularly. Why? You need someone to go to a funeral with you?"

"Worse. Prom. I'd like to just not show up, but I have to go to humor Mom. Before you answer, you should know that I am planning an extravagant bribe."

"Ooh! Tell me more."

"It involves frozen yogurt."

I consider this. I'm pretty anti-prom, but at least I won't be attending my own. And I don't know anyone at Micah's school, which makes the stakes seem lower somehow. "Add sour gummies and I'm yours."

* * *

"Can I borrow the Barbie dress?" I ask from the doorway of Saff's room.

The clingy fabric accentuates both the ample and small areas of my frame. I begged to buy it from Saffron after I tried it on the first time, but she shut me down. Then I tried to steal it, but it's impossible to hide a dress that amazing—even if I hang it at the very back of my closet. So I'm resorting to borrowing it.

"Sure," says Saff, who's sitting on her bed reading.

"Thank you. That dress is magic. It sounds corny, but it makes me feel like a woman."

While Saff belts out an old Shania Twain song, I sift through her closet until my hands land on fabric so smooth that it feels like satin (although it clearly isn't). I step into the Jack-and-Jill bathroom that connects our bedrooms and slip off my T-shirt. I catch sight of myself in the mirror, in my black push-up bra.

I'm not the kind of girl who spends hours staring at my body in the mirror, searching for fat deposits or critiquing the shape of my thighs. So sometimes I sort of surprise myself. Like, "Oh, hi—there you are." Sometimes I don't even recognize myself right away. And today's one of those times. The soft fullness of my breasts surprises me, the contrast of my collarbone against the curve of my flesh, against the flatness of my midsection. A study in contrasts.

And for a moment, even without the magic dress, I strike myself as beautiful. Not in a conceited way, just in an observant, self-removed way. Like it's not even me in the mirror. Just some girl I don't know. Would Saff think it's wrong to admire my body? She's so focused on "what's on the inside," but she'd probably also say that I should love all the parts of me.

I turn sideways, a profile of my curves and lines. I pause again, and then turn nearly backwards. In this twisted position, I can see the way my shoulder blades jut out, and slight muscles in my back, along with my face. Saff has a lovely, delicate appearance, but my features are stronger, more unusual.

Saff keeps on singing "feel like a woman," all dramatic. *What makes me a woman?* My body, lean and curvy? The way my breasts bloom from my bra? Is it my face—my chestnut eyes and full lips? My ovaries? My womb? Or is it all within? Is it my mind? My soul? Some combination that I choose?

Maybe removing my breasts or my ovaries wouldn't make me less of a woman. I don't mind keeping them for now, though.

I shake the magic dress out and lift it up to slip over my head. I watch myself in the mirror, how my skin shifts as my arms move.

Wait.

What's that? I freeze, arms up, dress suspended above my head.

"Saffron." My voice sounds strangely calm, but there's an energy underneath it that Saff must hear right away, because she stops singing.

"What's wrong?" Almost instantaneously she edges in behind me.

"Look. When I lift my arms. What is that?"

Saff reaches for me, her fingers cold, and presses on my skin in that area. The chill of her fingers startles me. "Does it hurt?"

"No. But your fingers are giving me frostbite."

Any possibility of humor falls flat. "Touch it," she commands me.

I move my left hand toward the top of my right breast, almost in my armpit. And press, working my fingers in a circle around the tiny area. Small. About the size of a raisin. Not totally hard, but a little firmer than the rest of my skin. Kind of a thickness, like a clump in my oatmeal. "That can't be possible, Saff. There's no way. I'm too young."

All traces of color drain from her face. "I'm going to look it up." She pulls me back into her room and sits down with her laptop. "What should I search for?"

"Earliest known case of breast cancer."

She types quickly, her fingers catching my urgency. And hits "enter."

"What?!" I fixate on the screen. "*Eight*? That's not possible. Girls don't even have breasts at age eight."

"Okay. Calm down. Let's look up overall percentages." She types again. "Okay. I found a graph. Uh-oh . . . 1.6 percent of cases are for people between ages sixteen and twenty-eight." She centers herself. "That's still really rare."

"But it's possible."

Saff scans the screen. "It says here that many masses are just cysts. Most of those are benign. It says that they can biopsy it to find out. Let's move up our appointment with the specialist. And if he can't see us, we'll switch and see someone else. I'll call right now."

I turn my gaze downward. Two minutes ago, I was admiring my breasts for their aesthetics. Now, examining the mounds of flesh pushing out from my chest, I suddenly understand how it's possible to hate them.

Chapter 38

Aunt Tee and Luke are at the zoo with the kids, and Dad's working, so we decide to handle this on our own. Since it's Saturday, the specialist isn't in, and neither is our primary care doctor. We leave a message on both of their after-hours lines. Technically this is not an emergency. But it sure feels like one.

Saff is holding it together better than I'd have expected, especially given her freakout when we first got our BRCA results. Her skin is pale and her hands are shaking, but her words are calm and simple. "Listen," she tells me. "It's highly unlikely that the lump is cancerous. You're super young. But we'll get this checked out ASAP, even if I have to camp out on Dr. Garcia's front lawn."

I toss the dress on the floor.

"Oh no you don't." Saff scoops it up. "You're wearing that dress and you're going to prom. Nothing's going to happen tonight, so you might as well be distracted."

"I can't go to a dance now!"

"Yes you can." Her voice is firm. She's in her take-charge mode. "And you will. I will not have you crushing Micah's childhood dreams."

"He couldn't care less about prom." I sink onto her bed, wishing the mattress would absorb me completely. "It's Alicia. She's reliving *her* childhood."

"I don't know, Cayenne. I think he really wants to go with you . . . as his date."

"You're the one who's always saying we should please ourselves before we worry about pleasing some guy!"

"You know, arguing with me would take a thousand times more energy than just going to the dance."

Unfortunately she's right, so I disentangle myself from the mattress and put on the stupid dress. Micah arrives while Saff is helping me fasten my hair into a twist on top of my head. I have to admit that the dangly silver earrings and my up-do make my neck appear ballerina-long.

"Wow, Cayenne," Micah stammers from the door to my room. He's wearing a classic black tux, with a deep blue silk shirt. "You look a-maz-ing," he says, accentuating the three syllables of the word.

"Thanks," I say, but my voice is tight.

"Micah, will you help me reach something in the kitchen?" Saff asks, a transparent excuse. She whisks him away, and when he returns, I know she's told him about the lump. For a moment, I'm irritated, because sheesh, my breasts are my own business! But on the other hand, I'm relieved. There's no way I can fake it through this night. If I'm going, and it looks like I'm going, he needs to know where my mind's at.

"Saffron," I say, reaching for a joke, "have you been describing my breasts to my date? Because perhaps he'd like a visual?"

I can tell they're both caught off guard by this, which is absurd, because they've both known me their whole lives, and by now they should know that this is how I roll.

Micah's face is so complicated—furrowed brow like he's worried, deepening of his dimples like he's amused by my joke, and eyes hinting at sadness. "Saffron. Can you excuse us?"

She's peeking around the door. "All right."

"Maybe we should ditch the prom tonight," says Micah. "Stay here and talk, or watch a movie."

"Your mom would never forgive you."

"We could take fake prom pictures and text them to her. She'd never know the difference."

"Tempting. But I'll go as long as you promise me one thing."

"Anythin—" he starts to say but thinks the better of it. "Wait. I know you too well to promise without knowing what it is."

"Oh, this is an easy one," I reassure him. "Just don't talk about my boobs."

* * *

Three things surprise me tonight. One is that Micah is a decent dancer. This is something I didn't know about him—I guess I've never had the opportunity to dance with him. I hate it when guys don't have rhythm. Micah, on the other hand, accentuates each movement with the beat, as if the music and his body are joined.

The second thing that surprises me is how little I think. My mind is full, bursting with the sounds of the music, Micah's clean cologne smell, and the texture of his hand in mine. I can almost forget about the tiny bump lurking in my skin.

And the third thing that surprises me is that neither Micah nor I want the evening to end. He parks in front of our neighbor's house, but instead of exiting the car we sit there in the dark, holding hands. He rubs his thumb on the space between my own thumb and finger. Back and forth. It soothes me at first, and then it makes me tingle.

"Thank you for tonight, Micah."

He's looking down at our hands. "Cayenne. I don't want to mess things up. So, you can tell me to back off and I will." "His eyes shift up to meet mine. "I know I'm not your type. But I'm pretty sure you're mine."

"Only one way to find out," I say, keeping my voice light. I lean in, catch his lower lip in mine, and turn my head to let my tongue enter his mouth. He tastes sweet, and he's gentle, tentative, following my lead. His free hand runs up the side of my face, tracing me, smoothing my hair away. When we pull back for a breath, his eyes are soft.

"Huh. That was nice. Maybe you are my type." I touch his cheek, feeling the slight stubbles on my palm. "To be sure, though, I need another sample." I kiss him again, deeper this time. No matter how long I've known him, he definitely doesn't feel like a cousin.

My neck is getting sore from turning in his direction. I scoot back my seat all the way and recline it. "Here. Come on my side."

"We could just go into the house," he suggests.

"And deal with Aunt Tee?"

"It's late. There aren't any lights on." There's eagerness in his voice. I imagine Tee or Luke discovering Micah in my room, and decide they'd be relieved it wasn't Axel. How did I not realize how much my family disliked Axel?

"Okay." He's right. The house is quiet. Even Saff's light is off. I lead him quietly into my room, leaving everything dark.

267

There's something exciting and sensual about having to feel my way with only touch. I ease my bedroom door closed behind me and guide him over to my bed.

He hesitates. "Let's go slow, okay? You're vulnerable right now—you just broke up with your boyfriend, you've got medical worries—"

I cover his mouth with my palm. "You promised! None of that."

He laughs, his breath hot against my palm. "I just don't want to get carried away. I really like you . . . so I need boundaries."

I consider being offended, but the truth is that I want to take it slow too. When I was with Axel, I kept second-guessing that instinct, kept wondering if I should push myself further for his sake. It's a relief that Micah and I are on the same page. "Just kissing," I tell him. "Lots and lots of kissing."

This seems agreeable to him. He lowers me onto my bed and starts in. First he kisses my neck, and gradually he moves to my ears, sending tingles down my spine. A warm buzzing of complete relaxation spreads across my chest and out to my limbs. By the time he gets to my lips, I'm more than ready to participate. There's something both gentle and strong in the way he kisses. I lose track of time. His kisses fill me up and make my mind hum.

Unlike when I was with Axel, I'm aware of the limits of what this feeling can do for me.

It can't fix all my problems. It can't cure me of my family curse. It can't erase this tiny mass under my arm.

But it doesn't need to. For now, I'm okay. For now, I'm alive.

Chapter 39

Apparently my situation is now "imminent," and my appointment with the specialist has been moved up to Tuesday. Tee keeps saying, "It's a cyst, it's gotta be benign" until I inform her that this mantra is not helping. She quiets down after that, so much that it surprises me. It occurs to me that our last heart-to-heart might've hurt her feelings more than I realized. She and Luke both seem more distant lately, and maybe it's not just from the stress of dealing with Tee's surgery and recovery. Maybe Saff isn't the only one I've been pushing away.

* * *

At the medical appointment, the specialist conducts a fine needle aspiration biopsy, which sounds way worse than it is. The specialist reassures me and Tee that the cyst is most likely benign, but he's doing the biopsy as a precaution due to our family history and the gene mutation. He adds that I should start getting an MRI twice a year to screen. Saff latches on to that idea like it's a life preserver, forcing me to make the MRI appointment even before we receive the biopsy results.

MRIs are supposedly more sensitive than mammograms and now that I'm in this "high-risk" category, I'll be signing up for MRIs every year, indefinitely—or as long as I have breasts. So today Saff and I are sitting in the waiting room at Spelman Imaging. This is only Tee's second week back at work, so I turned down her offer to take a day off and come with me. And Dad texted me this morning too, asking if I'd like a ride to the imaging center, but he's my dad and they're screening my breasts . . . it just feels weird. Same with Luke, who was also willing to come. In the end I decided I'd prefer to just go with Saff. She doesn't have the gene mutation but she'll still need to go through all these screenings at some point, so this is valuable preparation for her.

I'm filling out my questionnaire, submitting my insurance cards, and signing consent forms for a variety of medical interventions.

My name is called. "Oh yay," I grumble, but good-naturedly.

"Have fun!" Saff says, like she's sending me off for a pedicure or a massage. She continues staring at her phone screen, but I know she's faking. She's every bit as nervous as I am. Maybe more. She'd have to be, to be willing to miss a chunk of school during the last week. She claims that two of her classes have final papers instead of tests, and that she finished them already. It's funny though—the more I stress about my own health, the more Saff seems to let go—a little. It's almost like she was carrying the burden of stressing *for* me, and now she's stressing *with* me.

The MRI nurse introduces herself as Kelly and leads me back into the office. Nurse Kelly's ruddy skin looks like it fries the second she steps into the sun. I wonder if she ever worries about skin cancer, if every time she doesn't bother to reapply sunscreen she feels like she's jumping off a cliff. Suddenly it strikes me that lots of people are walking around with genetic risk factors of various kinds. Maybe I'm lucky that mine is something I can actually do something about.

She hands me a gown and a key on one of those scrunchy wristbands. "You'll need to remove everything except for your underwear, and make sure that nothing you're wearing has any metal in it, including any piercings. The gown opens to the front. Place your clothes in the locker and secure it."

The dressing room holds a bench and a full-length mirror. I slip off my stretchy T-shirt, unhook my bra, and slide out of my shorts. I examine myself for a moment. I stand as I did the other day in the bathroom, the day I found the lump. Weird how I can be an observer of myself, totally bare, without criticism or pride. This is just me.

I turn my back to the mirror and then twist my neck. I observe the dimple above my butt, the way my spine pokes through my back, the slight redness from where my bra pressed against my skin. I square off in front of the mirror again, pulling my hair back into a low ponytail. My breasts, round and full, not yet pulled downward by gravity or aging. Whether or not Saff would agree, they meet every standard of attractiveness I can think of.

But these things may kill me. They're parasites embedded in my skin. They may hijack my body and consume me. I don't care how attractive they are. In a weird, dissociative way, I want them off my body. I don't think I'll ever look at them in the same way again.

Once I'm gowned, Nurse Kelly takes charge of me again. We pass a technician station where a tech is typing. I hold onto the fabric of my gown so that I won't accidentally flash him.

He offers to hold the locker key for me before we head into the scanning room.

It's freezing in here. Nurse Kelly has me lie down on a flat surface, directly in front of an enormous tube.

"I'm going in *that*?"

"Mostly. About two thirds of the way in, just to get you far enough to examine your breasts. First we'll set up an IV for me to administer contrast. That's a dye that will course through your blood stream and allow us to get better images. Let's get that IV started now, and then I'll help you set up."

Seeing as how people get mostly naked to climb into these machines, one would think the room would be less frosty. I'll have icicles forming on my nose before I know it.

Nurse Kelly pricks me twice. She says the vein on my left arm rolls, whatever that means—I think it's just her excuse for stabbing me repeatedly. Maybe she has bad aim. So she moves to the vein on the right. I can't look, but I feel the needle enter, and it must be right this time, because she tapes it there. "We'll start the contrast in a bit. It might feel cold as it enters."

I just nod, focusing all my energy on keeping my teeth from chattering.

"All right. I'm going to have you lie face down here." Nurse Kelly gestures to a flat cot that has two holes. "I'll help you place each breast through an opening."

"Seriously?" So this MRI will be done on my stomach, with my breasts hanging through two holes. A joke would work well right now, but for the life of me, I can't come up with one.

"Yep. This is how it's done." Nurse Kelly offers me a small smile. "It won't be too bad. But here's the trick: you have to be entirely still while this MRI is taking place. If you change position, or really move at all, it'll take much longer."

"How long will it take?"

"About a half hour, if we're lucky."

"I can't move for a half hour?"

"Nope." Again, the small smile. Apologetic but uncompromising.

I give up questioning her. Everything I ask just makes me feel worse. Nurse Kelly maneuvers my breasts into these holes. Her hands are so cold she may have had them shipped from Antarctica. Next she helps me adjust a face cushion and covers my ears with noise-blocking headphones. "It'll be loud," she warns me. "Just try to relax."

She steps away. Then the platform moves backward, slowly, sliding me into the tube. Shifting, repositioning. The clicking and beating noises start, deafeningly loud. Thank god I have headphones. I focus on trying to find the pattern in the noises, and just when I think I have it, the constellation changes. I slide in farther, and suddenly I feel trapped. In a tube, strapped to an IV, unable to move for fear of screwing the whole thing up.

A voice comes in through speakers. "Okay, Cayenne, we'll be administering the contrast at this time. You might feel a slight cold sensation." Almost immediately, I do. My heartbeat triples, banging around in my chest, keeping time with the battering sounds of the machine. Sweat gathers along the cushion. The urge to readjust myself, to pull out the IV, nearly overwhelms me, because I know I can't. I suck in a breath, trying to catch enough air, and force myself to think of something else.

Perhaps because of the anxious adrenaline surging through my veins, I picture my last jump with Axel. Hanging in midair, hand in hand with Axel at first, falling fast but in a frozen moment of time, losing my grasp on him, my heart surging.

Crashing into Axel's body, plunging deep into the water, and then losing him.

I shake, everything shakes, and it's not from the machine. The physiological memory of those moments takes over, and I feel like I'm back there.

"Don't forget to hold still in there," the otherworldly voice says. "You're shifting just slightly. Try to relax. It'll go faster."

How long will this take?

I grasp for a more relaxing image, and the day at the beach with Micah surfaces. The crashing waves, the salt in the air, the gentle breeze that ruffles my hair, the feeling of not being alone. I visualize the rhythm of the waves as they break and force my breaths to slow in time with them.

The surging of adrenaline dissipates.

When it's over, Nurse Kelly slides the needle out of my arm, and Band-Aids a cotton ball against my skin. "Not bad." She pats me. "You'll get used to it."

I guess I'll have to.

* * *

I'm actually starting to look forward to writing my journal entries. Everyone's asleep, and I can use those quiet moments to sift through my scattered thoughts.

WHAT'S IN A LIFE —CAYENNE

I get it. I get that it can happen to me.

But how do I ride the middle on this? I know it can happen, and I know that I have to take precautions, but I don't want to be paralyzed by fear that it WILL happen.

Because what kind of life is that?

*I don't want to miss out on the Minions' lives.
I want to be here for every school play and
science fair. I don't want to leave them the way
Mom left me.*

*I don't want to have regrets. No regrets
that I didn't do more to take care of this. But
also no regrets that I did it too soon. That I
limited my options in my life.*

*I'm not sure if this information is a curse or
a blessing.*

* * *

The biopsy results come back negative. Benign cyst.

But it's strange. I'm not as relieved as I thought I'd be.
So . . . I dodged the bullet this time. What about the next one?
I'm starting to understand why Tee did the preventative surgeries. She was tired of waiting around for bad news. I have a
follow-up appointment with the specialist next month, and I'm
compiling a list of questions.

In spite of my huffiness with Tee during our last heart-to-
heart, now I kind of do want advice. So I offer to treat her to
a chai latte. We sit with our hands wrapped around steaming
mugs in the dark corner of a coffee shop.

"Have you ever felt like, no matter what you do, no matter
how many precautions and preventative measures you take . . .
you might still get cancer and it will all have been a waste?"

Tee nods slowly. "Sure. But honestly, Cay, I could get hit by
a bus tomorrow. I could die in an earthquake. You know what
I mean? Life and death can be completely random. So all I can

do is try to give myself the best odds possible, based on what I know and what I'm able to control. That's all any of us can expect of ourselves."

"I think I need someone to tell me what to do," I admit.

"Oh, Cayenne." Tee places her hand on mine. Her skin has been warmed up by the tea mug, and it feels nice. "Usually, I'd say that's music to my ears. Do you know how many times I wished you'd come to me? And at least be open to my advice or feedback? But in this particular situation, I can't tell you what to do, or when to do it. I can only offer my own experience."

I deflate. I really just want her to make an executive decision for me. Parents are supposed to be good at that. I think I know what I have to do, but I still have to figure out when. How long I wait. Should I have an MRI every year and set a reminder in my phone for when I'm thirty? Do I dare wait that long? I hate the question marks of life.

Tee squeezes my hand. "That's why I want you to come with me to a BRCA support group. There's such a range of risk management options. The women and men in this group have so many different perspectives. No one will tell you what to do. But after hearing all their views, I think you'll have a better sense of your own."

The idea of sitting in a support group circle talking earnestly about my cancer-related feelings makes me gag. I push away my chai, but leave my other hand in hers.

Tee must see the emotion in my face. "Here's what I can tell you. That we can never be sure we're making the right decision or choosing the right timing for something like this. All we can expect of ourselves is to do our best with the knowledge and tools we're given. And then we have to let go of judging or second guessing ourselves. We have to make a decision and then find peace in it."

Now that she's given me an opening, I have to ask. "Are you at peace with your decision?"

"I am," Tee responds quickly. "Now. If you'd asked me right after surgery, I might have had a different answer." She simultaneously laughs and grimaces at the memory. "Sure, it hurt, and it takes time to heal, but this decision has brought me incredible peace of mind. I'm not sure I realized how heavily the fear of cancer weighed on me. For me, preventative surgery was so worth it. But clearly, my age and life situation are way different from yours. I can't tell you what to do or predict how you'll feel about it."

I let out a long sigh that's meant to be dramatic but actually gets a little shaky. "I guess I could go to one support group even though I'll hate every second of it."

Tee gives an approving grunt. "Coming from you, I'd say that's enthusiasm. Saff and I will go too. We're all in the same club—even if she doesn't have the gene, she still has the family history. We're in this together." She extricates her hand from mine and pumps her fist in the air as she adds, "Silk family strong."

"Corny." I swat at her, but I'm smiling.

Chapter 40

On graduation day, in the midst of flying mortarboard hats, all I can think about is Mom. I miss her in a way I haven't before. I wish she was here.

Still . . . Dad is in the audience, along with Saff and the Chowders. The school has limited seating, so Tee and Luke volunteered to stay home and let my grandparents come. Luke gave me a crushing hug today, something he hasn't done in a long time. Typically, I'm not a big fan of crushing hugs, but this time it felt nice.

My classmates are jumping around, like graduating high school is this major accomplishment. Or maybe they're all just looking forward to post-event parties. I try to get pulled into their excitement.

I'm saving my graduation hat for the Minions. For their preschool graduation last week, they made adorable caps out of cardboard, and now they're obsessed with them. It's funny how much I relish each of their milestones. It's almost as if I experience those moments for myself *and* for Mom, as compensation for all my milestones she missed. My new phone screensaver is of the Minions, wearing their cardboard caps, with their arms slung around each other.

Tee, Luke, and the twins join us for a celebratory dinner that the Chowders insist on buying.

"I hear you're dating Alicia Johnson's son," says Nonna before we've even ordered our food.

"You hear correctly," I say with a smile. Micah and I are now an official item. But we're both a little scared of ruining a lifelong friendship, so we're taking it snail-pace slow. I actually love taking it slow with him. Each step feels new and fresh and worth waiting for. I can only compare it to being super hungry and then getting a favorite candy bar. I can either cram it into my mouth and barely taste it, or I can nibble it down and savor every bite. Micah is the savoring kind. And he makes me feel like I'm worth savoring too. There isn't the lusty intensity I felt with Axel, but I don't really miss that. And I definitely don't miss agonizing over whether I should escalate things to please someone else when I know I'm not ready. To be honest, I feel like I'm at my best with Micah. Like I have multiple selves and he brings out the self I'm proud of.

"He's always seemed like such a fine young man," says Nonna.

"He's an upgrade for Cayenne, for sure," Saff chimes in. I roll my eyes, but thankfully the conversation moves on without any further allusions to Axel. Our relationship has had zero closure, except for him placing a cardboard box of my random possessions on my doorstep. All things I've left at his place or in his car over the last year.

As I'm stuffing my face with onion rings, Dad leans over and says, "So I've been thinking . . . the summer term at Coast starts in three weeks, right? And they let you apply online?"

"Yeah. I was going to work on my application tomorrow,

actually." I've decided to get my Gen Ed requirements out of the way at community college and then try to transfer to Cal in two years. Micah promises he'll at least try to make friends before I get there.

He nods. "I was thinking the same thing."

"No way!"

With a sheepish shrug, he explains that he'd like to get his associate's degree and veterinary tech certification, so that he can work as an assistant in a vet's office. He's enjoying the pet care component of his housesitting business, and being a vet tech would have insurance, benefits, and consistent pay. With that kind of job he might finally be able to move into his own apartment.

"That's awesome, Dad," I say. It's weird—I've stopped thinking of him as Ryan/Dad. Now he's just Dad. "Wanna be application buddies tomorrow afternoon?"

I haven't seen my father smile very often, but I love the way it softens his face. "Thought you'd never ask."

* * *

"Why is this so complicated?" Dad grumbles, hunching next to me at the Chowders' computer.

"Maybe they figure if you can't complete the application, they don't want you in their school." The application process really isn't that hard, just time-consuming. I can't believe I might be attending the same school as my dad.

"I need a break. Want a snack?" Dad suggests.

"Sure. Something salty." He heads to the kitchen while I browse through my social media accounts. I roll through different posts, enjoying the distraction, until something snags my attention.

Axel has posted: "Today! The biggest rush of my life. It will top EVERYTHING."

The next big jump. Pinnacle Peak. The one we were building toward this whole time. And although I was supposed to be right there by his side, now the thought of it makes me physically ill.

It's not my business. But no matter how hard I try, I just can't shake this feeling of obligation that I should help him. Or try to help him. Try to stop him. What if he hurts himself or even dies . . . and I'm the only one who knew he was planning to do this? The only one who could've talked him out of it?

I message him. *Please don't jump.*

His reply is prompt. *What do you care? Don't you have a new boyfriend already?*

I don't want you to hurt yourself.

You're a hypocrite. We've been doing this together.

I know. I regret it. Please listen to me now. It's not worth it.

None of your business, Cayenne. Go complain to your boyfriend.

I must be groaning, because when Dad comes in with a bowl of pretzels, he asks, "What's wrong?"

I tell him. That I can't shake this feeling of responsibility. That I can't bear knowing Axel's out there doing something dangerous, and all by himself. It's not like he has parents or siblings or even responsible friends who watch out for him. His roommate is practically a non-entity, and Axel wouldn't listen to him anyway. There's nobody I can go to for backup.

It's strange—never in my life would I have thought I'd be asking Ryan-the-Reject for advice. But there's something comforting about his checkered past. He knows the impact of things going bad. He understands regret. And he won't pass judgment on me for the mistakes that led me to this moment, the choices that put me in this position.

"Go with your gut, Cayenne." For once, Dad doesn't hesitate. He slips right into the fatherly advice role like it fits him. "You gotta think ahead. You have no control over what he does, but you gotta be at peace with your part of it. If you think you need to go stop him, then you should. Because no matter what happens, you have to find peace within your own choices."

* * *

An hour later, five of us are winding along the road near the Bluffs. Micah, Saff, Fletcher, Dad and me. "Thanks for the moral support," I tell them, not sure if my nausea is from the twisty path, the crowded car, or intrusive mental images of Axel splattered along the rocks. I hope we get there in time.

"I think what you need is physical support." Saff sits to my right in the back seat. "Your ankle can't be ready for a hike just yet."

"I don't have to climb up, we'll just park and walk in on ground level by the water." My ankle doesn't hurt anymore, and the walking cast has been off for a while, but I've lost a ton of strength and mobility. I lean forward to direct Dad toward the best parking area.

Within the first ten minutes of walking, it's clear that I miscalculated. There's a short path from the parking area to the water, but the ground is uneven and rocky. Micah winds up carrying me on his back half the way, and I can't decide if I feel like a little kid or a princess.

"What's your plan, exactly?" Saff turns around to say. Wispy little flyaways have escaped from her ponytail and circle her face.

"We just watch him jump." I tighten my arms around Micah's neck and try to hold myself stiffly so that I'm not too heavy for him. He smells clean, with a whiff of vanilla and coconut—probably sunscreen. "Make sure he's okay. If anything goes wrong, at least we'll be here."

"And then after today?" Saff presses. "You going to follow him around the rest of his life? Like a guardian angel?" I can almost feel Micah's ears perk up. He's been a trooper about all this, but I'm sure he's ready for me to cut Axel loose. Nothing like asking your current boyfriend to help you protect your ex.

"No. Just this jump. We planned this one together. I'm a part of it. I was supposed to be up there with him. If something happens during this jump, it'll be on me." I rest my chin on Micah's shoulder. "After this . . . he's on his own. I think."

We set up camp near the water's edge. Fletcher and Saff came prepared, cramming one backpack with a blanket and another one with drinks and snacks. While we're waiting, Fletch teaches us all a disappearing penny trick so that we can entertain the Minions later. Only no one has a penny, so we use the dried cherries he packed. I pop mine in my mouth when he's not looking and really make it disappear.

I keep peering up at the ledge above us, but there's no sign of Axel. After a while, I start to suspect he isn't going to show. He might have changed his mind.

Micah and I find a shallow area and wade in the water up to our thighs. The rocks poke at my feet and the cool water laps at my legs.

"Maybe your rescue isn't necessary," Micah suggests.

"Maybe. But I'm still glad we came."

"I know."

He reaches for my hand, and I intertwine my fingers with his. Dad watches us from the shore. Before I knew he was my dad, I wouldn't have thought anything of it, but now it makes me feel strangely self-conscious. Dad turns away. I wonder about the thousands of times he must have had fatherly feelings without my knowledge. And how many times I hurt his feelings without even realizing. I have the urge to hug him, and I decide that I will—I'll hug him when he drops me off at home tonight.

A handful of high school kids approach, calling to each other and joking around. They storm into the water, splashing and yelling. I recognize a couple of them vaguely.

"You all here to watch the jump?" a thick footballer type asks us.

"The jump?"

"Yeah, this dude's taking a dare. He's jumping off Pinnacle Peak backwards."

"*Backwards?*" My voice is shrill.

"Yeah." His eyes spark with excitement. "I'm gonna try to catch it on video and I'll post it later. I bet I'll get a thousand hits in a day."

"Where is he?" Micah asks, shading his eyes and looking upward.

"Betchya he's up there already." The footballer type readjusts his cap. "He's supposed to jump any time now."

I turn to Micah. "I gotta go up there and stop him."

"Cayenne." Micah pulls me away from the footballer and holds both of my hands in his own. "I know you want to end this, but you already tried to talk him out of it. What, do you think you'll walk up there, remind him that this is dangerous—and he'll just climb down? With all these people watching? He's doing this *because* it's dangerous. He invited people here because it's dangerous. All we can do is watch and be ready in case he needs help."

I know he's right, but I push away from him and try to haul myself up the mountain path. I've only gone a few steps when I hear Axel whooping from above. Something churns inside me.

There's no way I can get up there in time. The crew of onlookers have all whipped out their phones and are set to record.

Axel's backed himself up to the edge of the bluff, his posture as perfect as a military sergeant's. I have no idea how he'll get enough distance to clear the rocks below.

I yell up to Axel, with everything in my being. I don't even sound human.

Axel gazes down. I'm not sure if he can see me, but I'm guessing he can. But after a moment he faces backwards, bends his knees, and jumps.

Out and back.

He's gotten more distance than I'd have thought, but I don't know if it's enough. He's falling fast and hard. What feels timeless when you're suspended in midair is only a fraction of a moment in real life. I remember that feeling of suspension, of the strange power that comes with choosing to be completely out of control, and for the first time I don't crave it.

The water swallows him up. His splash is insignificant, and I wonder if that's a metaphor for his contribution to this world. He's only focused on his next big rush. Not what he can possibly do with his life.

He's under for a long time, but I feel nothing. Something shifts inside me. While moments ago I was screaming for his life, now I feel detached from it. He is an idiot. An *idiot*.

Micah and Fletcher climb on rocks near his entry point, peering into the deep water. "It's taking too long!" Micah yells to Fletcher. "He should be up by now."

"Give it another minute," Fletcher yells back. But Micah's diving already, near where Axel entered. Fletcher stands on a rock, shading his eyes so that he can see deeper.

Around me, the high schoolers are hooting and aiming their phones toward the sparkling water, like this is the best show on earth. Like they don't understand that someone's life could be on the line.

I am sick to my stomach. How is this entertaining to them? How can this possibly be entertaining to anyone?

A head pops up. Axel. Sucking in breaths, eyes blank, as if all he can focus on is the oxygen around him. I hate him. And I hate the part of myself that ever found this fun.

Axel climbs out, dripping and still gasping, the high schoolers whooping and running toward him with their phones pointed. He lifts a thumbs-up and nods in a self-congratulatory way, like he's accomplished something amazing.

I am flooded with something red and hot. Fury. I barrel over to him. "FUCK YOU, AXEL!" I've never been physically aggressive in my life, but all of a sudden I'm pummeling him. He's so much bigger that he swats me off like a fly, but I don't care.

"Cayenne!" Saff screams, and it's the panic in her voice that makes me pause.

I swivel.

Fletch and Dad are dragging Micah out of the water, one under each arm. What the hell—? I rewind my brain. What happened? He dived in to go after Axel, and then moments later Axel's head popped out. Did Micah never come up himself? How long has he been under?

He's bleeding from his forehead. There's a gash. Dripping down the side of his face. Did he, in his rush to help Axel, dive into a rock? His body is limp. Is it limp because he was under too long, or because he hit his head?

Saff's dialing 911.

I am frozen.

My brain is frozen. My body is frozen. I cannot think or feel. All I can do is watch.

Fletch and Dad are laying Micah out on the sand. Fletcher strips off his wet shirt and holds it to Micah's head wound. Listening for breath and heartbeats, tipping Micah's head back like we learned to do in CPR.

I stand, like a freaking Popsicle, and watch.

Before they even start the mouth-to-mouth, Micah's coughing and puking up water. A warm thought permeates my glitched-out brain. *Thank god. He's not dead.*

I lose time.

Everything that happens is a fog.

No clear memory of hiking back to the car. Or the emergency room visit for Micah. Or climbing into bed. I don't think I've spoken. I remember Saff helping me change out of my clothes and into sweats. Kind of tucking me into a bed that's not my own. Telling me it will be okay.

I wake up in the middle of the night in Micah's guest room. I wander the house in a trance, finding Saff on the couch and Micah in his own bed. I stand there watching him sleep, watching the gentle rise and fall of his chest. I can't believe I pulled Micah into that nightmare. Axel isn't his problem to fix. He's not mine either. Because I'm done. Axel's on his own.

Before I can change my mind, I message Axel, and I tell myself these will be my last words to him. Symbolically, I'm sealing this chapter of my life.

Remember my worst fear?

He must be up too, because he responds quickly. *Yes. Losing someone you love.*

That almost happened yesterday. Never again. I'm saying goodbye.

I had no control over your boyfriend jumping in, you know.

I know. That's just it: you can't control how your actions might affect other people. And even if you could, you shouldn't be putting yourself in so much danger. I hate you right now, but I still don't want anything to happen to you. Please stop with all this daredevil crap.

I'm tempted to suggest that he think about some kind of counseling, especially since he doesn't have the kind of support network of family and friends that I've got. I've always scoffed about the therapists Tee dragged us to when we were younger, but maybe they did more good than I realized.

I start to type another text, but the longer it gets, the more convinced I am that I can't offer Axel a solution to his problems. He's got to be the one to figure this out.

I remember the way Saffron drew a metaphorical line in the sand, saying she could no longer invest her heart in me if I wasn't going to take care of myself. This is the best I can do. For him and for me.

I delete the draft.

No guarantees, he texts in response to my earlier message.

Well, I hope you'll think about it.

Right before I power off my phone, one more text rolls through. *I'll try.*

* * *

I climb back into bed and pull the covers up to my chin. Before I know it, I'm sinking deep into my mattress, sleep sucking me down. I sense Lorelei hovering. Perhaps it's the stress of the day, but I have no tolerance for her taunting, tempting ways.

I reject you! I scream in my mind. *You tell me the game is over, and yet here you are, refusing to let go. So now I'm saying it—the game is OVER. I'm calling it off on my own terms, so back off. I will handle my gene mutation, I will go to that support group, I will do what I need to do, okay?*

Lorelei interlaces her fingers as if she's holding on to herself.

I don't accept you lurking at the edge of my reality, dangling my impending death under my nose. I'm done.

Finally. Her lips tilt upward in a tiny smile. *You needed me for a long time.*

This pisses me off, even though I understand. I needed to feel alive, I needed to know what to push against, I needed to test the limits.

And it's funny. Because I know I created Lorelei. She's been a part of my mind, a way to justify my death-defying stunts. Now that I'm no longer clinging to that illusion of control that our rivalry once offered me, maybe I'm outgrowing her.

I have never been out to trap you, Cayenne. I've been out to save you.

I nearly laugh. She's got a freaky sense of humor. *Save me? From what?*

From yourself.

I slowly digest this idea. Perhaps Lorelei has never been Death, hungry for more. Perhaps I created her to tether myself to my life rather than to torture myself with the fear of losing it. Perhaps she's been helping me survive, until I could see another way forward.

Chapter 41

Saff and I settle in to watch our final video. We've been helping Micah organize his mom's house by packing her abun-
dance of art supplies and knickknacks into enormous plastic
containers—his pre-college gift to Alicia. Now we're taking
a break.

The video image focuses on two little girls swinging in the
backyard. The sunlight makes the image hazy at first, but as
the camera focuses, I recognize the yard as Alicia's, and the
girls as myself and Saff.

"*Doesn't that look fun?*" Mom's voice comes in, hoarser than
before. "*You've been out there for an hour, and I've been watching
you from this loveseat on the back porch. You've taken turns pushing
each other on the swing, twisting the swing and spinning, lying on
your tummies to fly like superheroes, and standing on the seat, tilting
your heads up to the sky.*"

I nudge Saff and point through the window. That same
swing still hangs from a tree in Alicia's yard, rickety and splintered from years in the sun.

"*I love you girls so much. It's a love I cannot put words to.
I wouldn't want to try—no words could do this feeling justice.*

Watching you play, and laugh, and love each other, this fills my soul in some all-encompassing way that makes me complete."

Someone has woven our hair into elaborate braids. I vaguely remember Alicia brushing our hair, sitting us in front of her chair, and wrapping strands over strands. I remember thinking that she must like braiding, that maybe a part of her wished for a daughter. Wisps have sprung free, circling our faces, and swaying as we run.

"You may have noticed by this point that there are only six videos, and seven clues. That's because I decided to combine the last two." Her voice cracks. *"There's not as much time as I'd hoped, and there's so much more I wanted to tell you. But I have to put all my remaining energy into the you I see now, not the you of the future."*

My little-girl self cups her hand over her mouth and calls, "Come push us!" Moments later, little-boy Micah dashes forward. I arrange myself on the swing, and Saff climbs on my lap, facing me, and wrapping her legs around my waist. We both hold onto the chains. Micah pushes from behind me, and we sail up high, screeching like happy birds.

"Mostly I've found peace in this. Mostly I believe that you'll be okay. But there are moments that I am so angry. Moments when I feel royally cheated. I'm trying my best to let go of those crappy feelings. They don't change the situation, they only zap my ability to enjoy the special moments I have left. I don't know if you have any of those toxic feelings, but if you do, try your best to release them. They do you no good."

Our little-girl selves are singing as we swing high out of the camera's reach. Micah shakes his head at us like we're ridiculous but he loves us anyway.

"All right, I'm just procrastinating. Follow my instructions. Carry this video into the bathroom, girls, and go together. These are your final two gifts."

Saff and I exchange perplexed looks, but I pick up the laptop and carry it into the bathroom off the enclosed porch.

"*Okay. Now set the laptop on the bathroom counter. And look in the mirror, girls.*"

Saff clears the counter with one sweep of her arm, sending an assortment of potpourri bags into the sink. I place the laptop there, tilting the screen upward so that we can see it better.

"*Take a moment and look at your sister. This is gift six. I give you each other.*"

Saff and I meet each other's eyes in the mirror.

"*Treasure this relationship. Don't let silly differences divide you. Stay strong and stay together.*"

Saff smiles with a spark of recognition, like some unconscious part of her has known this all along. The bridge of my nose stings, and her image in the mirror blurs. I think of all her sticky note notes in the journal, and all my responses to her, still hidden away.

"*And now turn to your own reflections. For gift seven, I offer you yourself. YOU are someone you can always count on. YOU get to decide what path you take and how you want to live. YOU are your own greatest gift.*"

Saff's eyes shift from mine and move to her own. I linger on her face, watching her gaze at herself in the mirror, her lips vibrating with emotion.

I peel my focus away from Saff and toward myself. I can't lie to my own reflection. My image contorts, and I realize that tears are blurring my vision. I don't bother wiping my eyes. Crying has never felt so good. Like someone has released a dam that I've been struggling to hold for too long.

"*I don't believe in goodbyes. I, for one, choose to believe that I'll be watching over you for eternity. That I'll cry with you and I'll laugh*" *with you. Speaking of which, I'm going to set the camera down, and just enjoy you. I want to catch every possible moment with you two."* The image jiggles as Mom sets her camera down on a table, lens still angled outward. *"Alicia, you ready?"* I see the edge of Mom sit down on a chair by the camera, watching us.

A youthful Alicia walks into the frame. She aims a hose at our little-girl selves, her thumb over the spigot, and sprays. We squeal as the water hits us, happy little-girl squeals. We run in circles, both into the stream of liquid and away from it. Water cascades down on us, sparkling in the sunlight.

We open our mouths to catch the water, giggling and coughing, taking turns. We tip our heads back, our hair wet, our soaked clothes molding to our little-girl bodies. The edge of Mom is shaking with laughter, and I'm reminded of what a musical sound that was. The image freezes there, in a moment that captures the water droplets midair.

* * *

I spend that evening compiling all my Minion videos into a montage for Tee. And when I'm done, I tape my own sticky-note responses into Mom's journal. I center the book on Saff's pillow before I go to bed. Some of my sticky notes don't fit quite right and wind up poking out of the journal, but it's okay. We can always reconfigure this later. For now, I just want Saffron to know how I feel.

Chapter 42

"All right, cooking fanatics!" says our professor, who has introduced herself as "Call-me-Carla." "You all are in for a treat—both literally and metaphorically." She pauses for emphasis, a slight smile curving her lips, as though she thinks she's hilarious but is trying not to show it. "Although I hope you all didn't sign up for this class thinking it'd be an easy A, 'cause it's not. It is, however, a wild love affair with food creation."

Uh-oh. I peek at Dad, who looks equally uneasy. We'd decided to sign up for this class for that exact reason. Easy A. Something we might be reasonably good at. A gentle introduction to the community college experience. No homework (hopefully). We've selected the same table, at the back—the perfect place for slackers.

"For your first assignment in Cooking with Herbs and Spices, you'll need to familiarize yourself with the breadth and variety of options at your work station." Call-me-Carla circles the room, drumming her fingers on countertops as she moves.

I study the overwhelming array of containers.

"I give you permission," Call-me-Carla says, raising her arms up high, as though conducting a savory orchestra. "Open the lids. Smell, taste, dissect them with your senses."

I hand a container of nutmeg to Dad. He unscrews the top and sniffs. Seeming unimpressed, he fumbles for his phone. I inhale the scent of cloves, and it makes me immediately think of gingerbread cookies and pumpkin pie. I move on to peppermint, tarragon and thyme.

About ten containers later, Dad messages me. *Carla really loves herbs and spices.*

Clearly, I message back. *We're already her problem students, on our phones during class.* Luckily she's more hands-off than a high school teacher.

You wanna drop the class?

No. You?

Only if you do.

You're such a bad influence, for a dad.

I haven't had much practice.

Lesson one: Do not encourage your slacker daughter to drop a class on the first day. Lesson two: Do not text during class.

Oops. Putting phone away now.

Call-me-Carla taps her fingers next to my peppermint container, so I slide my phone under my arm. "Next, I'd like you to wander the room, to examine the herb and spice collections of your fellow students. You'll notice that the same spice can come in different forms. There's ground nutmeg. There's whole nutmeg. Et cetera, et cetera."

We begrudgingly stand up and mill around the classroom to other students' work stations, sniffing on command. I feel a bit like a puppy, walking around the room, smelling everything.

"Over the course of this class, we're going to explore different flavor profiles." Call-me-Carla raises her voice to be heard over the low tones of conversation. "Then we're going to experiment. Which spices can be combined for more intricate flavors. Which supplement each other. Which don't pair well."

Dad taps a bit of thyme into his palm and tastes it. "You know what your problem is?" I say. "You've got too much thyme on your hands."

He breaks into a smile. "Very funny."

Call-me-Carla continues to speak, loudly, so we quiet down to listen. "In this class, I'm going to educate you about the rules of classic cooking. And then teach you how to break them." With that, she gives us another assignment—to pick our favorite three spices and describe their flavors on the index cards she's placed at our stations. Meanwhile, she'll stop by each station to meet us personally.

A minute later she's strolling over to us. "Hi, you two. What're your names?"

"Ryan." Dad reaches out to shake her hand.

"And I'm Cayenne," I pop right back, trying to act as saucy as my name sounds.

"Cayenne?"

"Yes." I smile brightly. "As in pepper."

Her eyes widen, checking me out, probably to see if I'm the type to mess with her. "Seriously?" She must not have read her roll sheet very carefully.

"Seriously. Blame my father." I grin and point at him.

Pause for digestion, while she looks back and forth between us. At last she surrenders to a smile, as if she's deciding not to care whether I'm giving her a hard time or not. "Well, in that case, you're both in the right place."

I smile at Dad. "Yeah, I think so too."

Author's Note

I inherited my BRCA gene mutation from my father's side of the family. His cousin died of ovarian cancer in her early forties. His mother and his two sisters fought breast cancer, and he had prostate cancer. My maternal side of the family is rife with non-BRCA breast cancer as well. While no one particularly wants to be told they have an increased chance of cancer, I consider myself lucky to have learned about my BRCA gene mutation through genetic testing. Information is power, and this information allowed me to make difficult but important decisions about my future.

This story was sparked by a "what if" that materialized in my psyche. What if I'd known my BRCA status before I got married and had children? What if I'd known during my vulnerable teen years? How might it have colored my life choices?

The field of cancer research and prevention is ever changing. BRCA 1 and 2 gene mutations account for a small percentage of breast cancer cases. For anyone with a history of breast cancer, a helpful first step is consultation with a genetic counselor. If your risk is high, consider joining an in-person or online support group to hear what other people in the same situation are doing. Surgery is one approach to prevention, but there are many others. It's a personal decision. I believe that the recommendations for those with BRCA 1 and 2 gene mutations will change dramatically over the next twenty years. If you are diagnosed with this mutation, consult with your doctor about your options.

Anyone can get breast cancer, not just cisgender women. In fact, although breast cancer is less common in cisgender men, the mortality rate is higher, since men often take longer to seek medical treatment. This may be due to lack of education about male breast cancer. Everyone with breast tissue can benefit from being vigilant and consulting a doctor about any concerns.

Regardless of whether you have a history of breast cancer in your family, educate yourself about your body. Self-examinations are helpful and if you notice any changes, consult with your physician. For more information, check out the resources on the next page.

Further Resources

Prevention

#KnowYourLemons Breast Health Education
knowyourlemons.com

Prevent Cancer Foundation
preventcancer.org/education/preventable-cancers/breast-cancer

World Health Organization
www.who.int/cancer/detection/breastcancer/en/index3.html

Managing Cancer Risk

beBRCAware
www.bebrcaware.com/brca-resources/support-and
-education.html

The BRCA Umbrella
brcaumbrella.ning.com

FORCE—Facing Our Risk of Cancer Empowered
www.facingourrisk.org/index.php

National Cancer Institute
cancer.gov/about-cancer/causes-prevention/genetics/brca
-fact-sheet

Cancer Treatment, Research, Resources, and Support
American Cancer Society
www.cancer.org

Center for Disease Control and Prevention
www.cdc.gov/cancer/index.htm

HIS Breast Cancer Awareness
www.hisbreastcancer.org

Male Breast Cancer Coalition
malebreastcancercoalition.org

National Cancer Institute
www.cancer.gov

Susan G. Komen Breast Cancer Foundation
ww5.komen.org

When Your Parent Has Cancer: A Guide for Teens
https://www.cancer.gov/publications/patient-education
/When-Your-Parent-Has-Cancer.pdf

Acknowledgments

I'm so grateful for the opportunity to publicly acknowledge, honor, and thank those humans who have touched my life. This is about so much more than my writing process. It's about the professionals who dedicate their lives to researching prevention and treatment. (Keep it up! We need you.) It's about medical staff—ranging from empathic receptionists, to mammogram techs, to genetic counselors, to ICU nurses and physicians. It's about the community of loved ones who wrap around us in support. It's about the lives lost.

My heartfelt thanks to the medical professionals who have supported me and my family over the years, especially the skilled medical staff at Kaiser Permanente, who educated me about my options and guided me through the process with respect. My complete gratitude to the following medical professionals: Dr. Gary Lieb, Dr. Lucila Ortiz-Barron, Mary Stephenson, R.N., Jasmine Jose, R.N., Dr. Dean Nora, Jayamol Pachi, R.N., Nora Rosario, R.N., Dr. Justin Kane, Dr. Sendia Kim, Dr. Jeffrey Martin, Dr. Sherri Meredith Cheatham, Dr. E. Kristina Kang, Dr. Stephanie Smith, Dr. Jonathon Lipana, Dezarae Rutledge, L.V.N., Dr. Goldin, Dr. Saul, Dr. Huynh,